Nuala Casey graduated from Durham University in 2001 and moved to London to pursue a career as a singer-songwriter. However, her experiences living in Soho where she chronicled the comings and goings of the people around her, took her life in a different direction. She went on to work as a copywriter and was awarded an MA in Creative Writing. Soho and the urban landscape of London continue to provide inspiration for her writing. *Soho, 4 a.m.* is Nuala's first novel.

NUALA CASEY

SOHO
4 A.M.

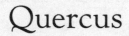

First published in Great Britain in 2013 by

Quercus
55 Baker Street
7th Floor, South Block
London W1U 8EW

A CIP catalogue record for this book is available
from the British Library

PB ISBN 978 1 78206 348 3
EBOOK ISBN 978 1 78206 349 0

10 9 8 7 6 5 4 3 2 1

Printed and bound in Great Britain by Clays Ltd, St Ives plc

Typeset by Ellipsis Digital Limited, Glasgow

In memory of Simon Kenneally

'Nothing thicker than a knife's blade separates happiness from melancholy.'

Virginia Woolf, *Orlando*

Chapter 1

It started with a low rumble, a faint voice on the periphery of a dream, a timpani drum buried deep underground, thudding fast then slow, the nervous heartbeat of an expectant city. It was in the split second between breaths that Stella heard it, felt its tremor beneath Trafalgar Square where thirty thousand people were watching a giant television screen and waiting on the words of a man with a card in his hand.

'London!'

The first syllable had barely left his mouth when the rumble exploded into a chorus of excited screams, so loud they drowned out the noise of the traffic; the black cabs and red buses stopped mid-flow in their circulatory route and the long, spidery hand of the Big Ben clock

1

paused too as it crept towards, then settled upon, a time: 12:49 p.m.

London had been chosen to host the 2012 Olympic Games; now the celebrations could begin.

Stella smiled as she made her way through the crowd, soaking up the happy faces, so many happy faces – where had they all been hiding? It was as though normal service had paused and the city, for a moment, had slowed down to a more leisurely pace. Like a sleepwalker, she could weave in and out of the empty spaces, safe and hidden in the eye of the crowd.

And now? Now, after four glorious hours passed in a blink, she is back where she started.

The elation of the square fades as she squints into the sun and sees him sitting on the step outside the flat. His reddish golden hair shimmers in the light of the sun and for a moment he looks like a statue, still and unmoving as he stares down at his feet. There is a beautiful stillness about the scene, the late afternoon sun pouring onto the street, bouncing off the windows of Bar Italia and Little Italy and bathing his small, sinewy figure in a sepia-tinted glow. As she approaches, she thinks how she would love to freeze this moment, to lock the happiness she had felt in the square inside some giant vault and keep it with her forever. If only they could stay at home tonight. If only there was no party to go to, then maybe everything would be okay. Maybe they could be happy.

'Stella!'

He has seen her. He jumps up from the step and runs towards her. He is smiling; it's a wide, happy smile. Stella used to say, when they first met, that his smile was like the sun coming out. Now the smile just reinforces her guilt; it slices through the happiness she has carried with her from the square and cuts it into neat little pieces of despair.

'Where've you been?' he asks as he hugs her tightly. 'It's almost five o'clock you know?'

Stella opens her mouth to speak then changes her mind. Instead she folds into his embrace, once again wishing she could pause the moment, put off the evening, the wretched party . . .

'I'm off to get some food. Do you want anything?' He untangles himself from her arms and slaps his taut stomach, the loose fabric of his T-shirt billowing like a deflated hot-air balloon. 'You really should eat something. We'll be doing a lot of talking at the party so there might not be much chance to eat, and you know what Warren's like, it'll be all macrobiotic rabbit food. Shall I get you a bag of crisps?'

'No thanks, Ade, I'm fine—'

'Are you sure? You'll be starving come eight o'clock. I'll get you some chocolate. You can stick it in your bag and have it later, yeah?' He pulls her towards him and kisses her on the top of her head. He has put his expensive cologne on, the one she bought him for his last birthday. It smells like orange blossom. She breathes in the scent as he kisses her. It doesn't smell like Ade, it smells like someone else. Then she remembers why she bought it, why she wanted to smell it every day. As she blinks away the thought, he whispers into her ear. 'Thanks for doing this for me. It will all be worth it, I promise you. I love you.'

A pang of guilt flutters through her chest as he kisses her cheek. She is always letting him down, always blocking out the sun.

'Oh, I've booked a cab to Warren's,' he says as she walks away from him towards the steps to the flat. 'We don't want to be stuck on the tube at rush hour. It'll be here in an hour.' He smiles again, the unsure smile Stella recognizes. He's worried about her, she can tell. That's why he's hesitating. 'Right,' he says, clapping his hands together, like he's snapping away his concerns. 'I'm off to the shop; I'll let you go up and get ready.'

'Ready,' she repeats, trying her best to sound upbeat,

but it is a resigned acknowledgement that comes out of her mouth; the ready of the patient as she waits for the injection.

She stands on the step, watching him walk towards Dodo, the off-licence on Old Compton Street, and feels empty, like every last ounce of hope has drained away.

An hour earlier, she had been standing among thousands of people, watching their faces, feeling their excitement and wrapping herself up in the novelty of an ordinary July morning that had stopped so abruptly in its tracks. She could breathe, she could think more clearly than she had for years. The constant interruptions, the demands on her time had paused, like a frozen screen, and though she could still see them, still sense them, hanging in the blue-grey sky above Trafalgar Square, they were out of reach, floating like a lost balloon over Nelson's head.

As she watched her worries flickering and scrambling, desperately trying to free themselves and return to her, she realized that in their absence she had become some-thing else, something she had always railed against. As she had patiently waited for the announcement to be made, she had shrugged off years of carefully honed nonchalance and taken on the guise of a tourist – wide-eyed and excited just to be in her own city. The tourists who, with their vacant expressions and over-sized kagouls, form part of the daily landscape of Soho, are so set apart from her own pace of life and yet so much a feature of it. How many times has she found herself joining in with the chorus of disapproval at Leicester Square tube, tutting as some hapless soul with a camera slung around his neck stands blissfully unaware on the left side of the escalator?

But that is the unspoken rule of daily life in London, the one that tourists never seem to understand but one that is imprinted onto the psyche of those who live and work in this city of dreams and dirt – you never, ever, get in the way of a commuter.

After the announcement had been made, the crowd had remained; people were dancing and singing, hugging their neighbours and waving their crumpled flags. Stella had stumbled out of the square intending to head home but, buoyed by the excitement of the day, had only got as far as the National Gallery. She sat on the low wall outside the stately building and watched as London spread out before her. The lions in the square looked as triumphant as the crowd, their steel-grey defiant faces standing guard over the minute figures scurrying beneath. After a couple of hours, the crowd seemed to tire and began, slowly, to melt away. Stella sat motionless, watching as the jovial mood carried the swarms of people like a giant wave into the winding streets that connected Trafalgar Square to Haymarket, to the river, to Charing Cross and Leicester Square. But as Big Ben boomed out the hour of three, there were still clusters of people in and around the square. For them, the party had only just begun. Stella stood up, suddenly aware of the time and all too aware of the party she had to get ready for.

But there was still time, she had thought, as she walked towards the pretty white church of St Martin-in-the-Fields, there was still time to light a candle. She could never pass that church without taking a peek inside. It was so still and quiet, a little pocket of calm right in the centre of the city. It was busier than usual, she had thought, as she opened the glass inner door and walked towards the candles. There were people sitting in the pews, some with their hands clasped in prayer, others looking up at the ornate baroque ceiling, perhaps noting how its gold chandeliers and balcony seats looked rather overdressed against the plain, puritan-style altar and pews. Stella had always liked the decadence of that ceiling, it was fitting for a church on the edge of theatreland, and wasn't religion just another kind of theatre? A show where the actors come on and say their lines, singing here and there and raising their arms to Heaven?

No voices were raised above a whisper inside the cool, airy building, and a lone verger strolled up and down the aisle nodding and smiling at the visitors like a benign host. Stella picked up a tea-light from the box and clasped it in the palm of her hand. Deep beneath her feet lay the remains of Nell Gwynn, outside the window, London was celebrating in its brightest colours and loudest voices, but there in that moment was peace and clarity, and as Stella leaned forward to light the candle from the burning wick of another, she closed her eyes, offered up a silent prayer and hoped that someone would hear.

She had walked home along Charing Cross Road, the streets opening up like a paper street map, bending this way then that, taking her into their confidence, daring her to keep going, to take that left turn towards Cecil Court, to have a look at the little second-hand bookshop, the one where she had seen a faded copy of her favourite childhood book in the window. Stopping outside the shop, she saw that the book had been removed from the display and she stood for a moment looking at her reflection in the shop window while the memory of a great open space, a barley field and the smell of autumn evenings, flipped back and forth in her head, like the pages of a book being turned too fast. She closed her eyes, wrinkled her nose and willed the memory away, and as it fell she walked on.

On past the old map shop and the new-age crystal shop, then back onto Charing Cross Road, where she took her familiar route down the little side street to Chinatown, past the Chinese grocery store where boxes full of lychees and kumquats jostled for space alongside red and gold ceramic cats and over-sized woks. As she stepped onto Shaftesbury Avenue, she smiled at the long queue of tourists that was snaking its way round the front of the Lyric, the plucky ticket touts threading in and out like hyenas encircling a herd of wildebeest.

'Come on, ladies and gents, who do you think you're fooling? It's the last night tonight, there ain't no tickets left, I'm telling you. Now, I can save you fifty, sixty quid. Come on, mate, don't shake your head, it's the last night, you'll never get to see this play again, it ends here.'

But nothing ends here, thinks Stella as she stands outside the flat staring at the coffee drinkers sitting around the flimsy metal tables outside Bar Italia. Nothing ends, it just reinvents itself as something bigger, better and stronger. In the small northern town she left behind, everything stayed the same, day after day, year after year; the same faces, the same expressions, the same problems passed down from generation to generation. It was as though life was defined by its limitations and boundaries. Whereas Soho, well Soho is infinite isn't it? There is no final curtain here. She continues to stand on the step hoping that by not going inside, she might somehow prolong the spell that the morning has cast on her.

Tonight's party has been planned for weeks and Warren Craig, the ageing Nineties pop star whose career Ade is helping resurrect, has assured them that it will be full of people worth talking to, people who can help him and Stella forge ahead in their careers: music industry heavy-weights, A & R men – and they are always men – on the prowl for the next young, pretty girl who can carry a tune and earn them enough money to buy another villa in Puerto Banús. Stella will be expected to flatter their egos, to see past their fine-weave hair implants, their man boobs and sexist jokes. She will have to smile, to answer their questions but not talk too much, just stand there like a geisha while Warren flits in and out of the conversation, peppering the 'man talk' with a burst of song, followed by his inane commentary: 'Can you remember that one, guys? Not one of my biggest hits but it's the one closest to my heart. You could say that is the song where I found my voice.'

'Think of the contacts.' Ade's pleading voice rings in her head. He's become obsessed with contacts, networking, introductions. While all Stella wants is to be inside, hidden away from everything and everyone, safe under thick linen sheets.

Damn it, he's played Warren's new album on repeat for a week now. Every day and night, his whiny voice, his turgid lyrics, suffocating her as she wakes up and choking her into restless sleep. Warren has infected their lives like a rash ever since Ade got involved with him. And why is he involved with him? That's what she can't get her head around.

When she first met Ade, the only things that mattered to him were making good music and the respect of his jazz peers. The likes of Warren Craig, when they appeared on Saturday morning kid's TV, had been a source of mirth for him and Stella, the kind of music that was destroying this country (Ade's words just a year ago). But fast forward twelve months and Ade is sitting on the promise of a co-writer credit on Warren's next album and a wedge of cash if it all goes according to plan.

It doesn't matter that Warren, by his very presence, makes the room ridiculous. Every word he speaks – so gleefully picked up on by his grinning band of hangers-on

– drips with cliché and bombast. Last time she saw him, he called her Stella Bella, put his hand on her shoulder and, in a tone of voice she guessed was usually reserved for a small child, told her that if she worked really, really hard then she could have it all, just like him.

She shudders at the thought of his breath on her face as she fumbles in her bag, trying to locate her keys.

'In this life, Stella Bella,' he had purred into her ear as she sat bored out of her skull in an overpriced Japanese restaurant, 'there are winners and losers, and in our business you have to choose which you're gonna be. You have to work your arse off and be prepared to sacrifice everything for the dream. Do you believe in the dream, sweetheart, do you believe?'

She looks at the row of black rubbish bags on the pavement, crammed with the detritus of the last seven days. One of them has been torn and the contents are spilling out onto the street. She can see the corner of a pizza box jutting out of the hole and the glint of a ring-pull from last night's tin of ravioli. It's making her feel repulsed; she wants to scoop up the bags and move them away from here, dissociate herself from them and their contents. It feels like everyone in the street can see them, knows what's in them, can see right through her and her guilty secret.

As she stands here, she thinks back to the first time she saw this street. This was once all she ever wanted. To be twenty-seven years old and living an eternal cocktail hour in a place where it would be rude not to, hadn't that been the dream? Soho. Even the name sounds like a suggestion, like an invitation to do something deliciously decadent. Neon lights bleeding onto a rain-soaked street, a stolen glance from a beautiful face in the crowd, the first few bars of the best song she would never write. She thinks of promises and hope and a young girl with everything to live for.

She looks up and sees Ade walking back. The clock outside Bar Italia displays the time in green and red neon. Ten to five already. She hasn't got much time so this will have to be quick. If she can numb herself, create a bubble around her that neither Ade nor Warren can burst then maybe, just maybe, she can survive the night. As she pushes the thick metal door and trudges up the stairs towards the flat, she knows what she has to do.

Outside the flat, Ade sits on the step and savours the first drag of his hand-rolled cigarette. A few metres up the street the hands on the big oblong clock outside Bar Italia creep towards five o'clock. All is calm, inside and out. Ade loves this time of day, when the big retreat towards evening begins; and best of all it's Wednesday.

Ade likes Wednesday nights in Soho. While the crowds stay in and wait for Thursday and Friday, the conventional party nights, the residents come out to play. Out of their bedsits, studio flats and penthouses they crawl, taking advantage of the available tables in the restaurants, the empty seats at the theatre and the clubs free of rowdy hen parties. There is only a small pocket of opportunity to reclaim their territory, as by Thursday the hordes will be back. Wednesday evening is when Soho takes time out to catch breath before opening its doors once more.

Any other evening, Ade would be in the pub, ordering his first drink and looking around to see who was in. He looks up the street towards The Dog and Duck that stands like a glowing beacon on the corner of Frith and Bateman Streets. As he sits there, sweating in the last of the afternoon heat, he tries not to think of the ice-cold pint of lager he could be holding in his hand.

He sneaks another look at the clock. No, he can't. Tonight is too important to mess up.

Without thinking, he rolls another cigarette, using the step to lay out the paper before carefully spreading a neat line of tobacco across the middle. After years of practice, he has it down to a fine art. The ceremony and precision that go into creating a hand-rolled cigarette make the end result all the more satisfying. He's supposed to be cutting down but he needs something to calm his nerves, and anyway the nicotine will help keep the beer cravings at bay.

A pint would be really good right now though. But then he would need another to get the conversation flowing and have a bit of banter with whoever happened to be at the bar. If there was a good crowd in and the talk was to his liking, he would have a third and by the fourth he'd be settled in for the night, feet up, beer in hand while all around him Soho's finest crept out of the shadows. The war correspondent with the sunken eyes just back from the front line and straight onto the sauce, the scarily thin models en route to something more exciting at The Groucho, the endless stream of artists, musicians, writers and entrepreneurs trying to sell their ideas to whoever will listen. From aristocrats to junkies, it's why he loves Soho, and the crazier or more unhinged the punter the better as far as he is concerned. Pubs like The Dog and Duck, the Carlisle on Bateman Street and the infamous Coach & Horses on Greek Street attract people with a few stories to tell, people who don't have to hide behind a veneer of respectability.

You can be yourself, whatever that may be. People come here on the way to something else, to fame, to money, to notoriety, all the things that Ade covets. He believes in the people he meets and, more importantly, they seem to believe in him.

It's a world away from the pubs he knew as a teenager, sitting in those dreary caverns of gloom while the landlord and a trio of old soaks served up a banquet of bullshit laced with the sorrow of lost hope and abandoned dreams; the turgid, ever present spectre of real life. As far as Ade is concerned, real life doesn't exist here, he is hidden from it, tucked away in the heart of a maze that generations of dreamers have fashioned out of blood and tears and neon, and in this strange, half-lit world, people treat him like he is cool, like he matters.

The pub doors open again and a man steps out. Ade looks up and smiles.

'Seb,' he shouts, as he gets up from the step and walks towards the tall figure making its way up the street. 'Alright, mate,' he says, then stops as the man looks up and Ade realizes he has been mistaken.

'Sorry, pal, I thought you were someone else.' He smiles and pats him on the arm. The man gives him a suspicious look and hurries on.

Ade shakes his head. 'Idiot. Did he think I was going to mug him?'

He stands impotently in the middle of the street, watching as the man turns the corner onto Old Compton Street. After a few moments, he resumes his position on the step, quite relieved in a way that it hadn't been Seb because then there would have been no question of staying out of the pub.

They first met a couple of months ago when Seb breezed into The Dog and Duck one evening with a couple of work-mates. Ade eyed him up suspiciously at first, noting the public-school drawl, the blond good looks and the expensive suit which all marked him out as a bit of a tosser. However, later in the evening, Seb asked him for a light and they got talking about football (Ade was a QPR man, Seb supported Spurs) and women (Ade liked beautiful women, Seb worked in a glamour model agency). Oh, and Seb liked a drink. He was no lightweight when it came to sinking a few while putting the world to rights and he was generous too, always making sure he got his round in. This final piece of informa-tion had sealed the friendship for Ade. The 'tosser' became a 'good bloke' and just the kind of drinking buddy he required.

'Alright, Ade?'

He looks up and sees Caleb, the doorman of Ronnie

Scott's, waving to him from across the street. He is pacing outside the club with a clipboard tucked underneath his arm – the all-important guest list for tonight's show. Ade watches as he takes it out and holds it in his hands, running his finger down each name slowly then pausing and looking into the middle distance, trying to memorize the long list of VIPs, to distinguish the aficionados from the first-timers, the PAs from the CEOs.

Ade smirks. He's a funny one, that Caleb. What a guy to have on the door of a bloody jazz club. He's like a nervous wreck, pacing up and down like that, the muppet.

Drawing his attention away from the doorman are the big white letters on the hoarding above the club door. Lucy Mancini, B2B's new signing who has made the crossover from jazz to pop, is showcasing this week.

'Oy, Caleb,' he shouts.

The doorman, now completely engrossed in checking his list, gives a start and looks up wide-eyed in the direction of Ade's voice.

'Is Lucy Mancini sold out yet?'

'Yeah it is, mate, but I can get you in,' shouts Caleb, with a wink. 'I mean you're more or less staff. Shall I put you down for Friday?' He smiles widely at Ade and nods his head.

Ade grimaces. Caleb can be such a prick sometimes.

Staff? A pleb in other words, is that what he means? And what's he grinning like that for? Fuck him, if things turn out well tonight, it'll be Stella's name up there with a set that he's written and produced. Then we'll see who's 'staff'.

'I'll put you down then should I?' Caleb shouts over the street impatiently.

Despite Ade's irritation, the anger and bluster stay contained within him and the face he lifts up to Caleb is one of affability and matey bonhomie.

'Nice one, mate,' he shouts.

'Shall I put Stella down too?' Caleb's thin voice competes with the noisy engine of a black cab that has pulled up outside the club.

Ade pauses.

'Yeah, go on then. I'll try to get her out.'

'Sweet,' shouts Caleb, quickly busying himself with the three middle-aged women who are climbing out of the cab.

'Ladies, ladies, doors open at six, you're gonna have to wait,' he shrieks as he flips the pages of his clipboard. 'Now, I need your names.'

Ade laughs at the flustered doorman, throws his cigarette into the street and turns to go back inside.

'Stella,' he hollers as he reaches the top of the stairs. 'Come on, sweetheart, it's time we were leaving.'

Chapter 2

The municipal-looking building on the corner of Shaftesbury Avenue and Charing Cross Road is often mistaken for a multistorey car park by those not in the know. Its glass frontage bears no company logo, no colourful hoardings, indeed gives no clue at all as to what goes on within. Passersby can't see inside as the glass is blacked out, like those glossy sedans that speed shaded celebrities through the streets of Soho, away from the pursuing paparazzi and towards their destination of choice – lunch at The Ivy, shopping on Bond Street or home to their gated north London mansions.

Inside the building, the ground floor is just as drab and anonymous as the exterior and, in keeping with the motor theme of the facade, gives the impression of entering a very large and very empty car showroom. In the middle of this vast empty space is a black oblong reception desk behind which sits an unsmiling security guard complete with hat, uniform and badge.

The only colour in this beige desert comes from six small squares of laminated MDF that are tacked to the wall above the reception desk. In a dark blue hospital-style font they whisper apologetically the names of the asset management and accountancy firms that reside on the first and second floors.

Next to these, like a party guest who has misinterpreted the dress code, hangs another, more elaborate, company logo – a beautiful pastel drawing of a 1940s Varga girl, clad in a black negligee, looking coquettishly over one shoulder with blonde Veronica Lake hair pouring silkily across one eye. A foot is visible beneath her gown and her pink polished toes point towards a name in scarlet and black lettering: Honey Vision.

The artist responsible for this homage to bygone glamour sits in his office on the third floor watching the clock as its fingers creep towards five-thirty. There are half-drunk cups of coffee, assorted pens, pencils and loose coins cluttering the desk and an in tray overflowing with photographs of semi-naked women. The office door is wide open and on any given day there will be a steady stream of people trooping in and out. Some will be asking advice, others presenting their portfolios or looking for work. More often than not they will be after a cigarette or a freebie. It seems everyone wants a piece of Sebastian Bailey, Honey Vision's newly appointed Creative Director.

As the clock strikes the half hour, there is a rumble of movement along the corridor. The exodus has begun. Chairs are scraped away from desks, female voices call out plans for the evening, mobile phones burst into life with a medley of competing ringtones and stiletto heels click-clack towards the toilets for a communal powdering of noses.

Though his bag is packed and he has switched off his computer, Sebastian, or Seb as he prefers to be known, remains at his desk waiting for the last footsteps to die away. He picks up a set of proofs from a recent photo shoot that has just been returned for checking. The model in the top photograph stares out blankly towards the camera. To Seb's artistic eye, the image is about as sensual as a block of wood.

He pushes aside the photographs and looks at the painting on the wall opposite. It shows the outline of a faceless dark-haired woman in a long scarlet dress walking barefoot along a desolate beach holding a bundle of rags in her arms. At her feet, in the foreground of the painting, lies a blond-haired young man with an oxygen mask over his mouth drawing shapes in the sand with one finger.

In a daze, he picks up his mobile phone and, without thinking, presses redial. He waits for the voicemail to kick in but instead gets a robotic female voice informing him that she is sorry but the number is no longer available. He panics. This can't be happening. He tries again.

'I'm sorry,' says the voice.

And again.

'I'm sorry.'

The voice is cold, it is harsh, it is anything but sorry.

As he clicks his phone off, an altogether brighter voice interrupts his dark thoughts. 'Poker?' He looks up to see the broad grin and wild curly hair of Henry Walker, his best friend, who also happens to be the boss.

'Poker night this evening at The Union,' he says breezily. 'I've booked the room. I thought we might make it into a celebration, what with winning the bid and all.'

Henry edges further into the office and sits on the soft chair by the door.

Seb smiles. You would think it was Henry who had won the Olympic bid. Never mind London, it is the Henry Walker Games 2012.

'No serious money involved, just a bit of fun.' Henry grins, flashing his newly whitened teeth. 'What do you say, you up for it?'

'Sorry, H, no can do I'm afraid.' Seb's reply comes out a little too quick, but he is relieved that this time he has a genuine excuse for turning Henry down, though he has to admit the alternative is even less appealing. 'Dinner at Mum's,' he continues, trying to sound suitably crestfallen. 'It's been planned for an age. You know what she's like. She says I don't see enough of her as it is.'

Curling up in the chair, Henry folds his arms and lowers his bottom lip in an expression of mock sadness. 'But I wanted Sebastian to come and play tonight,' he whines.

Seb shakes his head. He has been to so many of Henry's 'evenings' he could write the script. There is always a different theme – poker just being the latest fad – but the people never change. Braying city boys and their vacuous girlfriends, double-barrelled aristos with hunting obsessions or terribly intense would-be poets who Henry steers towards Seb because 'he's into art, you know'. Tonight, it will be sports stars and people connected with the Olympic committee as Henry is determined to get a slice of the 2012 pie. Seb endures these gatherings by making small talk but after a few drinks he usually ends up insulting some Henrietta by rubbishing her Art History degree or asking her boyfriend how much of his bonus comes from dodgy dealings in underdeveloped countries. Then he has to make a hurried escape to avoid a punch up. Henry, though, has always made concessions for Seb's dislike of their old school friends. He views Seb as a bit of a novelty, a strange, artistic specimen he likes to show off. It has always been this way.

'Are you sure I can't twist your arm, maybe just one teeny weeny little drink before you head off to your mother's?' Henry looks at him with that puppy dog stare, the one that women seem to find so alluring.

'Honestly, Henry, as much as I'd love to, by the time I get out of here . . . and anyway you know what she's like. Another time, yeah?'

'Oh well, suit yourself,' says Henry, cheerily. 'But do give Lady Liz a big kiss from me won't you? How's she coping with her newfound freedom? Loving it, I'll bet. Has she settled into Knightsbridge okay?'

Seb is willing Henry to go. All he wants is a quick pint in The Dog and Duck to calm him down before the ordeal of dinner with his mother. He tries to hide his impatience. If Henry senses he is on edge he will start to fuss, ask questions and probably suggest tagging along with him to the pub and that is the last thing he needs.

'Oh yeah, she's loving it,' he replies brightly. 'She's in her element, just round the corner from Harrods. You know it's always been her Mecca.'

'I'll bet she still gets them to deliver her groceries in their big green vans even now they're virtually on her doorstep,' says Henry, shaking his head. 'God, we used to have some fun up at your house.'

He leans back into the chair, folds his hands across his stomach and stretches his long legs out in front of him, warming to his theme. 'Do you remember that time she had too many G and Ts and jumped into the swimming pool in her evening gown?'

Seb winces at the memory. It's funny how other people find his mother's behaviour endearing while he has always been mortified by it. Talk of her antics is making the prospect of dinner even less appealing.

'Yes, unfortunately I do remember,' he sighs. 'If I recall, we were expecting my Art teacher to arrive for supper and she greeted him at the door, dripping wet, with mascara running down her cheeks.' He shakes his head at the image.

'Priceless,' Henry laughs, wiping his eyes. 'I bet old Armstrong thought she was a piece of performance art. Crazy times, crazy times. I must pop in to see her sometime, take her out for dinner.' He stands up and walks towards the door.

'She'd like that,' says Seb, pretending to work by pressing the 'return' key on the switched-off computer.

'Excellent,' replies Henry. 'Anyway, I'd better be off. Cocktails to imbibe, wagers to win, deals to be done.' He pats the door frame. 'And if you leave your mother's in time, we'll be at the club until closing.'

Seb ignores this second invitation and smiles at his friend. 'Have a good evening, H. Win big or whatever it is they say.'

'You're hopeless, Mr Bailey,' says Henry, looking around the walls at the assorted artwork. 'But one day, my investment in you might just pay off.'

'Bye, H,' mutters Seb as he continues to fake-type.

'*Au revoir, mon ami*,' Henry calls as he disappears down the corridor blowing kisses.

It has been six months since Henry created this job for him and still he feels like he could fall apart any minute. Henry had come to his rescue again, just like when they were teenagers. He had swept in and picked him up, bought him an expensive suit and put him on a forty-grand salary, found him a flat to rent in Camden and filled his head with talk of opening an art gallery and displaying his work on the walls. 'This is it,' Henry had told him. 'This is your new start.'

Seb exhales deeply, leans back in his chair and stares up at the strip-lit ceiling. His creativity has deserted him and all he can cope with is the monotony of this job, of designing web layouts and Photoshopping the models' bad bits. He can't afford to let his mind wander, to entertain thoughts beyond the mundane nine-to-five of his existence, because that would only lead to thoughts of her, and if he lets those in he will start to fall and never stop.

In a small waiting room, three storeys high, Zoe Davis looks out onto a London sky that is changing from pale blue to pinky gold, and wonders, for the hundreth time, if they've forgotten about her.

She checks her watch. It is twenty to six. *'Wait here in this room,'* they said, *'and she will see you, Becky Woods will see you.'* So she has waited. She has watched the traffic stop and start on the street below, she has seen the morning delivery trucks bringing crates of beer and boxes of crisps to the Duke of Cambridge pub on the corner over there. She has walked down the corridor three times. The first time she stood for ten minutes at the reception desk but no one came, so she returned to the waiting room and saw the lunch hour come and go, watched as busy office workers queued up at Mario's café for takeaway sandwiches and bottles of water. The second time, she was told by the receptionist that Becky must be running late but to feel free to wait a bit longer. So she has sat in this room for the last hour, looking out of the window at the afternoon lull, the coffee run and the steady stream of assistants and PAs running out to grab giant polystyrene cups of strong hot coffee.

She turns away from the window as two women walk into the room. They are dressed in pastel-coloured velour tracksuits and huge furry boots. One of them, a tall, slim black girl with waist-length braided hair, walks over to the vending machine and starts feeding coins into the slot.

'Oh my days,' she says to her companion, as a packet of crisps and two bars of chocolate land with a thud at the bottom of the machine. 'John Cooper. I am shocked and stunned. Can you believe it, Leila?' She takes the food and walks over to the citrus-coloured sofa right in front of where Zoe is standing by the window. The other girl, a curvy redhead, follows her to the seat, her eyes wide. 'It's amazing, Kel, it's like a dream.'

The black girl opens her bag of crisps and offers one to her friend.

'No thanks,' says the girl, waving them away. 'I've got a bikini shoot on Friday so I'm off carbs for the week.'

The black girl laughs as she tucks into her crisps. 'I'm gonna need all the carbs I can get this week, I need my energy.'

'Yeah, but you're lucky, Kel,' says the redhead. 'You can eat what you want and not put on weight. I'd be as fat as a house if I ate like you.'

'Good genes I guess,' says the black girl as she licks her fingers and throws the empty crisp packet into the waste-paper basket right by Zoe's feet. 'Sorry, love, didn't see you there,' she says with a smile. Zoe goes to say it's okay but the girls have resumed their chat.

'So who's the photographer, do you know yet?' The red-head pulls her knees up to her chest and starts scrutinizing her nails.

'It's Ben,' says the black girl, rolling her eyes. 'I hope he don't give me grief. I just wish he'd get the message. I'm not interested and he weren't that hot in bed either.'

The other girl gives a shrill laugh. 'Yeah, well he's had most of us. Not me though, I'm too choosy and he looks like a weasel.'

'I don't give a shit, love,' says the black girl, shrugging her shoulders. 'It could be Saddam bloody Hussein photo-

30

graphing me for all I care. What matters is that I am going to be modelling John Cooper.'

The other girl shakes her head in wonder. 'It's amazing, Kel, it really is. I've been saving my arse off to buy that peekaboo dress of his and now you're going to be bloody paid to wear loads of them. But don't get me wrong, hon, I'm so proud of you.' She leans across the sofa and hugs her friend.

'Oh, bless you darling,' says Kel, as she gently shrugs away the embrace. 'So, what's the plan for tonight? Are we going to this Space launch at JoJo's or what? See, I've promised my friend Saul I'd try to pop into Boujis to see him – it's his twenty-first. I mean, you're quite welcome to come but there'll be a strict guest list and I don't know whether they'll be your type of people.'

Zoe stands by the window, trying to take it all in. John Cooper dresses, Boujis, Ben the photographer, carbs and bikini shoots. She feels self-conscious, like a scared eleven-year-old trapped in the upper-sixth common room with the cool girls. As the girls stand up to leave, she looks at them. They look polished and confident, everything a model should be. They will walk into their parties tonight with their heads held high. That was how Zoe used to feel in the clubs back home, like a queen gliding through her domain. Here, she just feels invisible.

She tells herself to calm down. She has an appointment with Becky Woods and the receptionist knows she is here. Becky is running late, that's all. It is fine, it is all going to be fine.

She walks over to the sofa that the girls have just vacated and puts her bag and the plastic wallet she has been carrying onto the seat beside her. She picks up the wallet and smiles. This is what she is here for. These are the photographs that will convince Becky Woods to give her a chance, to send her out on modelling jobs like those two girls. The photos may not be professional but they look great. It was so good of Dina to take them for her, and the black and white film just makes them look even better.

She puts the wallet back onto the coffee table and looks at her watch. Quarter to six. She will give it until six and then . . . then what? Back to the flat, an evening of mind-numbing television and a bowl of whatever Dina's been cooking.

The door opens and another young woman walks in. She is tall and slim with a strikingly beautiful face, sharp cheekbones, deep green eyes framed by thick curled lashes and a mane of baby-blonde hair tied back with a hairband. For a moment Zoe thinks it is another model until she sees the black bin bag that the girl is holding in her hand.

She walks across to the waste-paper basket on the far side of the room and empties the various crisp packets and squashed plastic coffee cups into the bag.

Zoe picks up a magazine from the pile on the table and pretends to read. To the girl emptying the bin, she wants to appear nonchalant, indifferent. The girl will not know that Zoe has read this particular copy four times today, that she can tell her everything she may wish to know about Victoria Beckham's diet, Brad Pitt's ankle injury and the drug Hell of an ex-*Big Brother* contestant. Yet when Zoe looks up, the girl doesn't look interested, she just looks tired and cross.

'It's closing now,' says the girl. Her accent is eastern European but she doesn't sound Polish like Dina. This voice has a sharp lilt to it that makes Zoe think of a Russian villain or a Bond girl. She imagines the girl saying the word 'vodka'. She giggles as the serious-faced girl stands at the door with her arms folded across her chest. 'The office will be locked in fifteen minutes; you should go now.'

Zoe smiles at her. 'I've got an appointment with Becky,' she says. 'The girl on reception said she was running late.'

'I think everyone is gone for the evening,' says the girl, tying the top of the bin bag.

'Gone,' says Zoe. 'Has Becky gone too?'

The girl shrugs. 'I don't know who you are talking about. I just come to clean up; my work starts when the office closes.'

'Then I'll wait till six,' says Zoe. 'Just in case.'

She hears the girl tut as she closes the door. Zoe wonders where she has come from, whether she has family here. She is so beautiful, what is she doing cleaning out bins? Zoe would love to be beautiful like that, effortlessly so – the girl had hardly a scrap of make-up on. She knows that she is not beautiful, that she never will be, but she is pretty and that is enough. To be beautiful is like winning the lottery, it's all down to chance and it doesn't necessarily bring you happiness. Yes, pretty is more than enough for Zoe. The magazine is still open on her knee and she pauses at the double-page photograph of the glamour model Anna B. She stares at the model's face, her arms, her legs, her stomach. Then she grabs her handbag, takes out a small, smudged mirror and starts to scrutinize her own face.

She gives the mirror a wipe with the back of her sleeve then puts it into the handbag. Closing the magazine, she picks up the plastic wallet from the arm of the sofa. With the image of Anna B's voluptuous body imprinted on her mind, she pulls out two sheets of A3 glossy paper and looks at the blurry images. She looks at the arms. Not too thin, but certainly not fat. Nice bit of definition at the top. The legs, curled around a thick wedge of fake fur rug, are short but the black and white film and the positioning of the rug create a sense of length; nicely trimmed bikini area, no embarrassing wisps of stray hair peeking out. Then, the main event, the secret weapon in every glamour model's artillery, the two things that can transform a girl's life. Zoe holds the photograph up to the light. She turns it this way then that, she squints, but whatever she does, however critically she looks at it, one fact remains, one glorious fact. Her breasts are big. They are very big. And big is what Becky wants. Big sells magazines, big opens doors and gets you into parties.

'Why won't she just come and see me?' Zoe exclaims as she jams the photographs back into the envelope and pulls her handbag over her shoulder. She takes a last look at her watch. It's six o'clock. Time has run out. First one in, last one out. She turns off the light, closes the door and makes her way down the silent, empty corridor.

Chapter 3

The lights have been switched off in the open plan office opposite Seb's and it seems like the right time to make a move. His mobile phone vibrates on the desk. He clicks to open the message and his heart sinks. It is just a text message from his mother. He shakes his head at the jumble of words in front of him. His mother's cocktail hour has been getting earlier and earlier since the divorce. As he reads the message, he can see her pouring herself another Martini as she squints over her ancient Nokia phone and begins to type:

> Dsling, dinks fr 7 supppr 8_30
> Claire in town so hve imvitd hr
> Hop you dnt mindd Mumm y X

Seb puts his head in his hands. Not Claire. His mother is one thing but an evening of his permanently pissed-off sister is just too much. He wonders what the occasion is. She hardly ever makes the trip up from her lair deep in the Gloucestershire countryside. The rare times she does brave the capital she is accompanied by her humourless husband Roger and Seb's nieces, affectionately known as the 'demon twins'.

He goes to reply then thinks better of it. He is in no rush. If he gets there in time for dinner at eight-thirty he will at least avoid an hour and a half of Claire bleating on about Daylesford organic chicken and Boden twinsets. He will still get the rest of it though. When she sees that he is relaxing, she will lean in towards him, put her head to one side and with her unique brand of condescension ask if he is still renting 'that little flat'. She will tell him how strange it is that he, just two years her junior, is not on the property ladder yet and how he should talk to Roger, the sage of the Cotswolds, who will happily give him some financial advice.

Sebastian will smile. He will pour his mother another glass of champagne, safe in the knowledge that he will not rise to his sister's venom but will remain perfectly oblivious. He has a trick he uses whenever Claire is

37

annoying him, which is often, and it involves summoning the memory of her getting her head stuck in the railings in Regents Park when she was ten years old. That image of her fat pug-like face, framed by a mass of tight black curly hair, screaming and hollering, is usually enough to let whatever bitter and twisted sentiments she wants to throw in his direction simply fall off him like oil from water. He will still be able to hear her voice droning on, but he will remain happily free in Regent's Park waiting for the park keeper to come and release her – the purple ball of fury.

Seb squeezes the skin in between his eyes. Tonight it won't be enough to deflect her rants with the Regents Park ploy. If he had known just a few hours earlier that Claire would be there he could have prepared himself, mentally. Now, his head is starting to throb at the thought of his sister's banal stream of 'Roger says . . .', his mother's suffocating attempts to sympathize with his 'situation' and the chip, chip chipping away at him, his life, his choices.

'Fuck it,' he says to the empty room. 'Fuck it, fuck it, fuck it!'

He pushes the chair back, picks up his bulky satchel and heads out of the door, locking it behind him.

Time for a drink.

He walks towards the lift, but before he gets there someone calls out.

'Excuse me.'

He turns to see a small figure coming towards him. As it draws near, he sees the heavy make-up, the lip gloss and high heels. One of the models? She is wearing a tight blue dress with a push-up bra, but she looks slightly awkward, like a little girl playing dress-up in her mother's clothes. Despite this, he smiles politely as she approaches.

'Can I help you?'

She brushes a hand through her short, spiky, cherry-red hair, pulls out a hairslide and secures it back into place with a heavy sigh.

'Do you know if Becky is still here?'

Seb goes to answer but she continues.

'I rang her last week to tell her I'd got some photographs done and her assistant – I can't remember her name, the one with the nose ring?'

'Callie,' says Seb.

'Yeah, Callie,' repeats Zoe. 'She booked me in for today at nine o'clock. It was definitely today, I wrote it down twice.' She opens her bag and Seb can see her hands are shaking as she pulls out a little pocket diary embossed with a stitched floral pattern of blue and gold thread.

'Here,' she says, pointing a finger at the small, scrawling handwriting, 'Wednesday the sixth of July – 9am, meet Becky at Honey Vision offices.'

She shuts the book and puts it back into her bag, then looks at him earnestly, as though he has the answer to all this.

'Look, I'm sorry, er, what is your name?'

'It's Zoe.'

'Zoe. Hi, I'm Seb. I'm the Creative Director here. Basically, I deal with web layouts and logos and brochures and all that boring stuff. I'm afraid I'm not the best person to help you. The booking of models and Becky's diary, and what have you, is beyond me.' He laughs, but she looks like she is close to tears, so he continues in a gentle voice. 'I know that Becky is a very busy lady and if she forgot her appointment with you there will be a good reason for it, I'm sure. It won't be anything personal.'

He smiles at her and she nods her head. She looks vulnerable, not like the other models in this place. The Honey Vision machine would eat her for breakfast. The models Becky deals with are tough, streetwise women. They know how to deal with leery photographers, some of them rather enjoy it, and then there is the side work that Becky never admits to but everyone is aware of – the 'light' escort jobs the girls undertake for Becky's banker friends. Before he started working at Honey Vision, he had never encountered such ambition, such merciless desire for fame. The girl standing in front of him has all the right assets but she just seems too innocent for all this, too nice.

'The thing is,' she says, as Seb impatiently taps his hand against his thigh, 'even though I haven't had much experience of big-time modelling, I'm a really hard worker. It's so frustrating; I just want Becky to see me, see my photos. God, what a waste of a day.'

Seb is growing more impatient; he really needs to get out of here. 'Listen, Zoe,' he says, 'the best thing to do is to give Becky a call in the morning. See if you can rearrange the meeting. She's obviously gone home for the evening; there's no point you hanging around here any longer.'

He smiles politely and goes to walk away but Zoe is not going anywhere. Her eyes well up with tears. She blinks and a tear escapes and trickles down her cheek, smearing her make-up and leaving behind a thin orange streak. She is a pretty girl, thinks Seb, but she would be a whole lot prettier if she toned down the make-up. She reminds him of a waxwork dummy and in his increasingly agitated state, the make-up, the tears and the raw desperation are making him feel claustrophobic. He has to get out.

'Zoe, I'm sorry to be abrupt, but I really have to get on,' he says, looking at his watch to emphasize his haste. 'I've got a bit more work to do in the office,' he lies. The last thing he needs is to drag this conversation out any further by taking the lift with her. 'Look it's not worth getting yourself so upset about. All you have to do is call and rearrange the meeting. Now, I must go. Have a good evening,' he says, and turns back towards the office.

'Wait,' she calls after him. 'Can I ask you a big favour?'

He turns to see her standing with a folder of some sort in her hands. She is holding it towards him.

'Can you give these to Becky?' She pushes the plastic wallet into his hands.

'What?' Seb holds the wallet between his finger and thumb like it's a ticking parcel.

'I just thought you could put them on her desk before you leave tonight,' she says, her voice suddenly sounding brighter. 'If she sees the photographs, I know she will call me.'

Seb could really do without getting involved in this. He goes to hand the photographs back to her. 'Listen, Zoe, it's not up to me to . . .'

'Please.' She wipes her eyes and smiles at him. Christ, he needs a drink.

'Oh, alright then,' he relents. 'I'll put them on her desk. Now, go on, surely you have somewhere to be, a home to go to, a life.'

She glares at him then looks down at her feet. Now he feels bad.

'Sorry,' he says. 'I didn't mean to be harsh, it's just been a long day and I've got a load of work to finish off tonight.'

She looks up at him and nods her head. Her vulnerability has gone; she seems older, stronger, all of a sudden.

'Thank you for doing this for me,' she says. 'I really appreciate it. And just so you know, I have got a life, a very busy life, like you. I just happen to think that people should honour their appointments, that's all.'

She turns and walks towards the lift. Seb looks down at the plastic wallet he is holding in his hand. Becky's office will be locked now; he will give her them tomorrow. Right now he has a more important appointment with a large glass of red. As he hears the lift doors click shut, he tucks the photographs into his bag and finally makes his way out.

Stella sits on the bed while Ade stands looking out of the window.

He has been there for the last twenty minutes. Ten of

these were spent supervising her as she flicked through the contents of her clothes rail. She had been trying to find something that would make the blue sequined dress he is insisting she wear look less tarty and more vintage. She had dragged out a battered black leather biker jacket, one of her charity shop finds, hoping that, underneath it, the dress might just look ironic. She went as far as trying on her scuffed biker boots instead of the high heels, but Ade vetoed them.

'Jesus wept, Stel,' he shrieked. 'What are you trying to do to me? The jacket's bad enough and you're taking it off as soon as we get to Warren's.'

'Ade, why are you making such a fuss? You never usually complain about what I'm wearing.' She had made a point of noisily flinging the boots onto the floor.

'Trust me, Stella,' he said, placing his hands onto her shoulders. 'If we get it right tonight, it could change our lives. Everything has to be perfect, including you.'

Now she is ready she looks at Ade and wonders why he bothers with all this. They have been to so many of these parties and each one he thinks is going to be the one that changes their lives. It never is. Sod it, she thinks, so she will have to take the jacket off when she gets there, so what. Is that the worst he can do? Inside she is angry with him for making her go to the party, angry for telling her what to wear, but just outside this ball of anger is a thin film of calm that cannot be penetrated, like a protective filter between the real Stella and the contained, Zen-like Stella that sits here now.

An hour ago, she had been far from calm. While Ade had smoked his cigarette outside, she had run up the stairs like a mad woman, grabbed a bag of food from the cupboard under the sink – her emergency provisions – and locked herself in the bathroom with it. Then, sitting on the edge of the bath, she had emptied the contents of the bag onto the floor and launched herself at the food.

Ripping open a gold foil wrapper, she had crammed a gooey, caramel-filled chocolate into her mouth. As the sugar rushed to her brain, she felt an almighty shot of adrenalin coursing through her body. She was floating on air as she made her way through three packets of crisps, a pre-packed chicken sandwich, three cheese and onion pasties and a huge pot of spicy pasta salad, shovelling it into her mouth with her hands. In between mouthfuls, she took big gulps of bottled mineral water to make the journey back up less traumatic. When the food was finished, a familiar feeling of panic washed over her like an icy chill. Why had she done it? She was supposed to be dealing with it, this habit, but it just won't go away. It has become a part of her daily routine, as normal to her as brushing her teeth.

The first time it happened was at university, at a formal dinner of all things. She got carried away that night and committed the cardinal sin of straying from her strict 600-calories-a-day regimen. For the first time in a year, she managed to make her way through a three-course meal. Soup to start, nice and healthy; she knew where she was with soup. There was no danger, it was just liquid. But then came the main course, a rich chicken dish drenched in cream. Cream. Even without consulting her trusty calorie-counter book, she knew that the cream alone posed a 500-calorie, fat laden threat to her rigidly controlled eating plan. Accompanying the chicken was a large helping of dauphinoise potatoes, crisp and tempting and oozing with calorific goo.

But it was pudding that really tipped her over the edge. She had been starving herself for over a year. It was a kind of self-imposed penance, a way to control all the things in her life that were chaotic and unfamiliar, a way to deal with the pain that gnawed into her every minute of every day. And not once, not once in her long year of monotonous restraint, had she ever succumbed to something as unashamedly filthy as a Mississippi mud pie with clotted cream. But that night, she really let herself go. She chatted to the other girls at the table, watching as they happily tucked into their food without a care. For a few hours she became one of them, relaxed and at ease. After all, food was just fuel, not something to get so obsessed over.

It was after the meal that the guilty voice started making its demands.

What have you done, Stella?

She felt so full she could hardly move.

You couldn't be strong enough, could you?

The voice was loud and insistent and as she sat there trying to listen to the other girls, trying to join in and laugh at their jokes, trying to ignore the heavy, bloated feeling in her stomach, the voice inside got louder and louder until she felt like her head was going to explode.

There was only one thing for it. She ran to the loo and regurgitated the whole lot. And the surprising thing was, it felt wonderful. All the pleasure of eating and none of the guilt; it was like discovering the meaning of life. Dieting made her miserable and neurotic, but bingeing gave her a high like nothing she had ever experienced before. It was better than drink, better than drugs. Better than sex and all the complications that came with it. But she knew what she was doing. This wasn't going to become a habit, of course not. It would just be an occasional thing, when she felt like giving herself a treat. It would be her guilty secret.

Now six years later, the guilty secret is taking over her life.

A car toots its horn outside and Ade, who has been nervy and on edge since he came back, grabs her by the arm. 'Come on, taxi's here. Let's go.'

He ushers her to the door, grabbing his cigarette papers, lighter and tatty old wallet from the table. The wallet is crammed with the business cards he persuaded Seb to design, in return for a couple of pints and forty Marlboro Lights. 'I'll settle up with you when *Soho Morning*'s number one, mate,' he had assured him.

The result was a simple but beautiful line drawing of Frith Street with a hint of red for the neon lights of Bar Italia. In the foreground, a dark-suited figure strides purposefully across the street carrying a music case on which is written, in the same white lettering as a jazz club billboard: 'Adrian Ward – Jazz Saxophonist/Music Producer/Songwriter'.

Seb tried to persuade Ade to drop one of these titles, thinking it looked and sounded a bit cluttered, but Ade was happy to leave it as it was. 'Says it all, mate, says it all,' he enthused when Seb presented the finished cards at the bar of The Dog and Duck. 'A man of many talents, that's me. Now, mate, what you drinking?'

'Stella, come on, we don't want to be late,' he says as she struggles to get the key into the stiff door lock.

'This lock needs changing, Ade, we'll have to ring the landlord,' she says wearily. When she finally gets it locked, she yanks the key out then falls backward into him. He catches her with one arm and whispers into her ear.

'Come on then, gorgeous, let's go and get ourselves a record deal.'

She lets him run on ahead to stall the taxi while she slowly walks down the stairs, one step at a time, trying to delay the inevitable. On the wall at the foot of the stairs stand a row of numbered postboxes, one for each of the flats in their building. Ade and Stella's looks to be full of junk mail but as she reaches the bottom she stops to have a look anyway.

As she opens the wooden flap of the box and pulls out a red 'final reminder' envelope, her mobile phone vibrates inside her jacket pocket. It's a text message. She presses the green button, reads it, and in that moment the world becomes another world. Ade, Warren Craig, the unpaid bill in her hand, all fall away as she reads the words. She feels her cheeks redden. The message is brief:

Hello, stranger. Caity said you were living in Soho.

Wondered if you were about. I'm in Charlotte Street Hotel

if you fancy catching up. Paula x

She's back.

The cab toots its horn and someone calls her name. In a daze, she walks to the front door and opens it to the noise and heat of Frith Street. She looks out onto the street and for a microsecond she is standing in a large expanse of garden bathed in golden sunlight. She blinks into the sun and suddenly all is street again. Standing on the top step, she shakes her head at Ade who is leaning out of the passenger side of the cab looking agitated.

'It's the bank,' she shouts, pointing at her phone.

'Stella, surely it can wait. This guy's got his meter running.' Ade is sweating and he loosens the collar on his close-fitting white shirt.

She walks down the steps and leans into the window of the cab. 'Apparently someone's tried to access my account,' she tells him, trying her best to sound pained. 'The bank says if I don't sort it out now they could empty the whole lot.' It sounds ridiculously far-fetched and she tries not to look him in the eye in case he can tell she is lying. Instead, she looks down at her phone. 'I just have to call this number and cancel my card but it might take a while. You go ahead and I'll follow on.'

This is enough for Ade. Anything to do with money is deadly serious. 'Jesus, Stella, I told you not to use that cashpoint on Dean Street. Fella in the pub got his card cloned after using it the other week.'

The cab driver shakes his head knowingly. 'It's those bloody Albanians. They want rounding up, the lot of 'em,' he spits.

'Too true, mate, too true,' agrees Ade. 'Now listen, Stella, you call the bank and I'll see you within the hour at Warren's.'

The taxi begins to pull away and he shouts out of the window: 'You've got the address, haven't you. It's . . .'

But Stella is already running up the steps back to the flat. Back towards Paula and glorious summer days and the light of a faraway place she has only ever returned to in her sleep. As the door slams behind her she feels something shift and even though she cannot allow herself to contemplate what all this means, she knows that something is ending and something beyond her control is about to begin.

Chapter 4

Zoe stands in the lift, twirling round and pouting at herself in the mirror. She pushes up her bra and squeezes her breasts together.

'Bloody Becky Woods, what does she know anyway?'

The lift reaches the ground floor with a ping and as the doors slide open, Zoe is still striking poses, leaning towards the mirror and wriggling her bum.

'Hey, gorgeous, whatcha doin' to me?'

She turns to see a stocky man with spiky black hair standing by the lift door. He is wearing a shiny grey suit and mirrored sunglasses.

She steps out of the lift and giggles. 'Cheeky! Are you going up?'

He shakes his head as the lift doors shut with a click.

'Now, where do I know you from?' His voice is deep and husky, cockney with a weird hint of LA. 'Don't tell me, you're one of them Honey Vision models, ain't ya?'

He laughs, revealing a sparkling ruby stud on his front tooth.

Zoe goes to say no, but then stops herself. If he thinks she's a model, why disappoint him?

'Er, yes I am, actually,' she replies.

'I knew it,' he says. 'Have you heard of Absolute PR?'

Zoe shakes her head.

'Well,' he goes on, 'we do a lot of work for Honey Vision – corporate entertainment, that sort of thing.'

'That's nice,' says Zoe. She walks towards the revolving exit doors. The man follows.

'Wait a minute, sweetheart,' he says, removing his sunglasses. 'Sorry, what did you say your name was?'

'It's Zoe.'

'I'm Jules.'

She smiles politely as she pushes through the doors and steps out into a packed, early evening Shaftesbury Avenue. The pavement is filled with people going home from work, running to catch buses, queuing up at the cashpoints, all with the same expression, the look of resignation at the long journey that lies ahead of them:

standing wedged into a stranger's armpit on some clammy tube or bus, then a long walk home to eat a hurried TV dinner before collapsing into bed ready to do it all over again the next day.

'Zoe!'

Jules tails her through the doors, shouting to make his voice heard above the traffic noise.

'Zoe, babe,' he calls after her. 'These parties I organize. They're big-time, you know, full-on glamorous affairs.'

He catches up with her and stands so close she can smell the cigarettes on his breath.

Zoe isn't listening. She is wondering if Seb has put the photographs on Becky's desk. He had seemed a bit vacant. She starts to worry. What if he forgets, what if he loses them; they were her only set. People are bumping into them as they stand on the busy street. Jules takes her by the arm and leads her round the side of the building.

'There, that's a bit quieter,' he says.

They stand in the little bit of no-man's-land between the back of the office and the first of the Chinese restaurants. It is quiet if not exactly fragrant. From the smell of it, this is where the leftover lunchtime 'All You Can Eat' sweet and sour pork balls end up, congealing amongst the prawn shells and rancid fish sauce.

'Oh God, that stinks.' Zoe screws up her nose. 'I hate Chinese food.'

'Sorry, babe, I won't keep you long,' he says, breathlessly. 'It's just I couldn't hear myself speak back there. Listen, what I'm trying to say is that I might be able to put some work your way if you're interested. You'd be doing me a huge favour. See, I got this big party tonight, it's a birthday bash for Dan Williams.'

He folds his arms and grins, waiting for her reaction.

'What, *the* Dan Williams, the footballer?'

'The very same,' replies Jules. 'When Dan's in town, he gives me a call and asks me to make his party fabulous.'

'How do you do that?'

'I organize the venue and supply the entertainment.' He says the last word slowly, with a smirk. 'And that's where you girls come in. You know Anna B?'

'Of course I do,' replies Zoe. She stands back and steps into a slimy pool of oil. 'Yuk, what was that?'

'Sorry, darlin', that was my fault. Come and sit over here while I tell you some more.'

He walks over to the red and gold pagoda by the Chinese grocery shops and sits down on the step. Zoe follows and stands scraping her shoe on the dragon's mouth.

'So, anyway,' says Jules, standing beside her, 'Anna B. You like her?'

'I'd like her career,' says Zoe. 'She's got her own TV show now on Channel 5. Have you seen it?'

Jules nods. 'Anna B is one of my success stories,' he says. 'She started off doing my parties. Nuff said, eh?' He laughs huskily.

'So what would I have to do?' she asks, sitting down next to him.

'Have a good time, drink some champagne and look gorgeous, sweetheart. There's nothing to it. Well, there's a hundred quid in it if you're up for it.'

'Are you serious? And there's nothing dodgy about it?'

'Dodgy, pah.' He swipes his hand through the air. 'This is serious business, my love, I ain't got time to fool around. If you're up for it, great, if not I'll find someone else. It's no big deal.'

Zoe looks at him. He looks cool, self-assured. She would be mad to let this opportunity pass her by. She thinks about those girls going off to Boujis and that comment Seb made. 'Haven't you got somewhere to be?' Well, no, she hasn't. So, it's either a night drinking champagne with Dan Williams or sitting watching TV with Dina.

'Okay, I'll do it,' she says. 'Now, where's the party?'

He stands up and reaches into his inside pocket. He takes out a piece of paper and a red felt-tip pen, then, resting it on the palm of his hand, he scribbles something down and hands it to her.

'There's no name,' she says. 'What's the club called? I'll never find it.'

Jules is looking towards Chinatown as though something of extreme importance is happening up there.

'It's a private venue, big flash apartment, belongs to a mate of mine.' He puts his wallet back into his pocket.

'Oh, okay. Sounds cool. And it's on Tottenham Court Road, yeah?'

'That's right, darlin'.'

'Okay,' she says. 'What time should I get there?'

'Turn up for seven-thirty,' he says, clicking his phone shut with a flick of his wrist. 'Laters.' He laughs his throaty laugh and turns to walk off through Chinatown.

'Wait a sec,' Zoe calls after him. 'What should I wear?'

'You just make sure you look the dog's bollocks, yeah. Wear something that shows off those fine bristols of yours.'

He gives a salute as he strides off into the queue of tourists waiting for the early bird specials outside the Golden Dragon restaurant.

Zoe waves towards his departing figure. Then, clutching the piece of paper in her hand, she walks home.

Seb has used the back stairs to make his getaway. He isn't going to risk another encounter with Zoe. Closing the fire door behind him, he takes a deep breath and inhales the distinctive smell of Chinatown. Stepping carefully over the cardboard boxes and rotten vegetables, he heads for the narrow passage that will lead him back onto Shaftesbury Avenue.

But as he turns the corner, he sees her standing at the far end of the passage talking to a man.

What the Hell is she still doing there?

Luckily Zoe doesn't see him, so he turns on his heels and speed-walks down Gerrard Street.

Crowds of tourists jostle him as he strides along the centre of the street. Pulling his bag over his shoulder, he walks through the past five days.

The previous Saturday, July the second, would have been her thirtieth birthday, and he had spent it standing in Hyde Park with Henry watching the Live 8 concert. It was another of Henry's attempts to cheer him up, but instead of helping to forget, it just brought back more memories. It made him think back to the time he had met her in Hyde Park for a picnic, when they had sat by the lido and he had sketched her. There was plenty of time: a long lazy Saturday stretched out ahead of them and the sight of her reclining on an old tartan rug, soaking up the sun, had made him pick up his pencil and start to draw her, to take in her profile. It was the best piece of line drawing he had done since college, pure and composed yet full of life, full of her life. The way her expression changed from minute to minute, the wrinkled nose when she caught his eye and giggled, the calm, serene half-smile when she regained her composure and settled back into the pose. It was all there in that drawing, everything she was that day and everything she would become, contained in a simple pencil sketch. She said she had never felt so happy, sitting there looking out over the Serpentine, and as he drank in every move-ment, every breath, he knew she was right. It was the ultimate happiness. The kind of day you look back on years later and berate yourself for letting it pass so indifferently. Just a day in the park with a sketchbook. Now it was, and always will be, his last memory of happiness, of feeling part of someone else, of feeling still inside.

In comparison, the return to Hyde Park one year on proved just too much to take and he left Henry dancing wildly to Madonna while he headed home to Camden.

Camden via Soho and The Dog and Duck, and when last orders were called and the four bottles of wine failed to obliterate her face from his mind, he had walked to Chinatown to find the drinking den that Ade from the pub had told him about. The one he is walking past now. The one that by day looks like a harmless chop-suey house with tourists standing outside reading the 'specials' board, oblivious to what lies deep in its bowels. He had woken up at dawn in an absinthe-induced haze, slumped over a grimy, drink-splattered table with no wallet and a pounding head. All those tourists standing gawping at the menus, they would never know what goes on in those places. To them Chinatown is fun and light and frivolous but Gerrard Street in the early hours is the bastard offspring of its daytime persona. It is a secret society with its own unique code of ethics and only true Soho night owls will ever know its darkest corners.

Henry does not know about the binge drinking. He thinks Seb kicked all that into touch long ago. They had gone their separate ways after school and while Henry wanted to build a business empire, all Seb wanted to do was draw. After he graduated from the Royal College of Art, he had rejected offers of help from his parents, got a job waiting tables at a Belgian restaurant in Covent Garden and spent his days painting in a cramped studio flat in Stockwell. He had freedom and the time to concentrate on his painting like never before; it was Heaven. But in the space of a few years, he had let it all go.

When he met her, he wanted to spend every spare minute with her. His paintings remained unfinished, but it didn't matter, she gave him all he needed. He knew it was foolish of him, but she was like some wonderful drug, one that he couldn't get enough of. When he was with her, he was sated and fulfilled, but those empty nights when she had to go home, he would sit in the flat staring at the blank pieces of paper on his drawing table, urging himself to do something. But it was no use; for two years, he didn't draw a thing. It was like all his energy was spent just being with this woman, just loving her.

It was a few weeks after it happened that he started drinking heavily. One night in the pub he met an old eccentric called Billy who regaled him with stories of his youth. He had been an artist like Seb, hung out at the Chelsea Arts Club until they barred him. One night, after drinking the pub dry, he had allowed Billy to bring him home. Waving a pencil in his face, the old man had implored him to 'draw it while it's raw, it's the only way you'll get over this. Trust me, son, you gotta paint the bitch out of your system.' To Seb's inebriated mind, this was the advice of the gods and Billy's voice rang out like an oracle from every corner as Seb picked up his pencil. While the old man sized up Seb's belongings, his semi-conscious host lay on the ground, coughing and wheezing and drawing himself into oblivion. The last he saw of Billy was an outstretched hand holding an old gas mask towards him.

'That'll stop yer cough, lad.'

Seb shudders at the memory as Chinatown becomes Wardour Street. He takes a sharp right and is met by a mass of red-faced people waving England flags and singing the national anthem. The party that began in Trafalgar Square this morning has spilled over into Soho. He pushes through until he reaches the relative calm of Shaftesbury Avenue. Standing on the edge of the kerb, he weighs up his options. To his left, the short walk to Piccadilly Circus tube station and the three-stop journey to his mother's flat in Knightsbridge, in front of him the neon lights of Soho and liquid oblivion.

It isn't a question of choice; his feet are leading the way. He looks straight ahead as he marches on; his head feels light, his heart pumps with adrenalin, a screech of brakes as he steps out into the road barely penetrates his trance. A beeping car horn and a muffled expletive fizzle out like spent bullets over his head as he reaches the promised land of Frith Street. As it opens up before him, the road elongates, teasing him, making him sweat for his prize.

This, the quiet end of Frith Street, usually deserted on

a Wednesday night, is alive with lights and noise and activity, and now from the direction of Cambridge Circus comes another bunch of flag-waving revellers. There are a dozen or more of them, walking in a broad group, taking up most of the pavement and the road.

He tries to get past but only manages to tangle himself up in their hot, cheerful bodies. One of them grabs his arm and starts to dance with him.

'Makes you proud to be a Londoner, mate, don't it?' The man thumps him on the back and grins, showing a set of sharp, tobacco-stained teeth with breath to match.

'Yes,' replies Seb, smiling politely. 'It's wonderful news.'

He disentangles himself from the man and crosses over to the other side of the street. His hands are shaking.

What's the matter with me?

It is the laughter, the dancing, the ordinariness of the revellers. It has left him feeling uneasy. They were not meant to be there. Now he is seeing her face, he is feeling the softness of her skin next to his, he is hearing her say, *'I love you,'* he is thinking about that phone call, everything that was left unsaid, and he has to get it out of his head right now.

All he needs is a big glass of deep red liquid to numb his mind and take the thoughts away and all he can feel is the complete absence of it in his bloodstream.

He tells himself it will be just one drink, as the lights of The Dog and Duck shine into his eyes like a probe. There will be no Chinatown tonight, just a glass of wine then supper with his mother and Claire. This is going to be a normal night. He can do this, he really can.

As he reaches the door of the pub he puts on his confident 'Sebastian Bailey' face. That's who they'll be expecting tonight.

Chapter 5

Back in the flat, Stella lies on the unmade futon and stares up at the ceiling. Her breathing is shallow, her eyes wide. The neon sign of Ronnie Scott's is casting squiggly red shapes on the ceiling, and as the sun gets lower, the room fills with a strange straw-coloured light. It reminds Stella of something, something she can't quite place, a memory of some pastoral scene, a field at half-light, the sound of swallows flying in and out of a barn . . . It is one of those momentary memories that spring up on her from time to time, have done since she was a child, and she has convinced herself they must be a glimpse into a past life, so swiftly do they come and go, like a calm sea, its waves coming in and out, in and out.

'Paula,' she whispers, still not quite able to believe that she is still here in the flat, that she is not in a taxi on her way to Warren Craig's house. Suddenly she realizes that, in her excitement, she hasn't replied to the text. She reaches for her handbag, takes out her mobile phone and opens the message. She stares at it unblinkingly, trying to think of a reply. It has to be light and she cannot seem overly excited. As always with Paula, she has to appear beyond all that. She begins:

Hello, Paula. What a nice surprise.

She reads it aloud, analysing the tone, wondering how Paula might interpret it, then removes the word 'nice', remembering that Paula always hated that word. 'Nice,' she would snort when she came up against it. 'What does it even mean? It's such a non-committal bloody excuse of a word.' After deleting it, Stella continues with the rest of her reply:

I'd love to come and meet you, shall we say

She looks at her watch. It is just coming up to 6:30 p.m. She will have to get changed and take off this stupid red lipstick. Oh, and she could do with having a shower, she has been so rushed by Ade she hasn't even had a wash. No, I'll have a bath, she thinks as she types in:

7:30pm? Stella x

She gets up from the bed and takes her dressing gown from the back of the door. Tonight deserves the right kind of preparation. It needs more than a thin trickle from the sorry excuse for a shower to commemorate it. She goes into the bathroom and turns on the light. Not that it makes much difference. The bathroom is dark. The walls are painted a deep brown and the only, tiny, window looks out onto a brick wall – the back of the Prince Edward Theatre. If you open the window you can hear the bitchy gossip of the cast members as they huddle outside for a cigarette break. Tonight, Stella will keep it shut despite the heat. She wants to hide in the silence, declutter her mind and think about what she wants to say to Paula.

She places her mobile phone on the top of the little wicker laundry basket that stands next to the sink, then turns on the taps and pours a glug of vanilla-scented oil under the running water. Candles. She needs candles for this. She unzips her toiletry bag and pulls out two white tea lights – not scented, just bog-standard, but they will do – then locates a lighter from Ade's stash on top of the fridge. After several attempts, she manages to get the ghost of a flame from it, enough to light the candles that she places on the side of the bath.

She can work things out in the bath. She likes to call it her 'think tank'. It is here that she has her brightest ideas, here that she finds solutions to problems that just minutes ago seemed insurmountable. She could write her life history just by looking back on her baths. There are the sad ones full of snot and tears and foam; there are the exhausted ones, the kind that go on for hours and end with her sitting in tepid water because she hasn't the energy to peel herself out; and then there are the pampering ones where the water disappears in a cloud of pastel-coloured bath bombs and expensive depilatory creams.

Oh and, whatever the weather, the bath has to be hot, really hot. She can definitely relate to Blanche DuBois on that score. If the shower is a three-minute ad break, full of bluster and shocks to the system then, for Stella at least, the bath is a three-hour Sunday evening melodrama, full of highs and lows.

Why, even her first taste of London had come through an immersion in water. When she was six, she, her mother and Caitlin had travelled down to London to visit their father who was working as an economics correspondent at the BBC. They had spent the day in Hyde Park and Stella had been mesmerized by a wedge of driftwood floating on the surface of the Serpentine. She thought it looked like a raft and wondered if she could reach it in one leap. She soon found out when she landed with a splash into the dirty, brown water. Her poor father had waded in wearing his expensive suit and pulled her out. The two of them had to walk the length of Hyde Park covered in duck shit and algae, trying to find the exit, while their mother and Caitlin stayed three steps behind, trying not to laugh. Stella has often thought about that incident since moving to London and wondered whether having such a baptism has connected her to the city and its lifeblood forever.

What with the banging and crashing, the screams and shouts outside her window, sleep is a rarity round here. Stella never gets the chance to dream. The closest thing she gets to a dreamlike state is lying in the bath, floating in that liquid space between this world and the next. She loves the silence that comes when she puts her head beneath the surface to wash her hair, the water lapping around her like waves as she lies there like an ancient fossilized creature. There is something primordial about bathing, cleansing the body and the soul, starting afresh. She often wonders if this is what death would feel like: the body disappearing into warmth and weightlessness, the water claiming back one of its own.

Tonight's bath will be her first since the 'incident' last month, the thing she never speaks of, her 'mad Ophelia moment' as it has come to be known in the dark recesses of her memory. Ade was at a gig and she had spent the evening working her way through three carrier bags of junk food. It had been a particularly bad day at work. A woman she had been at university with had come into reception. A marketing manager, she was there to meet Stella's boss. Stella had wanted to crawl underneath the desk and hide but instead she had to smile and ask her if she wanted a coffee. The woman had looked at her pityingly, like she was a joke, a failure, a washed-up receptionist with no prospects.

The only way to make herself feel better was to comfort-eat, and as soon as she got home she had crammed the food down her throat so fast she had forgotten the golden rule: you always drink enough water to bring it all back up. She had stumbled to the toilet and put her fingers down her throat but the familiar rise of substance in her windpipe didn't happen. She had started to panic. There was no way she could leave a family-size pizza, six bags of crisps and three doughnuts in her stomach. That was thousands and thousands of calories and fat and sugar and God knows what.

Her heart was racing as she started to contort herself into all sorts of positions, stretching her arms up to the sky, touching her toes, anything to get the food to budge. She had shoved her fingers down her throat violently. If she could have got her hand all the way down and into her stomach to grab it all out, she would have done. Instead she stabbed her fingers down her windpipe again and again until at last something started to come up.

But the force of her fingers must have scratched the back of her throat and blood came up with the vomit, splattering the toilet bowl. It looked like an operating theatre but she didn't care; as long as the food came up she could deal with the blood.

It was when she had finished, after she had flushed the chain and gone to wash her hands, that it began to sink in.

She looked in the mirror as she cleaned the mess from her hands. Her face was swollen and red, her eyes were bloodshot and her mouth was stained pink with blood. It gave her such a fright she did something she had never done before – she called the Samaritans. It was the only thing she could think of. So she sat for an hour and poured her heart out to a Welsh woman called Hayley who listened patiently but said she wasn't allowed to give any advice. Though before she hung up, she did suggest Stella refrained from brushing her teeth after vomiting to stop the enamel coming away.

Stella had been hoping for clarity, she had been hoping for kind words, but all she got was dental advice. Putting the phone down, she walked into the bathroom and ran herself a bath. She let it run and run until the water almost overflowed. Climbing into it, she felt herself letting go, felt herself disappearing. It was coming. The little death she had glimpsed so many times was becoming a reality.

But then Ade had arrived back and burst into the bathroom. She remembers feeling the muffled thud of his shoes through the floor, then a whoosh as he pulled her head out of the water. 'Stella,' he screamed. 'Stella, baby, what are you doing?' He was trembling as he brought a towel over to her and guided her out of the bath. 'Don't you do that to me again,' he said as he held her to his chest and stroked her hair. 'Don't ever do that again.' He held her so close, she could feel his heart thudding against her head. As his shock subsided, still holding her, he sat down on the damp floor and started to sing, gently, the tune to Gershwin's 'Summertime'. They lay like that all night, him propped up against the bathroom wall kissing her head and rocking her like a baby, her folded into the warmth of his jacket, like a small animal burrowing for shelter in the depths of the earth.

Enough, she tells herself, enough of all that. Tonight is a happy bath, it's a getting ready for Paula bath. As she takes off her clothes, the phone beeps. She picks it up and reads the message.

7:30 sounds perfect. I'll be in the bar. See you soon, P x

By the time Ade arrives at Warren's house in Highgate, he is sweating heavily. He walks up to the black gates and presses the bell. After a minute or so, a female voice crackles through the intercom.

'Yes?'

'Oh, hi,' he shouts. 'It's Ade, er, Adrian Ward?'

There is a pause and a crumpling noise, like the shuffling of papers. After another minute the woman's voice returns.

'Come through,' she crackles.

With a metallic whirr, the gates slowly draw open. Ade

walks across the gravel driveway towards the front door. He is about to knock when the door swings open. A small, dark-haired woman stands there. She is in her mid-thirties and wearing black velour tracksuit pants and a sparkly silver vest. Around her head is a thick headset and she is clutching a clipboard to her chest. Ade recognizes her as Vanessa, Warren's Australian PA.

'You're band,' she drawls as Ade steps inside the house.

'Sorry?'

'That's why I couldn't find your name. You weren't on my main guest list. You're on the other list, for staff and band members.'

She stares at him blankly.

Ade takes a Starbucks paper napkin from his pocket and begins dabbing the sweat from his forehead.

What's the miserable cow talking about?

The intercom rings again and Vanessa leaves him standing in the entrance hall while she goes to answer it.

He can hear music and voices coming from outside. He has to walk through the kitchen to get to the garden. The kitchen is open-plan and white, like everything else in Warren's house. White floors, white sofas, white candles, the only room with a bit of colour is the games room where the walls are covered with Warren's gold discs and framed magazine covers. Tonight, the kitchen is full of beautiful young men and women dressed in white. It is all very Calvin Klein circa 1995 but then that *was* Warren's heyday. The surfaces are covered in platters of sushi and trays of drinks ready to be taken into the garden. Ade smiles at a girl with red Pre-Raphaelite hair as he walks through, but her face barely cracks.

'God, I could murder a drink,' he mutters as he makes his way through the French doors and out onto the immaculately landscaped lawn.

Paper lanterns are strung around the neatly clipped triangular conifer trees and clusters of tables are draped in white linen with elaborate centrepieces of lilies and white roses. There are thirty or so people milling around, chatting in groups of three or four. At the far end of the garden is a giant pagoda decked in white netting and silver fairy lights. Inside it stands Warren Craig in a peach satin shirt and silver PVC trousers. He has dyed the tips of his short spiky hair with peroxide and his face has been freshly Botoxed. He catches sight of Ade shuffling across the lawn and rushes to greet him, grimacing at the casual white shirt.

Warren would prefer it if Ade played the game more, if he read the dress code at least. Last month, he had invited him to a business meeting at Nobu and Ade had turned up looking like he had just got out of bed. Warren had arranged for them to go shopping, hoping that he could point Ade in the direction of some well-cut suits, but Ade had shunned his suggestions, saying that he couldn't afford Paul Smith, and they ended up in some surf-wear shop in Carnaby Street where Ade bought a pile of T-shirts and cargo pants. But that's jazz musicians for you, Warren tells himself, and he tolerates all of this because Ade has a talent that Warren does not possess – he can write great songs. And more importantly, as far as Warren is concerned, Ade is hungry enough to forgo the credits of the songs he writes in return for the promise of a record deal for his girlfriend. It's a win-win situation. Well, it is for Warren.

'Ade, you made it!'

A smile is about the only thing that can move on Warren's face.

'Only just, mate,' says Ade with a smirk. 'Your PA almost turned me away at the door.'

Warren frowns at Ade's sweating face and clicks his fingers at a passing waitress.

'You need a cool drink,' he purrs, taking a cocktail glass from the tray and handing it to Ade.

'Ah, cheers, mate, I've been looking forward to this,' gasps Ade. He takes a long swig. 'Fuck me, what's this?'

He spits the liquid out onto the grass, narrowly missing Warren's diamante-encrusted loafer.

'It's one of my favourites,' says Warren, jumping out of the way. 'Elderflower cordial, soda water and peach puree. I like to call it my Baby Bellini.'

As another supermodel waitress passes by, Ade puts the half-empty glass back onto the tray.

'Not really my cup of tea, Warren. You got any beers?'

Warren is busy telling the waitress to take Ade's glass back into the kitchen. When he has finished, he turns to him, puts his head to one side and smiles as though he is about to address a child.

'Now, Ade, I thought you knew this was going to be a dry party. No alcohol allowed. It's my anniversary today.'

Ade braces himself for the long night ahead without booze. He digs into his pockets and pulls out his cigarette papers.

'What anniversary's that then?'

He starts rolling a cigarette and Warren looks at him with disgust.

'It's my fifth year of sobriety,' he mutters through gritted teeth. 'Look, Ade, if you want to smoke that cigarette, then

I'm afraid I can't stand near you. One lungful of that filth would obliterate my vocal chords for the rest of the week.'

He starts to back away.

'Alright, alright,' snaps Ade, putting the unlit cigarette back into his pocket for later. He takes Warren by the arm and whispers:

'Is he here yet?'

'Who?' replies Warren, removing his satin-clad arm from Ade's grip.

'Robert Anderson,' says Ade, 'the guy from B2B Records you were going to introduce me to.'

Warren pauses, as though weighing up whether to unleash Ade onto one of the most influential men in A & R. Then, maybe encouraged by the look of expectation on Ade's face, he agrees, for there is nothing Warren likes better than to show these young session musicians how well connected he still is. He smiles benignly at Ade.

'Oh, you mean Rob? He's just over there by the Buddha.'

He points to a sinewy, tanned figure with shoulder-length grey hair, standing beside a silver Buddha statue. He is flanked by two emaciated creatures with unnaturally large breasts and poker-straight dark hair.

'God, I didn't realize he was *that* old,' gasps Ade.

'Well, he's been around since the Seventies,' replies Warren. 'He worked with Fleetwood Mac. That's how he made his money. C'mon, I'll introduce you.'

Warren strides across the lawn with Ade following, undoing the top button of his shirt and wiping his trousers with the paper napkin. The cocktail he spat out has left a sticky orange mark on the front of his cargo pants.

'Rob, I'd like you to meet Ade,' says Warren, brightly. 'He's my sax player. Ade, this is Rob Anderson.'

Ade is just about to say that he isn't *just* Warren's sax player, he's also his producer and songwriter, but then thinks better of it.

He grasps Rob Anderson's hand and shakes it tightly.

'It's *so* good to meet you, Rob. I'm a huge fan of your work,' he gushes. 'All these young A & R kids coming up now, I bet you could show them a thing or two.'

He can hear himself wittering on. He sounds like a bloody idiot. Come on, Stella, he thinks, where are you?

Rob Anderson removes his hand from Ade's and wipes the clamminess on his handkerchief. 'Hi,' he mutters, then turns back to his model companions.

Warren is already heading across the lawn to greet a guest, jumping up and down as he runs.

'Oh my God, it's Sandy! Look at you, my African princess,'

he shrieks, holding out his arms to embrace Sandy Williams, the voluptuous American soul singer who supported his last tour. Sandy floats across the lawn in a huge silver kaftan, the beads on her braided hair jingling as she moves.

Meanwhile, Ade stands looking at the back of Rob Anderson like a spare part. He takes a deep breath and taps him on the back.

'Er, Rob, I just wanted to tell you about this song I've written.'

Rob Anderson turns around with an expression of undisguised irritation.

'It's called "Soho Morning",' says Ade.

Rob looks at him blankly.

'Anyway,' Ade continues. 'I think you'll love it. It's got a real Kylie vibe to it.'

He winces, imagining what Stella would say if she heard her homage to Joni Mitchell being compared to cheesy pop, but sod it she's not here and he's got to speak this man's language if he wants to get them a deal.

'Look, why don't you pop it into the office, leave it with my PA. She deals with submissions,' replies Rob.

'Well, the thing is,' says Ade nodding like he is about to impart the secrets of the universe. 'I've got this girl, fantastic vocalist, she's on her way here as we speak. You've got to meet her. She sings on "Soho Morning" and she's just got the most amazing look, completely unique like . . .' Ade is clutching at straws now. '. . . like Stevie Nicks,' he blurts.

Rob Anderson shakes his head.

'I mean, you discovered Fleetwood Mac, didn't you?'

'I didn't discover them as such, no.'

'Yeah, but you know about finding the right girl to sell records and Stella's that girl, I'm telling you.' Ade can hear his voice getting higher, feel the desperation rising in his throat.

'I don't think Stevie Nicks would take too kindly to being referred to as a girl,' spits the music mogul. 'Anyway, Al, as I said, put the CD in the post and my PA will give it a listen.'

'It's Ade, and I can do better than that.'

He reaches round to his back pocket and pulls out a CD.

'I've got one here,' he says, thrusting it towards him.

'Oh for Christ's sake,' Rob cries, holding his hands in the air. 'This is a private party and I'm trying to talk to my friends here.' He nods towards the women. 'Now please, either post the thing to my office or bugger off!'

He turns his back once more and whispers something to the nearest of the two girls who looks at Ade and shrieks with laughter.

Ade's head starts to thud. He can feel an old rage stirring inside. He looks around at the sparkling lights, the silver Buddha and the elaborate drapes.

What is he doing here? This isn't him. This is bullshit. This is all just bullshit.

Rob Anderson, oblivious to what is stirring behind him, turns to leave. The girls walk ahead and, as he edges past, his elbow lodges in Ade's side.

In an instant, Ade's fury is unleashed. He grabs Rob Anderson's throat. 'Who the fuck do you think you are, you old coffin dodger? You think you can treat me like a piece of shit, you washed up old pervert.'

The older man's face is turning beetroot as he desperately tries to prise Ade's fingers from his neck. The girls suddenly find their voices and start to scream. The noise alerts Warren who has set up a microphone in the pagoda and is about to launch into his new song, 'Daddy Didn't Love Me'. He runs across the lawn, a vision in peach.

'Ade, stop!'

For all his campness, Warren is a solid guy and he grabs Ade around the shoulders, hurling him onto the grass.

'What are you doing?' he shrieks, wiping down his silver trousers as he gets to his feet.

Rob Anderson has recovered quickly and is striding across

the lawn to the house. 'Where's security?' he bellows. 'I want this nutter arrested.'

Warren takes Ade by the shoulders.

'Come on now, buddy, pull yourself together.'

Ade is already walking away from Warren, his fists clenched by his side.

'Adey, come back. We can sort this out. I'll get Magda to fix you an iced camomile tea,' calls Warren from the now deserted lawn.

Ade stops then turns round to see the frozen-faced creature he had sold his soul to.

'Fuck off, Warren,' he shouts. 'And stick your camomile tea up your arse.'

Chapter 6

It is just coming up to a quarter to seven when Zoe arrives home to her flat on the top floor of a grey 1960s tower block behind Carnaby Street. It's not ideal but she puts up with it by telling herself that this is just a stopgap, that one day, when she is a successful model, she'll be able to buy herself one of those luxury apartments in the Docklands.

When she can't sleep at night, when she lies there listening to the street cleaners screeching and clattering outside her window, their flashing orange lights blazing through the flimsy curtain, she imagines that she is lying in a huge bed with linen sheets and soft cushions – like the one Anna B was reclining on in her 'at home' magazine shoot – while outside the gentle splashing of the river rocks her to sleep. She loves the water, be it the sea, the river or even a little duck pond; she feels at ease just being near to it, like she can breathe. Her mam says it's because she's a Pisces – the two fish swimming in opposite directions. And it's true, her life has always been one of extremes – she is either rapturously happy or hideously depressed; if she is hungry, she is ravenous; if she is ill she is at death's door. At school she had been brilliant at certain subjects and utterly hopeless at others. There is no in-between state; she is either rising to the top or sinking to the bottom.

She's not quite sure what she is at the moment. Six months ago, when she had looked out at London from the window of the National Express coach, it felt like she had broken the surface of some mysterious, exotic pool. Everything around her seemed hyper-real, like a giant TV advertisement. The Houses of Parliament, the open-top buses, the underground signs: these were things she had seen countless times before on television, but observing them up close was another thing entirely. London looked like a sprawling mass of cardboard cut-outs, like one of those huge film sets they construct at Universal Studios. Despite its history, despite the ancient buildings and bridges and monuments, it looked fragile and transient, like it was set adrift on its own, set apart from the rest of the country, a floating city drifting out to sea. Zoe couldn't help but think that it would take just one strong gust of wind to capsize the whole thing.

Arriving at Victoria Station, she had seen people getting off the bus that looked like they were sinking, like they were drowning right there on dry land. Lost, solitary figures with dead eyes and creased clothes stumbling into the artificial light of the bus concourse like moles emerging from deep underground.

There was the family of eight – a mother and father and their small children – who had been wedged into the three rows of seats opposite Zoe. It looked like everything they owned was crammed into the frayed rucksacks and plastic carrier bags they had with them. They were already on the coach when Zoe got on it at Middlesbrough. As she squeezed down the aisle to get to her seat, she accidentally stood on the father's foot. He frowned, and muttered something to his wife in Arabic. Zoe apologized as she settled herself into the seat opposite and the man had smiled. He's just tired, poor man, she thought, looking at the bundle of sleeping kids.

If her brother Mark had been with her, he would have made her sit elsewhere. As far as he was concerned, anybody of Middle-Eastern origin was a nutter with a bomb.

He had always been a small-minded little sod, even when they were kids. He wouldn't speak to this child because he had ginger hair, wouldn't sit next to that one because she was fat. And as he got older, he got worse. Three of his school friends had joined the army, two of them had been out to Iraq, and when they came home on leave they would fill Mark's head with their stories of 'shooting mad rag-heads'. Mark suddenly became a mouthpiece for these zealots, shouting obscenities at burkha-clad women in the street and heckling Muslim students outside the mosque on Southfield Road.

It worried Zoe, what her brother was turning into, particularly after that Asian lad was stabbed outside the Empire last year. He had ended up in intensive care and for a while it looked like he might die. It was in all the papers and they still hadn't found out who had done it, but Zoe was sure Mark and his friends had played some part. She noticed the way they behaved in the days following the attack, the looks that passed between them. It was just a feeling, you could call it sisterly intuition, but Zoe knew he had done something.

It felt good to get on the coach and leave all that behind her. As Middlesbrough became a dot in the driver's windscreen, she had been struck by an overwhelming sense of purpose, a feeling that she was plunging into a whole new life. When they reached Nottingham, with three hours to go until they got to Victoria, she fell asleep, slumped in her chair with her arms folded across her chest. As they pulled out of the bus station she felt a tap on her arm. She opened her eyes and saw one of the little girls from the family standing there, wide-eyed and serious, holding a piece of paper towards Zoe. 'For you,' she said, in a slow, precise voice. Zoe took the paper from her and opened it out, smiling at the little felt-tip drawing of a stick person with spiky red hair, a yellow dress and a big handbag. 'Is that me?' she asked. The little girl nodded, then leaned in towards Zoe and whispered, 'You pretty.' Her mother called her back to her seat and Zoe folded up the little picture and smiled as she put it into her pocket.

She saw them again when they reached Victoria and she was waiting her turn behind the exhausted father as he hauled more of their luggage from the hold in the side of the coach. Then, after retrieving her modest two bags, she watched them walk away through the concourse, laden down with the weight of their baggage and whatever horrors had brought them here, to try to start all over again. She often wonders what became of that family, particularly the little girl, whether things worked out for them.

As for her, after spending her first night in the capital in a grotty bed and breakfast in Victoria, she spent her second morning sitting in Starbucks on Victoria Street, sipping a 'venti' hot chocolate and flicking through the 'rooms to let' section of *Loot*. She was about to leave when a stout, ruddy-faced woman sat down opposite her.

'You're looking for a room? I have a room.' She spoke with a slight accent that Zoe later discovered was Polish. Zoe had gone to view the flat that morning and was nicely settled in by the evening. She couldn't believe her luck, and Dina didn't even ask for a deposit.

Since then, her landlady has gone out of her way to make sure Zoe settles in. She certainly makes life easier for all the tenants – sorting post, checking the electrics and cooking up huge vats of food for them. It is rather like having a kindly housekeeper and Zoe has struck up a friendship of sorts with her. Dina seems to enjoy hearing Zoe's stories of her days as a teenage clubber and will often quiz her on boyfriends and relationships. Zoe likes having Dina around. It is nice to feel there is someone there, someone solid and tangible, someone who cares.

The flat is clean and spacious and most of the time she has it to herself as her flatmates work nightshifts in restaurants around the West End. She rarely sees them, except for the brief glimpse of a shadow crossing the darkened bedroom at some unearthly hour, the sound of hurried footsteps on the stairs or a reticent key in the lock. Sometimes, she wonders if they even exist, and if they do, then it must be in some grey, halfway state somewhere between the twilight and the morning. But everywhere she looks there is evidence of them: three flimsy dresses hanging on the curtain rail, limp and lifeless; make-up and lip balm on the bathroom shelf with orange fingerprints embedded on the tubes, a chipped cup on the draining board with 'Number 1 Daughter' printed on it in thick black lettering. They are everywhere yet they are nowhere. As Dina says, 'It is what it is.'

The loneliness is starting to get to Zoe now and as time goes on, her reasons for being in London are starting to wear thin. She tries not to show it but it's crushing her, all this waiting and wishing, but she's started this journey and she has to stay on it. And tonight could be it, life could finally be opening up for her, and goodness knows she could do with the money. She had just about managed on her wages from her reception job in Covent Garden but then Eve, her hard-faced frumpy supervisor, told her that she could no longer tolerate her unexplained absences and that was that. So now she goes along twice a month to the job centre in Victoria to sign on. It's funny, she once thought that London was the busiest place on earth but all she has done since she moved here is sit still; it's like she is locked in a vast, never-ending waiting room.

As she unlocks the door, she hears the muffled sound of the television coming from inside. A voice calls out from the sofa.

'Is that you, Zoe?'

'Oh, Dina, you'll never believe it. I've got my first assignment!' Zoe shrieks as she bounds into the living room.

'Doing what?' Her landlady pulls an oversized brown cardigan around her bulky frame and stretches her legs out across the sofa.

'I bumped into the guy who does the PR for Honey Vision. Anyway, he's having this corporate party thing tonight for Dan Williams.'

Dina takes off her spectacles and starts to clean them with a tissue.

'Who is that?'

'He's just about the most famous footballer in England.' Zoe throws her coat onto the armchair.

'Oh, he'll be stupid then,' says Dina. 'All those football players, they are very stupid.'

'I don't care how stupid he is, Dina, he's gorgeous and I'm going to be the star guest at his party.'

'Where is this party?'

'It's a private venue on Tottenham Court Road,' replies Zoe, brusquely. 'Listen, I can't chat, I've got to be there for seven-thirty.'

She runs into the bedroom then reappears, hauling her make-up case towards the bathroom.

Her landlady sighs. 'I cannot believe how long it takes you to get ready, Zoe. It is insane. Oh, I almost forgot.' She heaves herself off the sofa and walks across the room to the little wooden sideboard by the stairs. 'I opened this by mistake.'

She holds out a green and white envelope with 'City of Westminster Council' stamped on it in red ink.

'It is from the Job Centre, they say they're going to freeze your housing benefit.'

'What? They can't do that, let me see.' She grabs the letter and begins to read but the words are a blur. She flings it on the sofa. 'I don't have time for this now,' she snaps. 'Anyway, bugger them, I'm going to get my big break tonight, then my worries are over.'

Dina takes the letter from the sofa, folds it inside the envelope and puts it back onto the sideboard.

'Maybe you're right but you're going to have to find some work soon so you can pay your way.'

She folds her arms and shuffles towards the kitchen.

'Oh, Dina, please,' says Zoe. 'You should be happy I've got a modelling job at last. Wahey!'

She shrieks excitedly as she hurries into the bathroom. Locking the door, she opens up her industrial-sized make-up box and starts the arduous task of 'putting her face on'.

First she has to remove the day's make-up with cleansing lotion, toning pads and handfuls of thick moisturizer, slathering it onto her face and neck. Then comes dark beige foundation and several layers of silver iridescent eyeshadow which she frames with four coats of 'Full Volume Double Lash' mascara. After blusher, dark brown lip liner and pale pink lip gloss, the job is done.

'I look too pale,' she says, frowning at her naked body in the full-length mirror.

So, after a quick shower in which she manages to keep her face and hair dry by leaning back in a position that would make a contortionist blush, she delves back into her box of tricks, pulls out a bottle of quick-drying tanning lotion and smears it liberally over her body.

While that is drying, she starts on her hair. Taking a big scoop of wax she vigorously pulls and twists it into the spiky style she saw on Posh Spice in *Heat* magazine last week. Once the fake tan has developed into a golden glow, she puts the finishing touches to it by dusting pink sparkly glitter from neck to ankles. Then she looks in the mirror again and smiles.

'Perfect.'

Wrapping a towel around her glittery, bronzed body, she unlocks the door and walks carefully through the living room, where Dina is back on the sofa watching the television and eating a bowl of spicy meatballs.

'Ha!' she shrieks as she catches sight of Zoe. 'You look like a Christmas turkey.'

'Shut up, Miss Piggy,' giggles Zoe. 'Have we got any wine?'

Dina points her fork towards the kitchen; her mouth is full of food.

'Is that a yes?' says Zoe, walking into the kitchen.

'There's some in the fridge,' calls Dina, swallowing her food. 'You can have some, but you'll have to buy a bottle tomorrow to replace it. We all pay our way you know.'

'Thanks, Dina,' says Zoe, as she takes the half-drunk bottle of Soave out of the fridge. She opens the cupboard and takes out a wine glass.

'Do you want some?' she shouts as she pours herself a large glass.

'No thanks, Zoe,' says Dina. 'I'm working tonight. Got to have a clear head.'

Zoe opens the cupboard next to the fridge. This is *her* cupboard – full of cans of beans and packets of sweets and crisps. She grabs a tube of Pringles and takes out a handful. 'God, I'm starving,' she says, as she walks back into the living room. 'I hope there's some food at this party, I haven't eaten all day.'

Dina looks up from the TV and frowns. 'You should eat something more substantial than a handful of crisps. Why don't you sit down and have a proper meal. I can get you a plate of this if you like.' She gestures to her bowl of meatballs. 'There's plenty in the pan.'

'No thanks, Dina, I'm fine,' says Zoe, taking a sip of wine. 'If I eat anything heavy, I'll feel bloated, and I want to look my best tonight.'

'Okay, suit yourself,' says Dina.

Zoe pats her landlady's arm. 'Thank you for offering though. What would I do without you? And, hey, if it all goes well tonight, I'll replace that bottle of wine with a crate of champagne.'

Dina shakes her head as Zoe walk out of the living room. Balancing the glass of wine in the crook of her arm, Zoe opens the bedroom door.

Two beds are crammed side by side under the window with a tiny gap in between. Zoe's clothes hang on a rail wedged behind the door. The girl who shares the room has left a pile of clothes on her bed: a green shirt and a pair of black trousers. The arms of the shirt are spread outward and the trousers still hold her shape. It looks like a body, like one of those bloated corpses that are fished out of the Thames, with no past, no future and no name.

Zoe puts the glass of wine down on the floor, leans over the beds and opens the curtains.

'That's better,' she says, as a shaft of pale yellow sunlight exposes a cloud of dust particles billowing towards the ceiling.

Right, what to wear?

She walks back to her clothes rail and begins to flick through the row of skimpy garments. She picks out a pale pink sequined dress with a built-in push-up bra and smiles. This is the one. Pulling it carefully over her head, she takes care not to get any streaks of foundation on the front, then reaches under the bed for her large fake Burberry suitcase. This is where she keeps her shoes. Sliding it out from the end of the bed towards the door, she opens the lid and inspects the contents.

'It will have to be the silver ones,' she says. 'Hope no one notices they're from Primark.'

Leaving the suitcase open on the floor and her towel crumpled on the bed, she picks up her wine and downs it in one big swig. 'I needed that,' she says as she walks to the bathroom to check herself in the full-length mirror. As she stands there clipping little butterfly slides into her hair, Dina appears behind her.

'Take your mobile with you, won't you?'

'Jeez, I thought I left my mam back in Middlesbrough. Do you want me back by ten as well?'

Zoe laughs as she squeezes past Dina to get her pink diamante handbag from the bedroom.

When she comes back into the living room, Dina is on the sofa, picking her teeth with a plastic toothpick. 'Just remember to take your mobile, yes?'

Zoe is too busy wondering if the hundred pounds will be cash in hand as she opens her purse. She pulls out Jules's piece of paper and puts it into her pink handbag, leaving the empty purse behind on the sofa, then she sits on the armchair and smiles at her landlady.

'Are you going anywhere nice tonight then, Dina?' She looks at Dina's cardigan and slippers and giggles.

'If you call dealing with life's waifs and strays "nice", then yes I've got a very nice night ahead of me, Zoe.' Her serious expression makes Zoe laugh again.

'Oh, Dina, honestly. You spend so much time fussing over those young runaways, you think you've got to do the same with me,' she says, shaking her head. 'If I want to make it as a model, I've got to get out and network.'

Dina rolls her eyes and flicks the television over to another channel.

Zoe stands up and stuffs her make-up into her handbag. 'I don't understand how you can live here in the centre of London and not be out partying.' As she squeezes the bag shut she notices her mobile phone on the sideboard. She'll need every bit of make-up with her tonight so the phone will have to stay. She slides it to the back of the sideboard so Dina won't see it. Then, picking up her black jacket from the armchair, she heads for the door.

'I'm off, Dina, see you later.'

'Goodbye, Zoe. Have a good night!'

She shuts the door, takes a deep breath and makes her way down the narrow stairs. As she adjusts the strap on her dress, her hand brushes the small crucifix that has hung around her neck since her Communion day. Wrapping her hand tightly around its stem, she closes her eyes and kisses the tiny amethyst stone at its centre.

'Wish me luck,' she whispers.

Stella smiles as she eases herself into the gloriously scented water and thinks about the first time they met.

It was the summer of 1994 and Stella was a shy sixteen-year-old when Paula had strolled into the garden with Stella's sister Caitlin.

They were both undergraduates at Oxford – Caitlin studying Law; Paula, English Literature – and they had come home to visit for the weekend. Home was a big converted mill on the edge of the North York Moors. It was a noisy childhood, full of visitors and animals and endless debate. Stella, as the youngest, tended to stay on the edge of the action, blushing if anyone asked her a question. She never really felt a part of the world which she inhabited. To her young mind, the fields surrounding her house were full of sugarcane not barley. It might have been Africa or the Deep South. As a child she would dream of other landscapes, other views, other skies. What would the moon look like as it shone on the River Ganges? Would New York rain feel the same as the rain in northern England? Her childhood seemed to be a series of daydreams and thoughts, so vivid that sometimes she could barely differentiate between the real and the imaginary.

The day was uncomfortably hot and she was sitting on the grass, huddled underneath a huge sun hat. Through the open kitchen window she could hear the sound of voices mingling with the Maria Callas album that was playing on her mother's kitchen CD player. She tried to ignore the voices and concentrate on the opening words of the Virginia Woolf novel she had just started reading.

'And last but not least . . .'

Caitlin's voice trailed down the path with the opening bars of 'J'ai perdu mon Eurydice', Stella's favourite track on the album.

'. . . here's Stella – if you can see her underneath that hat.'

Stella looked up into the sun. A shadow crossed the lawn and slowly came into focus. The girl standing in front of her was thin and wiry with black, cropped hair and she had the most beautiful eyes, deep green and slanted like a pixie. There was a look of mischief in her eyes that made it look like she was going to burst into fits of laughter at any moment.

Stella thought about standing up but then remembered the white cotton dress she had on was a bit too short to be wearing in the presence of someone like Paula. Caitlin had talked about her incessantly for months, this new best friend who had won all sorts of prizes for her writing, who was on course for a First and about to take one of her plays up to the Edinburgh Fringe. Stella didn't want this wise woman of letters to think that she was a silly little girl in a silly little dress so she stayed where she was.

Caitlin lumbered over, all long limbs and messy hair.

'Stella, this is Paula. Paula, this is my baby sister.'

With that, Caitlin ran over to the shed to bring out more garden chairs, leaving Paula standing there.

'Hello,' she said, shielding her eyes from the sun with one hand. 'I must say, you don't look like a baby sister.'

Stella laughed. 'Oh, I think Caitlin will still be calling me that when I'm eighty; it's the role I'm destined to play forever.'

With anyone else, she would have been reticent. She always spoke in a near whisper back then, afraid of fully committing herself to a person or conversation by speaking up. But there was something different about Paula, this dark shadow that had walked into her world without warning. There was something about her presence that calmed Stella, made her want to tell her things and made her believe that she would listen.

'So, are you the writer?' she asked.

Paula was standing in the sun again.

'Something like that,' she answered from the shadows.

Caitlin appeared with the chairs.

'Here you go, Paula, have a seat. I'm just going to run inside and grab some drinks. Dry white okay for you?'

'That would be lovely, thanks, Caity.'

Stella was shocked. She had never heard anyone call her sister 'Caity'. As long as she could remember, her parents had insisted on using their full names and her mother had a deep-seated aversion to nicknames after spending an entire childhood having her name shortened from the refined and elegant Marjorie to the short but not so sweet Marje.

Paula took the chair and placed it on the ground near Stella. As she sat down, the air filled with her perfume. It was delicate and sweet, like orange blossom.

'What's that you're reading?'

Stella handed her the book and she took it carefully as though it were a fragile piece of glass, keeping her page open with one finger. 'Oh wonderful. I love this book, don't you? "Mrs Dalloway said she would buy the flowers herself." Isn't that the most wonderful opening sentence? Just throwing you straight into the story; you can almost smell the flowers. I love it.' She smiled exuberantly as she handed the book back to Stella.

'I've never read any of her books before, but I'm enjoying this one,' said Stella, taking the book from her and putting it down on the grass.

'Good, though I can't imagine how anybody could not enjoy it,' Paula replied. 'It has everything you could possibly want from a novel; a whole life condensed into one day.'

She had gone on talking, but Stella didn't really take in what she was saying, she just sat there transfixed by this magnificent girl. And the most wonderful part of it was that she had treated Stella as an equal. Having to spend most of her days at school trying to hear the teacher over the noise of a rowdy class of kids throwing rulers and shouting obscenities, Stella had longed for the day when somebody other than her father would sit beside her and enthuse about literature. She wanted Paula to stay sitting there forever; she wanted to listen to her voice, to look at her beautiful face and imagine how full and exciting life could be. Her parents may have believed in state education but all she could think of was getting out of there and finding a space of her own where she would be able to immerse herself in Virginia Woolf to her heart's content. She would go to Oxford too; she would study the great writers and read books all day, luxuriate in other people's words, and one day she would be confident and eloquent enough to write her own. Paula was only twenty, a second year English Literature undergraduate with holes in her jeans, but to Stella she was the future.

Chapter 7

Ade pounds the pavement along the northern end of Tottenham Court Road, furiously chain-smoking as he goes. He managed to afford a cab as far as Camden High Street but has had to walk the rest of the way. His big night has been ruined. He takes out his phone and calls Stella's number. It goes straight to voice mail.

Where the Hell is she? If she had turned up, none of this would have happened. He wouldn't have lost his temper like that if she had been with him. She knows he's no good at all this networking stuff, that's why he needs her. She's his greatest asset. If she had been there tonight, she would have charmed Rob Anderson, there is no doubt. She knows how to deal with people, important people, she knows what to say. When he was a teenager, he had eaten his meals in front of the TV with only the dog for company, whereas Stella, well, she had grown up with a famous father, a reporter for the BBC. She had told Ade about the elaborate New Year's parties her parents would throw, where she was allowed to stay up late and talk to the likes of Kate Adie and Michael Palin. Rob Anderson would have loved her and Ade could have stood back while Stella sealed the deal for them. He needed her to be there tonight; without her he just doesn't make sense.

Taking a deep drag of his cigarette, he recalls the skinny girl in the fake fur coat and trainers who stood at the door of his messy Soho studio flat one morning in 2000. It was January, just after Christmas, and freezing cold. Despite this, the front door was open, letting out the thick smoke from Ade's constant stream of cigarettes. He was crouched on the floor looking for an errant piece of wire when he heard a voice.

'Hello?'

He lifted his head and saw a figure in the doorway. She was early. He wasn't expecting her until one o'clock.

Registering him, she edged further into the room.

'Sorry to interrupt – the front door was open. I'm looking for Adrian Ward. Have I got the right place? It's about the advert for a singer in *The Stage*?'

He picked himself up from the floor and came towards her, extending his hand.

'I'm Adrian, but call me Ade, everyone else does. You must be Stella, right? Come in and take a seat, if you can find one.'

He hurriedly moved pieces of clothing off the rickety wooden table and chairs and threw them onto an unmade bed that was rammed up against the far wall.

As he shook her hand, he was sure he saw a flicker of disappointment in her face. He wasn't what she was expecting, he felt certain of that. He became aware of his scruffy T-shirt and wished he had worn something a bit smarter. Back then, he used to eat, sleep and work in that little flat and he would be so immersed in whatever song he was working on that he'd lose track of time. He sometimes had trouble remembering what day it was, never mind what clothes he was wearing.

When he put the advert in *The Stage*, he was expecting the usual response from session singers, experienced women who had done the rounds a bit. All he had in mind was a voice, a voice to put to his music that would sound strong enough to send off to record companies. He wasn't expecting someone like Stella.

'Here you go,' he said, pulling out a chair.

'Thanks.' She took off her coat and draped it over her knee as she sat down.

'Is that your demo?' He reached for the CD she was clutching in her lap.

She suddenly seemed alarmed and clasped it to her chest as though she didn't want to hand it over.

'Erm, yes it is but I'm afraid it's not very good quality. I mean, it's a bit unprofessional,' she said, staring at the floor.

'I'm sure it's fine,' Ade reassured her, still holding out his hand. Her reticence made him more curious.

'Don't play it now,' she pleaded. 'I can leave it with you and you can listen to it when I've gone.'

He wanted to put her at ease, to take the tension out of the situation and – to be honest – he really wanted to hear her sing. He knelt down beside her on the pretext of turning on the mixing desk and smiled.

'I'd love to hear it with you, if that's okay,' he said gently. 'Then we can talk through what needs to be done.' He raised his eyebrows pleadingly.

She passed it to him reluctantly, like a child handing over a hidden stash of sweets.

As he fiddled with the mixing desk she let out a loud sigh. He turned and saw that her head was bowed. She was staring intently at her lap, twisting her hands like a piece of dough.

'Okay, let's see what we've got here,' he muttered, as the opening bars of a simple piano melody started up.

He nodded as he heard a clear mezzo soprano voice sing the first verse:

> *Softly, softly,*
> *Catch a heartbeat,*
> *Then let it go*
> *And fade away.*

He was already mentally taking notes: Nice phrasing, bit of a flat note at the end but that can be dealt with. I'd like to overdub it a bit, a few strings would work really well.

The chorus was more uptempo and he nodded his head to the beat:

> *I woke up to a Soho morning,*
> *Everything was clear inside my head,*
> *Nothing more to say, it's all been said.*
> *I'll start all over again*
> *Today.*

He looked at Stella as the song came to an end. Her head was still bowed and she was digging her nails into the palms of her hands. He had never seen anyone have such a reaction to hearing their work. It felt like, in playing her CD, he had somehow violated her.

It confused him. As a musician and producer, he listened to music objectively, taking the melody apart, listening out for a flat note here or a loose piece of phrasing there. It was like a jigsaw puzzle or a piece of design, a series of parts that had to be brought into line to make it work. He wasn't really interested in lyrics or stories. It was the beauty of a song's construction that brought tears to his eyes, not the words. To him they were incidental, just fillers. Take one of his favourite songs, 'Yesterday' by The Beatles. The beauty of those chord progressions makes him weep. The words could be anything. In fact he remembered reading somewhere that when Paul McCartney wrote the melody, he sang it to John Lennon using the line 'scrambled eggs' over and over. To Ade, music was everything, the only language that mattered. All the rest – poetry, books, words – was just scrambled eggs.

'So, what do you think?'

Ade sat back in his leather chair feeling more and more like the producer he knew he could be. He lit a cigarette, took a deep drag and blew the smoke up to the ceiling, aware that she was waiting on his response. Folding one arm across his chest with the other still raised holding the cigarette, he nodded at the young woman whose whole future seemed to depend upon what he was about to say.

'That was . . . good, Stella,' he said, finally.

She began to apologize. 'I know it's not very professional but I'm willing to really try . . .'

'Stella.' He stopped her by placing his hand, still holding the cigarette, on her shoulder. 'We can definitely do something here,' he said firmly. 'It's funny, when I put that ad in *The Stage*, I wasn't looking to make someone into a superstar. I just wanted someone who could sing my songs. You see I'm trying to get taken on by B2B Records as a songwriter. It's tough to get in but once you are, you can make a fortune. My mate Dean's just written one for Kylie. Don't know whether it'll be a hit but bloody Hell he'll be set for life if it is.'

Stella looked at him blankly.

'Anyway, that's not important right now. What I'm saying is, you've taken me by surprise here. It's like you're the full package. I think we could work together, definitely. It's a tough project if I'm honest, but I'm prepared to put the work in if you're prepared to learn from me. You say you've written some more lyrics, yeah?'

Stella sat up in her seat. 'Yes, I've got about twenty songs that I wrote at university. They've got basic melodies, but it would be great to work with you to put them to music.'

Ade stood up. He was excited now; he was starting to make plans. How the Hell had this fallen into his lap? This girl was perfect.

'First up,' he said. 'I'm going to lend you some CDs. I want you to take them home and listen to them, learn the words, imitate what you hear. I'm thinking, for you, we should be going with Carole King, Joni Mitchell . . .'

She perked up at the mention of the latter.

'Oh yes, I love Joni Mitchell. I've almost worn out my copy of *Ladies of the Canyon*, I've listened to it so much.'

'Not one of her best in my opinion,' he interjected. 'You would do better to listen to *Blue*, that's her strongest album.'

He stood up and walked over to a large bookcase by the window. It was crammed full of CDs. He picked one out and handed it to her. 'Here we go, take this home and study it, particularly 'A Case of You'. That's a great song and the kind of style I think we should be working towards.' Reaching up to the top shelf where more CDs were piled up, he grabbed another couple. 'These are some more of Joni Mitchell's, might be worth listening to. Here, catch!'

He threw the CDs at her then watched as she scrutinized the covers, reading the track list carefully.

'*Hejira*,' she said slowly, holding up one of the CDs for him to see. 'I've never heard of this one. Did I pronounce that right? Is it *He-jee-ra* or *He-jy-ra*?'

'It's *He-jee-ra*,' he answered confidently. 'It's an Arabic word. It refers to the journey made by Muhammad to the city of Medina.'

'Really? The journey. I like that,' said Stella, sitting up in her chair.

Ade looked serious for a moment then he started to laugh.

'I'm sorry,' he said. 'I was trying to sound all clever there. I'm not an expert in Arabic, I just read about it in *NME* or something.'

She looked up at him and smiled, then they both started to laugh.

'Well, you impressed me,' she said, shaking her head and smiling. 'Shows you how much I know.'

He watched her as she started reading the track list again. Her eyelashes were long and black and they fluttered against her cheek ever so lightly. She was the loveliest thing and he was mesmerized. Where had she come from?

She looked up at him and smiled. 'Would it be okay to listen to a few songs now? I mean, that's if you're not too busy.'

He took the CD from her outstretched hand.

'Yeah sure,' he said. 'Any excuse to listen to it again. Sod Medina, this is a stunning album. Can I get you a drink? I've got some wine in the fridge.'

'Thank you, Ade,' she giggled. 'That would be lovely.'

He went into the kitchen to pour the wine and when he came back she was standing by the window looking out.

He pressed play on the CD player, then walked towards her and handed her the glass.

She took the wine and walked back over to her seat while Ade sat down on the edge of the bed.

'So you play the sax,' she said, nodding her head towards the tenor saxophone that stood in the corner, wedged on a black shiny stand.

'Yeah. That's my main thing really, but there's no money in it,' he replied gloomily. 'At least, not serious money; that's why I started this studio up. Music production, songwriting, that's where you make your millions.'

He noticed this hadn't really impressed her so changed tack.

'But, yeah anyway, the sax,' he continued. 'It saved my life really. I got booted out of school when I was sixteen and there was nothing else I could do. I went to an audition for this guy, Lenny Morris, when I was seventeen. He was a legend, a massive name in jazz, and he was putting together a session band. The rest of the guys were all from the Royal College so I thought I had no chance, but Lenny put me through. I think he liked the fact I was a bit rough around the edges; he used to say I was pure jazz. I couldn't read music, not a bit, I just used to improvise; that would wind the college boys up something rotten, but Lenny used to laugh and tell me to crank it up. You see that's jazz, that's what it's all about. I owe that man so much; he set me up for life really, got me my first gigs, made sure I could earn a living, then he left me this flat when he died . . .'

He cracked his fingers and stared at the floor.

'Jazz sounds really cool,' she said. 'I don't know too much about the music but I've always liked the idea of the jazz club, all gingham tablecloths and candles in wine bottles. Like that film with Liza Minnelli and Robert de Niro, what is it called again?'

'*New York New York*,' he answered, perking up at the mention of jazz clubs. 'I know loads of clubs like that in London,' he said excitedly. 'I've played most of them. In fact, I can get you onto the guest list of pretty much any club you like. You would love the 606 in Chelsea, it's smaller and more intimate than, say, Ronnie's, which is getting a bit commercial now. Yeah, the 606,' he muttered to himself. 'I'll have to take you there one night.'

He stopped suddenly. Was that a bit forward? After all, he'd only just met her. She might think him a dirty old man. Christ, she looks so young.

'So then, how old are you, Stella?' he asked, trying to sound casual. 'If you don't mind me asking.'

'Oh God,' she groaned, pulling a face. 'I'm twenty-two, just gone. I can't believe it, I'm getting so old.'

'Twenty-two. What a great age,' he said, shaking his head.

She looked at him blankly.

Nice one, Ade, now you really do sound like a dirty old man. Though he was just twenty-eight, he felt almost grandfatherly next to this girl.

'So, tell me about yourself. Where do you live?'

Stella rolled her eyes. 'Well, I'm living with my sister, until I save up enough to rent somewhere. She lives in Clapham, which is fine for now, but I'd love to live closer to the centre of town; it feels more like real London. Caitlin, that's my sister, says I need a reality check.' She shrugged her shoulders and smiled.

'I know what you mean,' said Ade. 'I'm spoilt living here, even though it's basically a shoebox.'

'It's lovely,' said Stella, looking round the room. 'It's got loads of character and it's Soho. I love Soho.'

'So, what do you do, work-wise?' Ade asked as he went into the kitchen to get more wine.

'I'm just temping at the moment,' she replied as Ade came back in and refilled her glass. 'My parents think I'm mad. They keep on telling me to apply for graduate jobs, to use my English degree.'

'And why don't you?' Ade could have listened to her talk all day.

She leaned towards him and smiled. 'You'll think I'm mad too,' she said. 'But, I have this morbid fear of being normal, of living a nine-to-five existence. Some days at work, I feel like I'm being buried alive and the thought of working like that for the next forty years makes me feel sick. I had some crap things happen to me back at home, well, at university, but living down here and singing helps me forget all that. London and music. That's all I need.'

Ade reached forward and held her hand and smiled.

'Same here,' he said, gently. 'I think we're going to get on, me and you.'

After a few minutes' silence she spoke, her voice reticent. 'So, am I what you're looking for?'

She sounded so innocent, it made him smile. He was used to good-time girls and desperate thirty-something singletons. This girl was like a gift from God. He stood up and rummaged in his jeans pocket for a fresh pack of cigarette papers. Then he sat down, rolled his cigarette and looked at her. Picking up his wine glass, he leaned towards her and clinked her glass with his.

'Let's give it a shot, Stella. Let's make you a superstar. Here's to London and music.'

'To London and music,' she repeated, clinking her glass back.

Her face was full of hope, full of faith in him, so much so that he could have kissed her there and then.

Instead, he stood up and retrieved his cigarette lighter from the overflowing ashtray that served as a centrepiece for the table.

He turned and looked at her sitting there like a little lost soul on the chair. There was a pause in the music, then Joni Mitchell's 'A Strange Boy' started up and filled the space in between them.

'I like this,' she said.

'Me too,' he agreed.

Something unspoken passed between them in that poky little flat. As they sat together, listening to *Hejira*, they seemed to know their lives would never be the same.

But now, as Ade blusters across Oxford Street, all sentimental thought drains from him. Some fucking journey, he spits as he waits to cross the busy intersection outside Nike Town. Warren Craig was his last chance to make something of his life, to get them out of that tiny flat and her out of that dead-end job. Now it's ruined, it's all ruined.

Stella wraps a towel around herself and steps over the crumpled blue dress that is lying by the side of the bath. She picks up her phone and looks at the time. Ten past seven. She will have to get a move on.

She walks through the galley kitchen and into the main room, the one that serves as living room, bedroom and music studio all in one. She crouches under the clothes rail that stands by the door, pulls out a battered pair of jeans and holds them up to the light. Too scruffy. She shoves them back under the rail and picks up a black tight-fitting Ramones T-shirt. It might look okay with the leather jacket but not for tonight, and anyway she's grown out of her indie-chick look. It is the kind of thing she was wearing the last time she saw Paula.

She was nineteen and had just completed her first year at Durham. Nineteen was a different country. None of the rules that had dictated her life until then applied anymore. Durham may not have been her first choice, but she had learned to live with it, and in place of Virginia Woolf and dreaming spires she had guitars and drums and a new means of expression. Instead of discovering great thinkers, she had found her voice, and it carried her on a wave of jangly guitar riffs from one world to another. Singing was the escape route she had been looking for. She could close her eyes and disappear into a song; she could create a new version of herself, one that didn't blush, didn't cry, didn't take life so seriously. When she sang – for the first time in her life – she felt strong.

That summer she came down to London to see Caitlin who, as a newly qualified lawyer, was living in a large shared house overlooking Clapham Common. Within a couple of years she would move to the other side of the world with Greg, her Australian boyfriend, but for now she and Stella were still as close as they had been as children. The plan was to stay for a week, but when Caitlin saw Stella dragging a huge suitcase along the platform at

King's Cross, she knew she would be with her until the end of summer.

One evening, Caitlin suggested going into town. 'We could go and have cocktails,' she said, trying to prise Stella away from the Sony Discman that seemed to be permanently attached to her ears. 'There's a great place in Soho; I think you will love it.'

Stella had been to Soho once when she was a child but had little memory of it beyond a vague recollection of falling asleep on her father's lap in a Moroccan restaurant during a family dinner. It may have been the same trip to London that she fell into the Serpentine, she could not be sure, though she remembers Caitlin telling her the next morning that she had missed a belly dancer and a snake. For years afterwards that image had somehow wound itself up in her memory so that any time she heard people talk about Soho she would imagine a mysterious dark land populated by belly dancers and reptiles.

Yet, when she and Caitlin walked into Frith Street that night, though it did feel like stepping into another world, it was a world of noise and light and chatter. The street was packed with people, some sitting outside bars and restaurants, others sauntering down the middle of the street. Rickshaw drivers weaved in and out between the pedestrians and a pack of gleaming scooters were parked up outside a café. But it was the colours that made the biggest impression on Stella. They were unlike any she had seen before. The effect of a darkening sky on rows and rows of neon signs gave the impression that you were walking through a half-remembered dream. It was futuristic and nostalgic at the same time. You could visualize the angry young men of the Fifties and Sixties huddled in their coffee houses just as clearly as you could a spaceship landing in the middle of Soho Square, though its flashing lights would pale into insignificance against the acidic pinks, blues, reds, greens and yellows of Westminster W1.

Caitlin pointed out Bar Italia. 'There you are, Stella. That's the one Jarvis Cocker wrote a song about.'

Stella nodded, her eyes wide, taking everything in.

Caitlin walked off in the direction of the cocktail bar while Stella stood in the middle of the street and made herself dizzy doing a three-sixty turn, looking up at the names on the hoardings: Little Italy, Bar Italia, Garlic and Shots, Ronnie Scott's.

She ran to catch her sister up.

'This place is amazing,' she whispered. 'Why don't you live closer to town, Caitlin?'

'Because, little sis, I would need about a million in the

bank to afford it,' she laughed. 'The only thing I could manage here would be a bedsit, and who wants to live in a room?'

After several cocktails and a greasy meal in Chinatown, they headed onto Shaftesbury Avenue and were weighing up whether to get a cab or make the trek to Waterloo Station when Caitlin saw her.

'There's Paula! Hey, Paula, over here,' she called to the small figure coming towards them.

As Paula waved and drew closer, Stella felt her stomach tighten. She looked older, better somehow, more assured, if that were possible. She was wearing a battered black leather jacket over a red flowery 1920s-style tea dress. Her hair had grown and it was cut into a sharp Louise Brooks bob. She looked amazing.

'Well well, look who it is!' She gave Caitlin a hug then turned to Stella.

'And look at you. You're all grown up.'

She leaned forward to plant a kiss on her cheek.

Stella tried to act cool by grunting, 'Hi,' then started to fiddle with her phone. She was thankful for the darkness; at least Paula wouldn't see her blush.

Caitlin asked her where she was going.

'I've been invited to a party over on Dean Street. A guy

I went to school with. You should remember him actually, he came up to Oxford a couple of times – Toby Lawson?'

'Oh yeah, I remember him,' said Caitlin. 'Huge guy, looked like a prop forward.'

'That's the one. He's just bought an enormous loft apartment on Dean Street. Listen, why don't you both come with me? It would be great to catch up.'

She looked at Stella who was still fidgeting with her phone.

'What do you think, Stella?' Caitlin asked 'You're not too tired?'

'No, of course not.' Stella rolled her eyes at her sister.

'Wonderful,' said Paula, excitedly. 'Now, shall we?'

She put out her arms for Stella and Caitlin to link then marched across the road towards Dean Street.

'Look at this. My two favourite people.' She smiled, looking from one to the other.

You barely know me, thought Stella as they made their way through the late-night drinkers clogging up the pavement on Wardour Street.

The loft apartment was breathtaking, an enormous space for Central London. Stella wondered what it would be like to live there, looking out onto the Soho streets and watching life in all its wonder and complexity as it passed by beneath.

You would have to be a musician or a writer to live here, she thought, as they walked from room to room.

Unfortunately, the gargantuan host Toby Lawson was neither. Like his father before him, he worked as an investment banker for JP Morgan and, from the sound of the music he played that night, appeared to have rather a thing for female soft rock. Stella was confused. He didn't seem like the kind of person Paula would befriend, in fact none of the people there that night fitted the creative, writer types she had imagined. The party appeared to consist of two sorts of people: loud alpha males in pinstripe suits snorting lines of cocaine off the enormous glass coffee table and skinny girls in loafers and gilets with strange backcombed hair draping themselves over Lawson's gigantic leather sofas desperately trying to bag a banker.

Stella spent most of the evening standing in a corner trying to shake off one lecherous cokehead after another. There was no sign of Caitlin, or Paula for that matter, and she really wanted to leave. She was about to go and look for them when Paula appeared and took her by the hand.

'I'm sorry about this. It's a bit crap, isn't it?' She had to shout to make herself heard above the shrieks of tanked-up Sloanes singing along to Bonnie Tyler. Taking Stella's hand, she led her into the vast living room. 'Too bloody packed,' she muttered, shaking her head.

Then something on the far side of the room caught her eye and she pulled Stella towards it. Stella stood back as Paula crawled under a large round table tucked away at the back of the room.

'Come on, Stella,' she said, beckoning her with her hand. Stella peered underneath the table and giggled. 'This is crazy,' she said as she crawled under to join her.

She felt slightly dizzy as she sat down. Three Blue Havana cocktails at the bar, three glasses of white wine with dinner and an enormous glass of what appeared to be neat vodka, courtesy of Toby Lawson, all helped to loosen her tongue and soon she was chatting merrily away to Paula about anything and everything.

At one point she told her about a story she had been thinking about.

'It's about a girl who finds an old vanity case in a flea market in Paris,' she said, exuberantly. 'Well, it turns out the thing is possessed and it gets the girl to do all sorts of things she would never normally do.' She could hear her voice getting louder and she stopped as her cheeks began to burn. 'It's not even a plot, just a bunch of ideas. I might write it down one day,' she said, quietly.

'Write it down now,' Paula urged. 'I'd love to read it when it's finished. It's funny, you've changed so much from when I first met you, sitting there all serious with your book. And look at you now, so confident and gorgeous.' She took hold of Stella's hand and kissed it.

Stella didn't know how to respond. She wanted to stop talking but her mouth carried on. 'I *will* write a book one day,' she said, with all the fearless assumption that nineteen brings. 'But right now I want to concentrate on my music. I've been writing lyrics and they're . . .'

She glanced at Paula. She looked different all of a sudden. Her eyes, always so animated, looked serious, glassy. She reached out and stroked Stella's cheek gently, moving her face so close, Stella could smell the wine on her breath. 'I think you are the most enchanting girl I have ever met. Whatever you want to do, you will do it, Stella, I've no doubt about that.'

Before she could reply, Paula kissed her. It was the greatest kiss, like the first breath of life; a kiss full of promise and excitement. As she pulled her near, she could feel Paula's energy pour into her, all of her strength surging into Stella's veins. Paula drew her closer and, as the kiss became more urgent, Stella felt the sharpness of Paula's teeth brush against her lips, felt the rough, hard wetness of her tongue as it pushed in and out of her mouth. Then her kisses moved to Stella's neck, gentle butterfly kisses that made her shiver with pleasure. She felt Paula's hand move from the nape of her neck towards the most intimate part of her; a soft, feather-like touch at first, then firmer, deeper. Stella thought she was going to burst with desire. This was beautiful, this was how she had always wanted to feel, this was what she closed her eyes and imagined when she was alone in her room. This was perfect and as Paula pressed her fingers deeper and deeper inside her, she closed her eyes and waited for the inevitable, the rush of pleasure that seemed imminent. But then:

'What's going on?'

Caitlin's face appeared and Paula quickly freed herself from Stella and started adjusting her skirt.

'Come on, Stella. You've had far too much to drink,' shouted her sister, pulling her by the arm. 'We're going now. I've got a cab waiting outside. And as for you –' she glared at Paula who was still under the table – 'what are you playing at? She's my kid sister.'

When she returned to university, Paula wrote her a letter, full of apologies, hoping that she hadn't got her into trouble with Caitlin. She wrote back, and there began a rather quaint correspondence. Unlike her peers who were frantically checking their email inboxes, Stella would trot down to the college post room like a romantic heroine waiting for news of her lost love. Paula always wrote in red ink and when she caught a glimpse of the spidery handwriting she would grab the letter and run back to read it in the privacy of her room.

After reading it once, she would reread it, looking for nuance and meaning. Sometimes the letters were weighty, three or four pages both sides, other times Paula would just send a postcard promising to write more next time. She was working as a production assistant in Soho then and she would write in detail about the people she worked with, the films they were making, where she had gone for lunch, what books she was reading, but the tone, though friendly, was rather detached, and she never once suggested Stella visit her.

Then the letters stopped. Stella heard from Caitlin that Paula had enrolled on a screenwriting course at the New York Film Academy. So she folded up the letters and put them away in an old shoebox with her school exercise books, her revision notes and swimming certificates. Maybe London had been a dream, it certainly felt that way, and Stella couldn't rationalize, in the clear light of day, what had happened that night. Caitlin had been horrified and refused to talk to her the next day. She couldn't live the rest of her life as a pariah, so she consigned the whole incident to the shoebox and set out to prove her heterosexuality with whoever happened to show an interest.

She spent the first few days of the new term lying underneath a greasy-haired guitarist who thought he was the reincarnation of Kurt Cobain, celebrated her twentieth birthday by bedding the editor of the college newspaper and ended her second year with a disturbing tally of conquests. But no matter how many men she slept with, it never felt right. Nothing ever came close to the feeling she'd had with Paula, the deliciousness of Paula's fingers inside her. Sex with men was just painful. Each time she did it, it felt like she was losing her virginity again, each thrust felt like a broken bottle being rammed inside her. She hated having a man on top of her, it felt like he was crushing the life out of her. Was this love? Was this the ultimate pleasure? Was this what people glorified in poems and songs and paintings – this agony? The sensation she'd had that night in London was like being submerged in a warm, safe place, while sex with a man felt like being caught in a freezing blizzard.

Yet, strangely, she found the attention flattering, and boy-girl was the norm, wasn't it? Despite her education and the liberal leanings of her parents, she had still been brought up a Catholic, still had the voice of the priest ringing in her ears, warning of Hell and damnation and breaking taboos. It really shouldn't matter to her, a modern girl who was supposed to belong to an enlightened generation, but she couldn't think of what she had done with Paula without feeling dirty and shameful.

The casual sex came to an abrupt end in her final year at university. She had gone home for the summer holidays. A group of friends had invited her to a party and it was there that she met Michael. He was sweet and funny and, unlike the rest of the men she had been involved with, she actually enjoyed his company, though on the surface he couldn't have been more different to her. He was a 'lad', right down to his expensive trainers, but she found she could talk to him and for a couple of months he became something of a confidante. He was kind and gentle and though he had tried really hard to understand her – he once sat and read 'He Wishes for the Cloths of Heaven' to her when she was ill – he was still part of that world, the world of being normal, of having a safe job and saving up to buy a house on the new estate. Those things would never be important to her and taking them away from him would be like taking away his lifeblood; without them he just didn't make sense. But in a strange way, she yearned for him and the calmness that filled the air whenever he was around.

She wanted to scoop him up and take him away, she wanted to laugh with him and hold him and have a life full of happiness, far away from Paula and dark, secret thoughts. For a few weeks, she had fantasized about travelling, just the two of them, to places where they could create a future. It was such a short period in her life and it blazed like a great warm fire, but no matter how much she may have wanted him to come with her, she knew that he never would.

So she enjoyed his company for the rest of the summer then returned to Durham to concentrate on getting a First. But something was not quite right. She did her usual trick of ignoring the 'problem' but then she had started to bleed heavily. A few hours later, in a bleak hospital room on the outskirts of Durham, she said a silent goodbye to her baby, then returned to university like a half-person, like a ghost floating between two worlds. She skipped lectures and scraped through her exams; she stopped reading her books and writing down her thoughts. Something inside her had died and could never be brought back. The only thing that made sense, the only thing that prevented her from turning inward, was singing. So armed with her second-rate degree and a copy of *The Stage* she boarded the train at North-allerton and headed for London.

She still couldn't bring herself to think about Paula. All that mattered was making music and showing her family that she could make something of her life. And then she met Ade and lived in his world for five years.

But things are different now. She is twenty-seven, a grown woman with a right to live the life she chooses. And she has to consider Ade in all of this. He is a good person, despite his bravado, and he loves her, she knows that. But he loves the person he thinks she is. She is deceiving him as much as she is deceiving herself. Why, only the other day he was talking about names they might give their children. She looks at his saxophone standing upright and proud on the far side of the room. He will have years ahead of him to find love, a love that he deserves. They can't go on ripping each other apart; it is time they let each other go, time they got the chance to find out what real happiness feels like.

Chapter 8

This must be the place, thinks Zoe, as she approaches a shabby-looking block of fast food restaurants and computer shops on Tottenham Court Road.

She checks Jules's note again. On the back he has scribbled: 'Top Floor, 41 Tott Ct Rd. Above MV Computers – first one past Burger King.'

She walks past the red and yellow BK sign with a gnawing in her stomach. The giant poster in the window of a Flame-Grilled Whopper with large fries is making her salivate. She almost succumbs, then remembers her empty purse sitting on the sofa at home.

She looks at her watch. Seven-thirty – she has made it dead on time. To the side of the computer shop is a steel door with six buzzers. She is about to take a chance on the top one when she feels a hand on her shoulder.

'Alright, sweetheart, you're keen, ain't ya?'

She turns to see Jules grinning at her, his ruby-encrusted tooth glinting in the early evening sunlight.

'Jules, you nearly gave me a heart attack,' she cries, holding her hand to her chest.

He waves a set of keys at her and grins. 'Shall we?'

She stands back to let him unlock the door.

'What is this place anyway?' she asks, looking up at the drab, grey building.

Jules is having trouble with the keys. He shakes his head and curses. He looks different tonight, more dishevelled, and he is sweating heavily.

'It's a flat, like I told ya,' he grunts.

'Well, it doesn't look like the kind of place Dan Williams would have a party,' she says.

Suddenly Jules spins round on his heels and pushes his face so close to Zoe's their noses almost touch.

'I never said he was, darlin',' he growls.

His pupils are wide and he looks menacing enough for her to back away.

'Oh, I'm sorry, I just thought . . .'

'What I did say was when Dan's in town, I make his

parties fabulous. You're the one who put two and two together and got sixteen,' he hisses.

'Look, I think I'd better go,' she whispers. 'I've got this all wrong.'

She turns to leave.

'Zoe, wait!' Jules grabs her arm and laughs manically. 'I'm playing with you, darling. Of course Dan's coming. You gotta get used to my sense of humour, doll.' He shakes his head and grins.

'Okay,' she says. She giggles nervously as Jules finally succeeds in opening the door.

The entrance is dark and narrow with peeling red and gold flock wallpaper and a threadbare inky blue carpet that has seen better days. There is a pile of junk mail and empty beer cans in place of a doormat and Zoe has to lunge to get over it.

The carpet stops at the foot of the stairs. Yellow linoleum creeps up the staircase like a damp stain with strips of metal intersecting the edge of each step. It reminds Zoe of the stairwells at school.

'Are you sure you've got the right place, Jules?'

'Oh, take no notice of this,' he replies as he makes his way up the stairs. 'This is a communal entrance; no one's in charge of it, so it goes to shit.'

Zoe thinks of the communal entrance of the flat she grew up in. Her mother had kept it immaculate with fresh flowers on the sideboard. 'Set your stall out right and everything else falls into place.' She hasn't even had the chance to tell her mother about the party, it has all happened so fast. Her mother loves hearing her news and when Zoe calls she tries to keep the phone calls upbeat, telling her how everything is going great. If she told her the truth, her mother would worry. She will give her a call tomorrow and, hopefully, she will have some exciting news to tell. She will want to know every last detail.

Jules has reached the top of the stairs and he looks over the top of the banister, beckoning to her with his index finger. 'Come on, sweetheart, two more floors to go.'

She follows him up, trying not to breathe in the rank smell of marijuana and stale urine that hangs in the air, which, along with her empty stomach and the narrow staircase, is making her feel increasingly nauseous.

She stops to take a breath on the small landing at the top of the stairs. It has three doors leading off it and, though not as bad as the ground floor, is still pretty grim. The walls are painted a sickly pink, like an old woman's bedjacket, and the floor is covered with soiled threadbare jute rugs. In between Flats 1 and 2 is a battered old bureau with a red fire extinguisher propped up against it.

Zoe stops as the door of Flat 3 opens with a loud screech. A red-eyed young man, in his late teens, stands in the doorway, smoking a huge joint. He stares at Zoe then blows a thick cloud of smoke towards her. The smell hits the back of her throat and she feels the nausea rise from the pit of her stomach. Holding onto the banister, she exhales slowly.

Jules, who has almost reached the top of the stairs, turns and sees her.

'One more floor and then we're there, darlin',' he chuckles.

She gathers herself and slowly walks up the remaining steps, which seem to get steeper the further she climbs. They reach a second floor with the same mawkish pink walls as the first but this time just two doors leading off it. A woman's voice shrieks behind the door of Flat 4 and a deep voice responds languidly:

'Shut it, you stupid bitch.'

Zoe hurries up the last flight of stairs, exhaling to stop herself throwing up.

'Come on, babe, we're here.' Jules stands at the top of the stairs, holding out his hand. 'You're a bit out of condition, ain't ya? You wanna get yourself down the gym.'

Ignoring his outstretched hand, she looks around at the white polished floorboards, the expensive-looking rugs, the funky black and white floor tiles, and feels slightly better.

'This is more like it,' she says to Jules who is standing outside the white panelled door of Flat 6, the only flat on the third floor.

'See, you gotta trust me, darlin',' he says as he tries to open the door with the wrong key. 'I wouldn't take someone like you to no shithole.'

Zoe pulls a face. The smell of the previous two floors is still fresh in the back of her throat.

After a second unsuccessful attempt at opening the door, Jules gives up. 'Fuck it, I must have the wrong set.' He shoves the keys into his back pocket and hammers on the door. As they wait, he turns to her and smiles. 'Let's get the party started, eh?'

He laughs at Zoe who is straightening her dress and pulling her fingers through her hair. There is no mirror in the hallway so she can't check if her make-up has survived the uphill trek. She hears footsteps from inside the flat and a heavy thud of drum and bass that gets louder as the door opens.

Standing in the doorway is a giant of a man, six foot

six at the very least, with a thin ratty face and long straw-coloured hair tied back in a ponytail. He is wearing a shabby dark blue sports jacket, tracksuit bottoms and a hooded sweatshirt with 'Raw Sounds '95' written across it.

'Jules, my man!' He holds up his can of Red Bull in greeting. 'You made it.' He speaks with a Scottish accent and the voice is surprisingly high-pitched considering his size.

'Marty blood, how ya doin?' sings Jules, patting him on the shoulder.

Then Marty spots Zoe and moves towards her, his arms outstretched.

'And you must be our girlie, eh?' He smiles, revealing a mouthful of grey, stumpy teeth.

Jules steps in between them. 'Zoe's kindly agreed to entertain us tonight, that's right, Marty. But listen, why don't we have a drink first before our guests arrive?'

He winks at Marty who shakes his head and laughs. 'Sure. Let's fix you a drink Zoe. Come on in, sweetheart.' He stands back and ushers her into the flat. Jules stays by the door, typing out a text message on his phone as Marty gives Zoe a guided tour.

'This is the living room, kitchen, games room, pleasure parlour,' he drawls.

The flat is large but it's no penthouse. The kitchen and living room are open-plan and there are no sofas or armchairs, just huge black leather beanbags and cushions scattered around the floor. A large glass oblong coffee table stands in the middle of the room and the far wall is dominated by a giant widescreen plasma television. Heavy grey blinds cover the windows but inside, the flat is brightly lit.

Almost too bright for a party, thinks Zoe. She stands by the door awkwardly and fumbles with her handbag.

'Have a seat, Zoe,' says Marty, gesturing to the beanbags.

Zoe smiles as she walks into the room.

'I'll get you a drink,' he says. 'What's your poison?'

Zoe is too busy trying to ease herself onto the squishy leather beanbag to hear what Marty is asking her. She tries lowering herself onto it but ends up with her knees stuffed into her chest. After a minute or so of writhing around like an upturned woodlouse, she takes one of the less scary-looking cushions and kneels on it.

'Here you go. I made you one of my cocktails.'

She looks up to see Marty holding out a champagne glass.

'Thanks,' she replies, taking the glass from him. 'What is it?'

'Oh, I don't know, a whole bunch of things, it's my bit-of-everything cocktail.'

He brings over another cushion and sits next to her.

Zoe takes a long sip of her drink. 'That's really nice, thank you.'

Marty sits silently, nodding his head and smiling at her. She sits up straight, wishing Jules would come back in. This guy is giving her the creeps.

'So, what time will Dan Williams get here?' she asks, taking another sip of her drink. She looks up as Jules comes back into the room.

Marty looks at her blankly. 'Who?'

Jules throws his mobile phone down on the coffee table. The noise makes Zoe jump.

'I've been telling Zoe about our friend . . . Dan?' He eyeballs Marty who looks up and makes an 'O' with his mouth.

Zoe doesn't notice. She is looking round the room and wondering how a man like him can afford to live in a place like this.

'I need a drink,' says Jules. He walks over to the kitchen and fixes himself a Jack Daniel's with ice. 'Don't worry, Zoe. He'll be here later,' he says. 'You know these celebs, they like to be fashionably late. Anyway, we got other people coming too. I think you'll like them.'

He brings his drink over to the living room and sits down on the edge of the coffee table.

'What other people?' Zoe drains her glass. 'Anyone I'd recognize?'

'Industry people, definitely people who could help your career. Wouldn't you say so, blood?' Jules raises his eyebrows at Marty who is scrutinizing Zoe's cleavage at close range.

'Oh aye, big time,' he replies, still staring at Zoe's chest. 'It all depends on how big a star you wanna be, how far you wanna go.' He takes Zoe's glass from her and goes into the kitchen to refill it.

Zoe perks up at this talk of industry people.

'I want to be the best glamour model in the business,' she says. 'That's why I came to London. I have a business plan set out. First, I want to get signed by Honey Vision, then I want *Nuts*, *FHM*, the lot. I want my own TV show and a column in *NOW* magazine like Anna B. I'm deadly serious about this; I'll do whatever it takes but I want to go all the way.'

Marty comes towards her with the topped-up drink and smiles slowly. 'That's what we want to hear, sweetheart.'

Zoe takes the glass and puts it down on the coffee table next to Jules.

'Now, where's your bathroom? I need to go and fix my face before all those people arrive.'

'First door on your left, sweetheart,' says Marty, as Zoe picks up her bag.

'Won't be a minute,' she says. Her voice comes out rather high. The drink has gone straight to her head and she feels giddy as she walks out into the hallway and into the bathroom.

Marty rolls his eyes at Jules.

'This is priceless,' he cries. 'Where the Hell did you find her?'

'Ssh, she'll hear you,' hisses Jules, standing up from the coffee table. He picks up his phone and dials a number.

'Alright, it's me,' he mumbles into the phone. 'Yeah, we're ready.'

In the end, Stella settles for a vintage cream linen dress and a faded denim jacket. She leaves her long black hair loose, just like it was the first time they met. It is a warm evening – July is coming into its own – and she feels light as she strolls through the early evening hub.

The air is ripe with a strange kind of energy. She can almost touch it as she crosses Oxford Street and on to Rathbone Place. There is a crowd of drinkers standing outside the Wheatsheaf pub as she passes. Flags are still being waved and toasts being drunk to the glory of Londinium.

2012. It seems like such a long way off and yet it is already a done deal and somewhere, in some distant country, a government-appointed group will be putting together their bid for 2016. Meanwhile, here in London, foundations are being dug in the east, new rail links will be constructed and ambitious parents will be pushing their offspring to go the distance. All in anticipation of a date that sounds more like an office extension number than a year.

Seven years. She'll be thirty-four by then. What a thought. At twenty-four, she had imagined herself ten years down the line with a couple of platinum-selling albums, touring the world and writing songs. Now she feels different. Five years of living with Ade has made her see the music industry for what it is. When she first met him, he was like a force of nature. He told her they could create songs together like Carole King and James Taylor, he lent her books about the music factory in New York and he showed her how to use her voice correctly. They had gone to jazz clubs together and met people like Herbie Hancock and Tony Bennett. Everyone loved Ade, people flocked around him. It was amazing, like being in some strange netherworld. It was the eternal cocktail hour she had yearned for when she was younger. And the first time she saw him playing in Ronnie Scott's felt like she was watching some kind of magic unfold. He was so talented, but his talent was edgy, unpredictable; he would take songs apart and make them his own, rip them up into new and crazy shapes and sounds. The first few years of their relationship had been wonderful and though the physical side could never fully satisfy her, it didn't matter because she was happy. But then Warren Craig came along. Watching Ade crawl up to him makes her feel sick. He has changed: the old Ade wasn't bothered about going to flash parties and sweet-talking record company suits, he used to say it was all bullshit. It's all about being desperate enough, unscrupulous enough and obsessed enough, and Stella is none of these things. The Ade she knew has disappeared; the life she loved has dissolved into sludge and nothing feels right.

The problem is, she doesn't know what she believes in anymore. All she has left are strange remnants of the past, forgotten dreams and distant memories of books and words and happiness, the things that had inspired her when she was younger, when music had been the background to her life, not her whole reason for living. She has two solid reasons for carrying on, for waking up every morning without fearing the future. One of them is just a bunch of words in her head, the other is waiting for her in the Charlotte Street Hotel.

She has this recurring daydream – it is actually more a meditation – that always comes to her on her early morning walks through Soho, listening to her iPod. Time after time, it is the same scene. A tree-lined street in New York. It could be Greenwich Village or even Brooklyn, she's not sure, and anyway, she's never actually been to New York. Still, it is so vivid she can almost reach out and touch the green and white street signs, the amber leaves on the trees, the fire escape with its black metal ladder. It is either a vision of the future, or she's been reading too many Paul Auster novels. Anyway, she gets to a brownstone townhouse and walks up the sandy-coloured steps, her arms full of groceries in brown paper bags (ever since she was a child she has wanted to buy groceries in brown paper bags). As she fumbles for her keys the door opens and Paula is standing there. She looks at Stella like she is the most precious thing in the world then takes the shopping from her hands and says, 'You're home.' There it ends, along with the closing bars of 'Morning Morgantown'. Her daydreams only ever last the length of the first song on Joni Mitchell's *Ladies of the Canyon* album but what remain are those words: 'You're home.'

She turns the corner into Charlotte Street and all the noise of the pubs on Rathbone Place evaporates. It really is a little piece of calm, right behind one of the busiest streets in the world yet a million miles away. The street is elegant and full of colour, from the bright pink of the Rasa Samudra Indian restaurant to the green and white awnings of the Charlotte Street Hotel. It is almost too perfect, too clean for London, like stepping into a Richard Curtis vision of how life should be.

The hotel looms ahead like a New England mansion with its sage green exterior and regal sash windows. Stella has been there once before, when she and Ade performed some covers for a fortieth birthday party. She loved the cool 1920s interior with its Vanessa Bell paintings and a chaise longue that was pure Gatsby. There had been a great atmosphere at the party and the guests seemed to like her rendition of 'The First Cut is the Deepest'. Of course Ade had to go and spoil it all by squabbling with the host over payment. He has this knack for causing trouble wherever he goes. Still, the hotel had left an impression on Stella and she knew that one day she would go back there without Ade.

Now is her chance, but as she approaches the entrance she starts to panic. She's had so many conversations with Paula in her head these past few years that now she's going to see her in the flesh she feels silly, vulnerable somehow.

'Be cool,' she tells herself. 'Be cool and don't say anything stupid.'

The entrance lobby is empty except for a curly-haired, rather earnest-looking young woman in a black trouser suit sitting on a purple velvet sofa reading a racked copy of the *Guardian*.

The bar, as Stella recalls, is through a set of glass doors to the left. She walks towards them and is about to go in when she pauses. She is not quite ready. Her mouth feels dry and she can feel her face burning. It's been years and now the moment has come, somehow it doesn't feel right.

She lingers. She even toys with the idea of walking out then back in again but that would be silly. As she stands there she is aware of someone looking at her and she turns to see the serious-faced woman on the sofa regarding her quizzically.

'Are you lost?' she asks, putting her newspaper down.

'No,' says Stella. 'I'm just thinking.'

The woman smiles at her.

Stella looks at her watch. She's late. She cannot put it off any longer and she pushes the heavy wooden door, trying to think mundane thoughts, telling herself that this is no big deal, it's just a drink with an old friend.

The bar, like the lobby, is quieter than she expected and as she looks around, she can just see a couple of middle-aged women sharing a bottle of champagne at a table in the corner and a heavily groomed woman in a baby pink pashmina sitting at the bar.

She stands there, not knowing quite what to do. Is Paula late or has she changed her mind and not turned up? She moves to go then someone calls her name.

'Stella.'

She turns to see the pashmina woman. She has jumped down from the bar stool and is smiling at her. She recognizes the eyes but that is about all.

'Paula?'

The woman walks towards her, her arms outstretched. She looks like a politician's wife. Her beautiful dark hair has been highlighted and cut into shoulder-length layers, and she is clutching a huge black designer handbag. It is like looking at a completely different person. This isn't Paula. This isn't the woman who invades her dreams every night, the woman who hid with her underneath a table in Soho and made her fall deeply and passionately in love. This is an imposter, someone claiming to be Paula. The real Paula is not a coiffed lady-who-lunches and she would never wear pink. She always hated pink.

'Stella, it's so good to see you,' she says. 'You look great, really great.'

Her voice is clipped and rather nervy.

'Thanks,' Stella replies. 'You look . . . different.'

'Ha, that's America for you,' she laughs. 'I couldn't get away with being a scruff out there. It's all teeth whitening and manicures wherever you go. I guess it was a case of, if I want to be taken seriously, I better smarten up.'

Stella smiles awkwardly and looks down at her feet. She doesn't know what to say.

'Well then,' says Paula. 'What are we doing standing here like lemons? Shall we have a drink?' She takes Stella's arm to guide her towards the bar, then stops. 'Nah, it's like a morgue in here tonight, and too bright. If I remember correctly, you always preferred low lighting, didn't you?'

'Yes,' says Stella. 'Bright lights show all your flaws.' She tries not to look at the pashmina as they walk out of the bar.

Paula turns to her and smiles. 'How about we head into Soho then? You can show me all the cool new bars. I bet you've been having a ball living there.'

'It has its moments,' says Stella, as they walk into the lobby.

The woman has vacated the sofa and the place is deserted.

150

Stella's head is spinning. This is all too much of a shock. She needs some space to think.

As they reach the main doors, she stops.

'Will you excuse me,' she says as Paula steps out onto the pavement. 'I just need to go to the loo.'

'Of course. I'll wait out here for you.' Paula smiles and strokes Stella's cheek. The intimacy of the gesture takes Stella by surprise and she looks at Paula's face. Her eyes haven't changed, they are still the same beautiful pixie eyes she fell in love with, but everything else just feels weird. It's like she's standing here with a ghost.

'It's so good to see you, Stella, it really is.' For a moment it looks like she is going to cry, her face looks so sorrowful. 'Go on then,' she says, sounding like a mother waving her child off to school. 'You go freshen up. I'll just be here waiting.'

As Stella walks back through the lobby it feels like her head and her heart are being torn in two. In the ladies, she rinses her hands with cold water then looks at her reflection in the huge oblong mirror that runs the length of the row of sinks.

It wasn't supposed to be like this.

She dries her hands on a blue paper towel and tries to think. She has gone off the idea of cocktails now, there doesn't seem to be much to celebrate, and cocktails would only make sense with the old Paula, the 1920s starlet with the laughing eyes, not this new laminated version. No, she will have to think of somewhere more low-key, somewhere casual and discreet and close to the flat so she can make a quick getaway if it all goes horribly wrong.

She knows just the place.

Paula is waiting in the lobby when she comes out of the toilet and as Stella draws near, she holds out her arm for her to link. 'Shall we?'

Stella takes her arm and smiles. 'I thought I might show you the street where I live,' she says, nonchalantly. 'There's a great bar just across the road from the flat.'

'Sounds good,' says Paula.

Stella lets go of her arm to open the door then turns and grins.

'It is. You'll love it.'

Chapter 9

It is standing room only in The Dog and Duck but Seb has managed to find a stool at the far end of the bar.

He looks at the large empty wine glass and feels warmth rising through his body. He got here in the end and now surely nothing can ruin the pleasure of this fine summer's evening. He has consumed just enough alcohol to feel vibrant, alert, every nerve in his body tingling with untapped energy. He can do anything, be anybody; he is in control. Now just one more glass will seal this feeling, give him the motivation required to make the journey to Knightsbridge and convince his mother and sister that all is well in his world.

Val, the fifty-something flame-haired barmaid, shimmies towards him, mouthing the chorus to 'Waterloo Sunset'.

It is clear she is feeling the heat and her gold satin vest is sticking to her body like cling film.

'You managed to get your CDs on tonight then, Val?'

'Too right, darling, nothing like a bit of The Kinks to get the night started, eh?' Wiping her forehead, she rings in an order on the cash register next to Seb. 'So how are you tonight, my love?' She doesn't look up as she slowly types in the numbers.

'I'm great thanks, Val,' he replies, leaning forward so she can hear him. 'Busier than usual, isn't it?'

'It's all this Olympic stuff,' she groans. 'Most of these clowns have been drinking since morning.' She stops to count the change in her hand then looks again at the illuminated numbers on the till. 'He gave me twenty pounds . . . two vodka tonics and a bag of Twiglets. Oh, Seb, love, I'm losing my marbles, I tell you. My head's pounding with this heat; I'm getting too old for all of this.'

'Nonsense, Val, you're in your prime,' shouts Seb above the shrieks of laughter from a newly arrived group of punters.

'Ooh, you're a charmer you are.' She leans towards him and pats his face. 'She's a lucky girl what manages to bag you, son, you know that?'

Seb's smile begins to fade. He needs that drink. 'Can I get another glass of Rioja when you're ready, Val?'

She goes to give the change to a man at the other side of the bar then turns on her heels to take Seb's order, ignoring the shouts from the lengthy queue that is now threatening to spill out onto the street.

'Same again, you say, love?'

Seb looks up as the opening bars of 'You Really Got Me' boom out over the speaker system.

He starts to loosen up again. Everything is fine; this is what is meant to happen, this is where he is meant to be, sitting here in Soho where the world begins and ends. It would be a betrayal to walk away now, to go and vegetate in Knightsbridge.

'Better make it a bottle this time, Val,' he says, pulling a twenty-pound note from his back pocket.

Val returns with the bottle and a fresh glass, clinking them down in front of him and swiping the twenty from his outstretched hand.

'Enjoy. I'll be back with your change when I've served that mob,' she says, rolling her eyes towards the queue that has now doubled in volume.

'Thanks, Val, and keep the change.'

She flashes a thumbs up as she disappears into the throng.

He pours the wine into his glass, feeling like a king

looking out onto his subjects. So palpable is this sense of completeness, he feels he could stand up on the bar and rouse all these cherry-faced drinkers into doing whatever he asks. If he could bottle this feeling, he would be able to conquer all that is holding him back.

He tells himself that tomorrow he will start drawing again, real drawing. His ideas are starting to flow as they always do after the third glass of wine. By the seventh or eighth, these ideas will evaporate and start flowing down Bateman Street, but for now he is energized and for the first time in ages he is actually making plans.

A female voice cuts through his thoughts.

'Excuse me, can you push your seat in?'

He turns and sees a flash of black hair and pale skin and feels his heart contract inside his chest. His face reddens and he can hear the blood pumping through his temples. It is only when he stands up and pushes the stool underneath the bar that he sees what is really there. The slightly crooked teeth, the round childlike face, of course it isn't . . . how could it be?

'Stella! How are you?'

He laughs: a hollow, guttural sound. Even after six months, the resemblance still sets off a series of little earthquakes in his chest when he bumps into her in here or in the queue at Tesco Metro on Dean Street. When Ade brought her over one night and introduced her as his girlfriend, Seb thought he'd had too much to drink. It was as though he'd been transported back in time – the hair, the skin, the movement, it was uncanny.

'Oh, Seb, I didn't know it was you,' she says.

'Is Ade with you?' asks Seb, looking towards the door. He smiles awkwardly.

'No,' she says, rather abruptly. She leans in towards him as a couple of overweight men squeeze past her to get to the bar. 'I'm just here with a friend.' Her voice is getting higher but Seb can't work out whether she is nervous or slightly drunk. She is standing so close to him, he can smell her scent, a strange mixture of citrus and sour milk. The two men decide to chance their luck at the other end of the bar and Stella takes a step back into the empty space.

'I hate it when it's like this,' she says. 'There's no room to move. I think I'll go upstairs, there'll be more chance of getting served.'

Seb nods, taking in her face. The full lips, the hazel eyes, the way her hair curls over one eye. It is like someone has cloned the DNA in some laboratory and then . . .

'It's a bit packed in here, Stella.' He looks up and sees a sleek attractive woman walking towards them.

'This is Paula,' says Stella. 'Paula, this is Seb.'

He extends his hand towards the woman. But instead of shaking it, she looks at it like it is tainted and, just to reiterate her disdain, folds her arms across her chest. She mutters a short, 'Hi,' before casting her eyes around the bar with a frown. 'It's so busy in here, Stella, do you think we should go somewhere else? I really wanted us to be able to talk but I won't be able to hear myself think.'

Seb notices the way she is looking at Stella, like a lioness with her cub. He wonders if they are related: could she be an overprotective elder sister, a cousin? No, Stella had referred to her as a friend.

'Honestly, Paula, it will be fine,' says Stella. 'We'll go upstairs, there's plenty of space up there.'

Seb is intrigued. Why is Stella so nervous?

'It's this way,' says Stella, leading Paula towards the glass doors and up to the first floor bar.

Seb sits back down, feeling unsettled by the encounter. She didn't even say goodbye. He feels tense again; the clear-mindedness has deserted him and he feels vulnerable, like he is stranded on some great windswept mountain with no hope of rescue. 'Oh, fuck it,' he mutters into his drink. 'Fuck it all.'

Someone taps his shoulder.

'What?' he snaps.

He turns sharply, ready to defend his solitude, ready to take on anyone who threatens to disturb it. Then he sees that face.

'Stella,' he says gently. He takes a sip of his wine and smiles at her, trying his best to appear sober and composed.

'Sorry to be a pest,' she says, 'but I just wanted to ask a favour.'

'Anytime.' He feels the wine flush his cheeks.

'If Ade happens to come in, can you not tell him I'm here? It might be a bit awkward you see, what with Paula and everything. Well, not exactly awkward, just, well you know what he's like. And, he's probably going to be pissed off, you see I was supposed to be going to this party with him tonight and I haven't and . . .'

She is speaking so fast, Seb can barely keep up. He places his hand on her arm, as much to steady himself as to calm her down. 'Don't worry, Stella, I won't tell him you're here.'

'Good; you know when he's angry he loses all reason and I couldn't face him making a scene.'

'Just relax and have a good night with your friend,' says Seb. 'And if he tries to make a scene, I'll pack him off to the zoo where he belongs.'

Stella's eyes light up and she looks like she is going to

laugh. 'I'd better get back upstairs.' As she heads towards the glass doors she turns and smiles. 'Thanks,' she mouths.

Seb stands up and stumbles towards her.

'My pleasure,' he slurs, raising his glass. 'And just you . . . just you behave yourself, you hear me.'

A group of women push past him, obscuring her from his view.

'You're too good for them,' he sighs. 'Too good for all of them.'

This last comment falls into empty space as the door closes behind her and he slumps back into his seat.

He has seen her sing. Three weeks ago. Ade had talked him into going to some dive on Denmark Street. It was a charity event. Tibet? What he can remember is walking through a half-lit gloomy bar to a poky back room where a small crowd had gathered. He heard it before he saw her: a beautiful sound, smooth and clear. She was singing something folky, something about the stars and the earth and falling, and he stood there with his mouth open, unable to reconcile the confident beauty on the stage with the shy, reticent girl he knew. She was on fire that night and Seb had fallen under her spell. Christ, he'd even, in his drunken stupor, told Ade of all people that he wanted to kiss her hand. But it was more than lust, it was the image of her standing under the green-

160

blue spotlight. For a second it wasn't Stella, it was someone else come back to visit him like a hologram and he'd tried to reach out, tried to grab her through the wires and the lights, tried to touch her skin, but he had stumbled into Ade who had laughed and offered to buy him another drink.

A chorus of cheers rings out as another group of revellers burst into the pub waving their crumpled flags. Seb raises his glass and toasts them.

'Here's to 2012,' he cries as he leans across the bar.

'And all who sail in her,' booms a voice from behind him.

'Alright, Seb, mind if I join you?'

Ade is already grabbing a stool from behind some unsuspecting drunk and walking back to the bar.

'Pass another glass will you, Val?' he shouts to the flustered barmaid who is busy grappling with a bottle opener.

Growing impatient, he leans over and grabs a wine glass from behind the bar, then fills it with the remnants of Seb's bottle.

'Now, comrade,' he leers. 'Let's get shit-faced.'

Zoe hears voices coming from the living room. She has reapplied her make-up twice but still isn't sure whether the red lipstick works better than the beige lip gloss.

'Important industry people', that's what Jules had said. She takes one last look in the mirror.

'Yeah, red lippy it is.'

The alcohol has made her head feel woozy and the harsh light of the bathroom is making her see white spots in front of her eyes. She leans in towards the mirror and holds the edge of the sink to steady herself as she runs a finger around the edges of her lips.

She smiles at her reflection in the mirror, half to check if she has lipstick on her teeth and half to see what she will look like when she introduces herself to the guests. 'Hi, I'm Zoe,' she says to the reflection, first with the smile, then with a more serious expression. 'Come on, you fool,' she says to herself, 'you can't spend the night locked in the bathroom.'

She opens the door and prepares to make her entrance. As she walks down the hallway, she sees that the living room lights are turned off. She can't hear any music or voices and she starts to worry: how long has she been in the bathroom? Has she missed Dan Williams? A thick cream-coloured cloud of smoke hangs in the air. It smells different to the marijuana she smelt on the way up, it's a more subtle smell: mustier and less sickly. Still, she tries not to breathe it in as she approaches the living room.

She stands in the doorway. The living room is in darkness.

'Ooh, you've gone for the vamp look. I like it,' Marty drawls from somewhere in the shadows.

Zoe tiptoes into the room. 'Er, why are you sitting in the dark?'

'Trying to make it more atmospheric, sweetheart,' Marty whispers. 'I'll turn on the light, if you want.'

She hears him tripping towards the other side of the room. 'Fuck! Almost kneecapped myself on that shitting table.' With a flick of a switch, his voice softens. 'There, welcome to my parlour, pretty girl.'

Zoe blinks as the light comes back. Is this the same place? The cushions and beanbags are gone, the table has been moved to the far corner and in the middle of the room is a huge rug with two naked women lying on it. Zoe gasps. One of them, a blonde girl, looks disturbingly young. She is thin and very pale. The other woman is much older. Her hair is long and greasy and she has dark circles under her eyes. They don't look up as Marty addresses Zoe. There is a bluish glow coming from the rug, and the silvery glint of tin foil. The blonde leans towards the glow and Zoe sees she has a glass pipe in her hands.

'Could someone please tell me what is going on?'

She directs the question to Jules who is sitting on a kitchen stool playing with his phone, but he doesn't answer.

Marty comes up behind her and massages her shoulders. 'Now, Zoe, you told me just now that you want to be a glamour model, am I right?'

'Yeah, but I never said anything about all this. I don't do drugs and I certainly don't do whatever they're just about to do.' She watches as the girl takes a deep drag from the pipe then tilts her head back.

'Ssh, now,' says Marty in a soft voice, as though trying to calm a nervous colt. He places his nicotine-stained finger to her mouth. 'You also said you wanted to be the best glamour model in the world, yeah? Well how do you think glamour models earn their keep, sweetheart?'

He lets go of her and walks over to the futon, squeezing between the two girls.

'Now,' he continues. 'Take Heidi and Rochelle here. They know what they've got to do to make it. And I'm telling you, love, you've got a long way to go till you get tits like this.' He cups the right breast of the blonde in his hand, then bends his head and runs his tongue along her nipple.

Zoe knows she should get out of there but she can't move. Her legs feel like they are weighted down. She stands there like a voyeur staring at the blonde's perfect breasts.

Inside, she is screaming, *Come on, Zoe, get out of here*, but her body won't respond. She wills herself to move but as she turns to go, Marty jumps up and comes towards her.

'Don't go, sweetheart. The fun's just starting,' he whispers, his face just centimetres from hers. 'Nervousness is such a turn-off. Now, come on, love, this is what you're getting paid for.' He roughly bundles her back into the room.

'Listen,' she says, trying to reason with him. 'There's been a misunderstanding here. I thought I was coming to Dan Williams's party. I think there's been a mix-up, you see I'm not a prostitute, I'm a model.'

'Wait, there,' says Marty, gruffly. 'I want to show you something,' He walks over to the kitchen and pulls open a drawer. Zoe's heart leaps. What's he getting? When he turns round, she sees he is holding a magazine. He comes towards her with a manic leery smile. 'Now this looks like a girl who's up for it, this looks like a girl who's just begging to be fucked.' He waves the magazine in her face and she sees a photograph of a woman splashed across the page. The woman is lying with her legs wide open, her head flung back. She is holding a man's penis to her mouth. 'Now, that's how glamour models earn their money.' Marty spits the words in her face; his breath is rank and she can smell stale sweat as he waves the page in front of her. 'Look at this whore, she's gagging for it.' He throws the magazine across the room and she watches numbly as it falls to the floor.

'Tell you what, Jules,' he says as he walks back into the kitchen. 'This one's got a lot to learn.' Jules doesn't respond. His head is slumped on the breakfast bar. Marty comes back out of the kitchen carrying a tiny silver camcorder.

'Didn't you say you wanted to get into TV?' he cackles. 'Now, you join in anytime you like, yeah?'

He walks over to the rug where the two girls are still taking it in turns to smoke from the crack pipe. 'That's enough now, lassies,' he says, taking the pipe from the limp hand of the blonde and putting it down on the coffee table. 'Now, I wanna see some action.'

He presses a button on the camcorder and places it next to the pipe. Then he starts to undress. The two girls druggily begin to perform. The older woman takes charge, straddling her companion, sucking hard on her breasts and grinding her like a dog on heat.

Meanwhile, Marty calls out instructions as he pulls off his trousers.

'That's right, Heidi, fuck her good,' he growls. 'Lemme see that arse of yours, baby. Oh Jesus, girls, you're making me fucking crazy here.' He crawls towards the girls on his knees, then grabs the blonde by the back of her hair and pulls her face towards his cock.

Zoe has slowly moved away from the centre of the room and is easing her way along the wall towards the kitchen. She hears the front door slam. Jules, roused from his stupor, stands up and walks across the room. Meanwhile, the floor show continues. The blonde has collapsed in a heap, her arms and legs spread out in a star shape. Beside her Marty is bent over the prone body of the older woman, roughly taking her from behind.

'Come on,' he howls. 'Take it like the bitch you are.'

Zoe looks at the open door. Now is her chance. She edges towards the kitchen and quickly slips out.

Jules is standing in the hall with a large woman who has her back to Zoe. They are busy dividing twenty-pound notes with Jules counting out her share one at a time.

'Come on, you dumb shit, I haven't got all night,' hisses the woman.

'Jules, I've got to go,' interrupts Zoe. 'This is not what I thought it was going to be.'

At this, the woman turns around and Zoe feels her legs buckle.

'Dina?'

She looks at Zoe blankly. 'What is the problem, Zoe?'

Zoe feels dizzy. 'Dina, what are you doing here? You . . . you should be at home.' She knows she is not making any sense, but nothing about this situation is sensible. Her head feels light and she feels herself start to sway.

Dina folds the cash into a wad and stuffs it into the top pocket of her jacket.

'I helped you, Zoe,' she says. 'This is good money for a girl like you. We all need to earn a living. We all need to pay bills, yes?'

'You set me up?' whispers Zoe. 'You planned all this?'

'Set-up, maybe,' grunts Dina. 'I see it as help. I help you girls out. You live in that flat for nothing, two-fifty a month in central London, it's a joke. You lost your job; I thought you would be grateful for the money.' She folds her arms across her chest and shoots a look at Jules who is staggering into the bathroom. 'Don't be too long in there,' she shouts. 'I need you to go and finish up the Goodge Street job.'

Zoe is trying to add things up in her head. This cannot be happening. She is thinking about the flat, about the room-mate she never sees, the girls who work all hours in 'restaurants', and she is thinking about Dina, her caring landlady, and tries to reconcile that image with the monster standing in front of her. Yet, still she tries to reason it.

'This is crazy, Dina,' she cries. 'I thought you worked for the homeless.'

Dina comes towards her. Her face is hard and indifferent. Where is the soft-hearted woman Zoe waved goodbye to just a couple of hours ago? Maybe she never existed, and Zoe has simply dreamed up a perfect image of a perfect landlady. Maybe it has all just been wishful thinking.

'You're right,' says Dina. 'I provide board and lodgings for all you homeless girls running away from your shitty lives. As you said, you left your "mam" in Middlesbrough.'

At the mention of her mother, something inside Zoe snaps. She doesn't know whether it is shock or anger but she knows it is all about survival now. Her heart is racing. She looks at Dina's mocking face; she looks at the twenty-pound notes poking out of her front pocket. The door is wide open and the two men are in no position to stop her; there is nothing to lose.

'Bye, Dina,' she says, putting her hand on the woman's shoulder. 'It's been nice knowing you.'

With a swipe of her hand she grabs the cash and before Dina knows what is happening, Zoe is gone.

Chapter 10

Upstairs in The Dog and Duck, Stella sits hunched over a low table watching Paula as she makes her way back from the bar with a bottle of champagne in an ice bucket.

'What are we celebrating?' she asks, as Paula sits down next to her and takes the bottle from its cradle.

'Seeing you again of course.' She lifts her voice over the noise of the room.

'I'm sorry it's so packed,' says Stella, holding out her glass for Paula to fill. 'It's not normally this busy on a Wednesday.'

'And what are all these flags for?' Paula grimaces as she pours them both a glass.

'Surely you've heard,' says Stella. 'London's just won the

bid to host the Olympics. I was in Trafalgar Square this morning. It was incredible, all the . . .'

'I can't stand sport,' Paula interrupts. 'All this communal flag-waving. Talk about the great unwashed. Although I do love hiking, strangely enough, but only when I'm in the mood, only in good weather.'

She takes a sip of champagne then smiles at Stella.

Stella feels like she is in some kind of parallel universe. Hiking? Is this really the same person?

'So,' says Paula, changing the subject. 'Who was the drunkard downstairs?'

'The drunkard?'

'Yeah, the pretty boy at the bar,' says Paula, narrowing her eyes. 'He was all over you, it was disgusting.'

'Oh, you mean Seb?' Stella is quite shocked to hear him being called a drunkard. Yes, she has seen him drunk more times than she has seen him sober, but she wouldn't call him an alcoholic, he just likes having a good time. 'Seb's not a drunk,' she says, defensively. 'Far from it, he's got a great job.' She tries to remember the title of this important job, but her brain feels like jelly. 'He works in the creative department of Honey Vision; it's a very senior role.'

'What's Honey Vision?' asks Paula. 'It sounds like an ailment.'

'It's a model agency I think,' says Stella. 'They're based on Shaftesbury Avenue. Really, Paula, I don't think he's a drunk, he's probably just had a hard day.'

'A model agency. How lovely,' says Paula, wryly. 'Well, he's obviously into you, big time.'

'What, Seb? I don't think so. I don't think I'm his type at all.'

Paula doesn't respond to this, she just nods her head vaguely. Her eyes are dead, thinks Stella. It's like the spirit has been sucked out of her. Stella is growing increasingly uneasy. She searches her brain for something to say while Paula stares vacantly at the champagne bottle.

'Anyway, what about you? How's the writing?'

'Oh that,' she sighs, topping Stella's glass up.

'You don't sound too enthusiastic.'

She is trying hard to ignite some flicker of the old Paula but it seems pointless. What is she expecting? Some kind of Wonder Woman moment when she will whip off her pashmina to reveal the gorgeous, cultured girl she once was?

'Well, to be honest, Stella,' she says, interrupting her thoughts, 'it just didn't work out. The TV industry over in the States is just manic, it's not for me.' She smiles weakly.

'What do you mean?' Stella's voice comes out louder

than she intended. 'That's all you ever talked about, all you ever wanted. What about all the plays you wrote at Oxford? What about the Fringe First?'

Paula stares into her glass then looks up and smiles at her, like a mother about to deliver a sermon to a naughty child.

'Everyone writes plays at university, Stella,' she says, rubbing the rim of the glass with her finger. 'Everyone acts, everyone writes, everyone sings. That's what's expected. You play-act for three years and then you go and live in the real world.'

'The real world?' Stella can't believe what she is hearing. 'So you're saying that writing and acting and singing and all those things we used to talk about in our letters, all those things you made me believe in, you're saying that was just play-acting? Come on, Paula, you were different, *we* were different.'

'Oh, Stella, calm down.' She pulls her chair closer. 'I'm not talking about you. I mean look, you're young, you're living in Soho and having a ball. I'm five years older and well, I'm just saying that when the fun and games of your twenties are over, you have to settle down and look at earning a living.'

'So, you're saying you can't earn a living from writing?'

Stella is trying, really trying, to bring the old Paula back, to reel her in like a fish.

'Well of course you can, of course you can, but I'm no bloody Stephen Poliakoff, and to be honest, Stella, I'm just happy doing bits and pieces now.'

Stella goes to say something then stops. What's the point?

'I still write,' Paula continues, 'but it's not the be all and end all anymore. I enjoy other things too. Sometimes, I think I was a bit too intense when I was younger, too moody and self-obsessed. Now I just think, Hell, there's more to life than all that introspection. You'll think I'm crazy but I've really got into gardening . . .'

Stella has lost track of what she is saying. She can just see a person she once knew fade slowly out of focus, until all that is left is a fuzzy pink outline.

'Stella? Stella, are you alright?'

'Yeah, I'm fine. Just daydreaming, that's all.'

She takes a sip of her drink and winces. Her mouth is dry and it is making the champagne taste sour.

'So why are you here, Paula?' she asks. 'Are you back in London for good?'

Paula looks serious for a moment, then sits up straight and puts her hands together as if she is about to pray.

'Yes, Stella, I am back in London now or, I should say, *we* are back.' She looks at Stella nervously.

'We? I don't understand.'

Paula sighs heavily then looks down at the table. She continues in a near-whisper. 'I mean, me and Ian. My husband.'

'Your what?' This cannot be happening.

'Oh, please, Stella, let me explain.'

Stella feels numb, like she is sitting at a wake while the dead person sits beside her digging their own grave.

'Say something, Stella, please don't shut me out.'

'What can I say?' She asks the question to herself. 'What do you want me to say, Paula? That I'm happy for you? Why the hell did you get back in touch? I was fine, I was getting by fine, and now you turn up and fuck with my head again, just like you did when I was nineteen.' Stella's hands are shaking. She places them on the table and tries to compose herself.

'Oh, Stella,' says Paula, putting her hands over Stella's. 'I knew I shouldn't get in touch, but when I spoke to Caity last week and she told me you were living here I just couldn't help myself. I kept imagining you, walking these streets, sitting in Bar Italia, doing wonderful things. I kept seeing your beautiful little face and I couldn't keep away.

You see, Stella, you and me, well we're not what I'd call conventional are we, though Heaven knows I've tried to be. The truth is I see you as my little . . . my guilty secret.'

Stella arches her back and pulls her hand away. 'What are you talking about, Paula?'

But she doesn't hear.

'You see, Stella, Ian's what I need right now,' she says, as though referring to an ISA or a time-saving kitchen appliance. 'He's a great guy, works in advertising, as ballsy as they come.' She gives a half-hearted little snort, then goes on. 'He's loud, funny, always the centre of attention. We're a good match.'

Stella just wants to run away, to bolt down the stairs, back to her life.

'Stella? Surely you can understand that this is what I need at the moment. That this is the place I'm in. Who's to say what might happen in a few months, a few years.'

Stella sits stony-faced, staring at the back of a red-haired woman standing at the bar. She has the straightest back.

'Backbone,' she whispers.

'What's that?' Paula asks, leaning in to hear.

Stella ignores her.

'Remember that song I sent you?' Paula starts to sing

off key. '*I wrote this song, two hours before we met . . .* That's you and me, Stella.'

'Oh shut up, Paula, please will you just shut up.'

She slams her fist down on the table with such force she surprises herself.

'Stella,' Paula cries, 'I thought you'd be okay with this. I thought you were like me.'

Stella looks up at her and realizes just how pathetic it all is. All these years of pining for her, analysing every letter for a hint of affection like a stray dog waiting for scraps of food. It's her fault. She had let her imagination run riot to create a heroine who doesn't exist. She is shaking and she can feel a familiar sensation in her throat. It isn't Paula she is crying for, it's the life she has always believed in. It's the brownstone in New York, it's a person who understood, it's *Mrs Dalloway*, it's all those expectations she nurtured back when Soho was just a word, before it became a way of life. Her life.

'Stella, this is crazy.' Paula stands up and knocks the dregs of her glass over her mobile phone. 'Shit!' She begins to wipe it with her sleeve. 'Stella, I don't understand this.'

'Just go home, Paula,' says Stella, wearily. 'Go and see your husband, enjoy your holidays and your glasses of wine and your gardening. I'm sorry but I'm not your guilty pleasure, I'm just a crazy person who thought you were something special. I was wrong.'

As Paula stands there, her phone starts to ring. She switches it off and stuffs it into her pocket. 'Stella, you have got to believe me, this is not what I meant to happen. There's so much you don't understand.'

'I understand all right,' Stella snaps. 'I understand that you're a coward. You haven't got the guts to be who you really are just like you haven't got the guts to be a writer. You're a fuck up, Paula, a total fake.'

Paula glares at her but her eyes are glassy with tears.

'Is that what you think? That I'm a fuck up? This, from someone who's living with a man – yes, Stella, I know all about the jazz man, Caity told me – and working in a minimum-wage job. What happened to *your* aspirations and dreams, Stella? What happened to that bright and gorgeous girl I knew? You expect me to be strong but look at you, you're a mess. All these years, I've credited you with a bit of maturity but really you're just a silly little girl.' She picks up her bag, pulls something out and goes to throw it towards the table but it misses.

'Goodbye, Stella,' she sobs as she makes her way out of the bar.

Stella is rooted to the seat. She can't move.

'Here, babe, she dropped this.'

She looks up to see the straight-backed woman holding something towards her. 'You want to get yourself another bottle of the fizzy stuff with this, calm your nerves,' says the woman.

Stella takes the piece of paper from her, trying not to look up. The woman walks away and Stella looks down at the crumpled twenty-pound note. She folds it over in her hands once, twice, three times, until it disappears into a tiny compact square. Then she opens her hand and watches it fall onto the sticky, drink-splattered floor.

'So, Ade,' says Seb, taking a large gulp of wine. 'Any plans for tonight?'

Ade is drinking the first, large, mouthful of his pint of lager. When he has reached the halfway mark, he wipes his mouth, looks at Seb and shakes his head.

'Plans? You're joking, aren't you? I had a plan. The plan was that Stella and I would go to Warren's party and get a deal.' He takes another swig.

'Oh,' says Seb, trying, through the fog of music and his own fermenting head, to focus on what Ade is saying.

'Did you get one? A record deal, that is.'

'Nah,' says Ade. He slams his pint glass down on the bar sending little drops of froth splashing onto his hand. He licks them off as though licking a stamp, not wanting to waste a drop. 'For one, Stella never showed up and for another, the bloke from B2B was a pillock.'

'Oh,' says Seb. 'I'm sorry to hear that.' He puts his hand up to attract Val's attention. He needs another drink.

'Don't worry about it, mate,' says Ade. 'I've calmed down a bit now I've had a drink. You wouldn't believe it: that fucking fairy throws a party then tries to give me a glass of sherbet. Said it was a "dry party". Yeah, as dry as his arse,' he bellows, slapping Seb on the back so hard, Seb almost falls over the bar.

'Jesus, Ade,' cries Seb. 'Take it easy will you.'

Is it him or is it getting louder in here, and where is Val? He leans further over the bar to try and attract her attention.

'Anyway, the fucker from B2B was laughing on the other side of his face when I finished with him.'

Seb can hear Ade's voice behind him rising and falling, like someone is playing with the volume control.

He feels a draught behind him and shivers as though someone has just walked over his grave. He turns and sees Stella's friend walking towards the exit. Shit, he has forgotten all about Stella. He needs to get Ade out of here before she comes down.

But Ade is still harping on about the party.

'You see, Seb, I had no choice, the man was blatantly disrespecting me. So I went at him, got him right round the throat; you should have heard him, squealing like a pig. I would have given him a kicking too, would have finished him off, if soft-boy hadn't waded in.' He nods his head and grins. It is the kind of grin Seb has become familiar with these past few months. It is the one Ade uses when describing feats of supposed masculine prowess – shagging women, giving someone a good kicking, pulling off a complex jazz tune on the sax with one breath then downing a pint of beer with the other, that sort of thing. It's a grin that demands a response, like a child wanting a pat on the head for doing something good.

'So,' says Seb, sounding anything but impressed. 'You hit him, the chap from the record company?' He has positioned himself so he can keep one eye on the glass doors while still appearing to give Ade his full attention.

'It was just a bit of a slap; he was asking for it, talking to me like I was a muppet.' Ade pats his pockets, trying to locate his wallet. 'Here, I'll get this,' he says, slamming a twenty-pound note onto the bar. 'Only meant to take out a tenner but after the night I've had I just thought, fuck it, I'm having a session tonight. VAL!' he hollers over the bar. 'Come on, love, what's it take to get served? Never mind that lot, we're your regulars.'

Seb cringes. He has to get out of here. The room is starting to feel oppressive, the gilt-edged mirrors that line the bar are reflecting odd shapes back at him, grotesque faces twisting and turning, like a Francis Bacon painting. The gold is peeling off, raining down like confetti and settling into a shape. He feels hot, but as he loosens his tie, the gold seems to takes form and walks towards him like a demonic high priestess.

'Same again, love?'

Whoosh!

Seb gathers himself by gripping the edge of the bar with both hands. He must look like a maniac. He straightens himself up and smiles at the frazzled barmaid. 'I say, Val, you're looking more glowing as the evening progresses.' His words come out slow and laboured; it feels like his brain is shutting down.

'I don't know about glowing, love, but I'm sweating buckets.' Val wipes her forehead then walks off to get the drinks.

'Yeah, nice to see you too, Val,' snaps Ade. 'Here, Seb, give her the cash while I nip to the loo.'

Seb takes the twenty-pound note and tries to focus his

eyes on the purple queen's face. Somewhere at the back of his brain, behind the blur of alcohol, his sober self remains. He can hear its voice, however faint, telling him to get out of there. When Ade returns from the toilet, Seb grabs his arm.

'Let's get out of here,' he says, as Val returns and sets a bottle of wine and a pint of lager down in front of them

'You what? Where do you wanna go?'

Val takes the twenty from his hand then smacks her hand down on the bar. 'Oh, bleedin' Hell, I've forgotten to open it. Two secs, darl', I'll go get the bottle opener.' She disappears into a crowd of hands, all holding out ten and twenty-pound notes like a guard of honour.

Seb hears himself mutter something about dinner at his mother's but his voice is drowned out by Ade's chatter and the opening bars of 'Song 2'. Soon the whole room is united in a chorus of 'woo hoos'.

'. . . and I'm telling you, I just don't know what's got into her lately. It's like she's in another world half the time. I love her, you know? I do. I would lay down my life for that girl, Seb. But there are limits, there are limits to how much I can give without getting anything in return. I mean, take tonight. Tonight was all about her. I had set up this meeting for her, to sell her song. All she had to do was turn up looking gorgeous and be herself and we would be in The Ivy celebrating with Rob Anderson by now. When I think of the hours I put into making that song sound like a hit, it's crazy. It was a poem, Seb, a bloody poem when she handed it to me. "Please, Adrian," she said, flashing those big eyes, "please help me." So I turn it into a song, autotune her voice – and believe me she ain't got the strongest of voices – and this is the thanks I get.'

Seb can hear Ade ranting, somewhere in the corner of the room, drowning out the other voice, the voice that is clawing inside his head, pleading with him to wake up. He looks at Ade and tries not to sway.

'Sorry, who? What?'

'Jesus, how many have you had?' Ade laughs. 'You're losing your touch, mate; once a man can't take his drink, he's finished. I was just telling you about Stella.'

'Stella?'

'Yeah, Stella,' replies Ade with a grin. 'Five foot six, black hair, also known as my girlfriend? I was just telling you what had happened at the party, how she didn't turn up.'

Seb stares at the glass in front of him and exhales slowly, willing his brain to focus, to slow down. He looks at Ade. He looks frazzled and suddenly Seb feels bad. 'Sorry, Ade, ignore me. I've had a bit of a hard day, that's all.' He picks up his glass and lifts it towards Ade. 'Cheers, mate.'

'Cheers, Seb,' says Ade, draining his glass. 'Look, sod it, we've both had a shit day, eh? Let's get another round in.'

Seb looks at Ade. He envies him. He envies the luxury of having a petty argument with his girlfriend. Ade will have a few drinks, he will curse and blame Stella for whatever happened earlier, but they will sort it out and tonight he will sleep next to her, he will feel the warmth of her skin next to his. Seb had always thought Ade to be brash, a bit of a lad if truth be told, but now he looks at him and thinks he is the luckiest man in the world. As he thinks this thought, a memory comes hurtling back with such force he feels like he has been hit in the back of the head. He can hear her voice, the voice he last heard on a telephone answer machine. It's as clear as day, like she's standing next to him, whispering into his ear. *There's no such thing as luck, Seb.'*

The intoxication of the last hour starts to fade. It feels like every last drop of alcohol has been drained from his veins. He can feel his feet coming back down to the ground. He is no longer the King of Soho, he is just Sebastian, sitting on a bar stool drinking himself stupid.

He feels empowered by the memory of her voice; it's

like she's travelled through time just at the right moment, to shake him out of his pathetic state. He looks at Ade and addresses him curtly. 'No, Ade, I don't want another drink.'

'Come on, mate,' says Ade, shaking his head. 'You're letting the side down.'

Seb sees a figure out of the corner of his eye. He turns sharply but it's just a couple of women coming back from the loo, wide-eyed and sniffing. He is getting more and more agitated, he can't spend the whole night watching the door like this. Sod it. He stands up and pushes his stool underneath the bar.

'Where you going?' asks Ade. 'I told you, tonight's on me.' He slides another twenty-pound note out of his wallet. 'I need someone to join me in my gloom,' he laughs. 'Come on, I'll give Val a shout.'

Seb can see Val over the other side of the bar chatting away to Ron and Pavla, two sozzled old barflies.

'Thanks, Ade,' says Seb, 'but really I'm going to head off.'

Ade looks confused. 'But it's only eight-thirty, still early.'

'I know,' says Seb. 'but maybe another time, yeah? Listen, I know you're angry with Stella, but you're not going to solve anything sitting here on your own, are you? Why don't you go and see if she's okay.'

Ade looks serious for a moment, like he is torn between the next pint and his concern for Stella. 'I don't know,' he says. 'I tried her mobile and it went straight to answerphone. I think if I go over there now, we'll end up arguing and I haven't got the energy. She'll be fine, she's probably reading or something. God, sometimes I feel like I'm living with a bloody teenager.'

Seb smiles. If he were Ade, he would treasure every minute of his time with Stella. He can see her lying on the bed flicking the pages of her book, lost in whatever story is unfolding before her while outside her window hundreds of other stories are beginning and ending.

'You'll sort it out,' he says, brightly. 'There'll be other parties, other opportunities.'

Ade doesn't say anything, just looks at him blankly, then he starts to laugh.

'It really is that simple to you, isn't it? Life is a breeze and we all go home happy at the end of the night. You see, Seb, I've never had these "opportunities" given to me. I've had to graft for every last bit of work I can get. Is that what they taught you at your posh school, eh? "There'll be other opportunities." Well at my school, we were taught that there are none, that life is just a bloody struggle.'

Seb grits his teeth. 'I'm sorry if that sounded flippant,

Ade. I was just trying to put this into perspective, that's all. You've got a beautiful girlfriend; life could be wonderful if you let it.'

Ade stares at him, then pats his arm. 'Nah, I'm sorry, mate. I'm just feeling sorry for myself. Sod it eh, let's have that drink. Val! Can we get the same again, love?'

Seb shakes his head. 'Ade, really I don't want another drink. Come on, let's get out of here,' he says. Then he laughs. 'Give your liver a rest.'

'Yeah right,' says Ade. 'I'll have a cup of Horlicks and paint my toenails as well, you daft sod. "Give my liver a rest." What do you think I am, some wino?'

Seb shrugs as he picks up his bag from the floor. The strap has got tangled round the leg of the stool and as he tries to release it he manages to tip out the contents of the bag.

'Shit.'

Ade jumps off his stool and comes to help. 'You clumsy git, it's all this talk of early nights; I'm telling you, mate, you're losing it.' He picks up a set of photographs from the floor. 'Who's this?'

Seb looks up. He had forgotten all about the photographs. 'Oh it's a girl I met in the office today. She's desperate to be a model but Becky won't give her the time of day.'

'She's nice,' says Ade. 'What's her name?'

'I can't remember,' says Seb, as he hurriedly grabs the photographs and puts them back in his bag. 'Chloe, I think, no, Zoe. That's right, Zoe.'

'Zoe,' says Ade, nodding his head. 'So, why have you got her photos? Aha, now I know why you're in such a rush to get off, you've got a hot date, haven't you?'

Seb can see Val walking back towards the bar. He wonders whether he's missed Stella. She can't possibly still be up there on her own. One last try, he thinks. And if he is going to get Ade out of there, he has the perfect excuse.

'Alright, you've sussed me,' he says, nonchalantly. 'I've got a date.'

'With the lovely Zoe?'

Seb nods. He can't believe he is doing this, but he just wants to get out of here and this is the ideal escape route.

'Ha,' says Ade. 'I knew you were on edge. So, where are you meeting her?'

Seb tries to think. 'Er, Knightsbridge,' he stammers.

'Knightsbridge! Christ, no wonder you're not buying the drinks tonight. So where are you going in Knightsbridge?'

Seb can feel this conversation going round in circles. He just needs to get out.

189

He leans in towards Ade and winks at him. 'Do you know what I think?'

'What's that, Seb?'

'I think you deserve a bit of TLC tonight after all you've been through,' he whispers. 'Go back to the flat, see if Stella's alright and leave Knightsbridge to me.' He raises his eyebrows and smiles.

Ade laughs. 'You dirty dog,' he says, slapping Seb's arm. 'I never thought you were into glamour girls, but nice one, mate. I might even be a tad jealous. You're right though, I should go and see if Stella's okay and there's nobody worth talking to in here tonight.' He picks up his pint and drains the last few drops of lager from the glass. 'Right, come on then.' He stands up and claps his hands together. 'You don't want to be late for the lovely Zoe.'

'No,' replies Seb. He picks up his bag and follows Ade out of the pub.

When they get outside, Ade starts rolling a cigarette. 'You going Piccadilly way, Seb?'

'No, no, I'm going this way,' says Seb, pointing towards Soho Square.

'If you're going to Knightsbridge you'll be wanting to get the Piccadilly Line, won't you?'

Seb looks at the drinkers huddled up outside the pub. There is still no sign of Stella. Why won't Ade just go?

'You get yourself off, Ade,' he says. 'I'm going to go back to the office first to drop my bag off,' he lies. 'You have a good night, yeah, and don't be too hard on Stella.'

'Don't worry about me and Stella,' Ade laughs and rubs his hands together. 'You just have a good night, mate, and I want to hear all about it tomorrow.'

Seb watches as Ade walks across Frith Street to the flat.

Great. Now what? There are more people going into the pub and if he goes back in now, he'll never get a seat. He fancies having a walk, see where he ends up. The night is young, he tells himself. There is no question of going to his mother's now. Not that there ever was.

As Ade walks up the stairs to the flat, his stomach lurches. He approaches the door and as he puts the key in the lock he becomes aware of the silence, a strange, heavy hush filling the air like gas.

He had been so angry earlier, he hadn't even thought that there might be something wrong, but now as he opens the door he feels unsure, feels a creeping dread of what might be waiting for him inside.

'Stella,' he calls, trying to keep his voice light as he walks into the main room. 'Stella, are you there?'

It's empty. The lights are switched off but the room is filled with the neon colours of the street outside. There are clothes strewn across the bed and a pile of CDs teeter precariously on the window ledge above the bed. He leans over and picks them up. They are the demos for 'Soho Morning'. He takes them and puts them on top of the bookshelf. Walking back to the bed he picks up the clothes, Stella's clothes, and folds them into tidy piles on the bed.

Outside someone screams and the sudden noise makes Ade jump. He finishes folding the clothes then walks slowly towards the kitchen, his heart thudding.

There is a pile of unwashed plates by the sink and he sees that the black bag they use as a bin looks fuller than it did when he left. He has begun to notice these things. To anyone else, something like that would not matter, but just by checking the size of the bin, Ade can see if Stella has had a good day or a bad day. He has become attuned to the little hints, the telltale signs such as a Tesco carrier bag stuffed with empty packets and cartons and crammed into the bin. He has had to become something of a detective these last few months. He had always known that Stella didn't eat properly, but he just thought that was a woman thing, watching her weight; it was only recently that he found out she was making herself sick. She had started to become careless – the toilet would often be stained with vomit when he came home at night or he would leave a pizza or chocolate in the fridge and it would disappear. And when he asked her if she had eaten them she would go mad and say that he was crazy and that he had probably come in drunk and forgotten that he had eaten them. Sometimes, he even questioned himself. Was he crazy? It certainly felt that way at times.

He steps over the bin bag and walks towards the bathroom. The door is closed but he can see a strip of light from underneath it.

'Jesus Christ,' he whispers.

His hands feel clammy as he approaches the door. He closes his eyes and sees blood splattered around the room; he sees vomit and gore, her thin body, pale and limp.

Open the door, he tells himself as he clutches the handle. 'Just open the bloody door.'

He pushes it and sees a flash of blue on the floor.

'Stella!' he shouts. His ears fill with a shrill, piercing noise, like tinnitus. He feels seasick.

As his panic subsides, he sees what is actually there. The blue dress he bought her for her birthday, the one he asked her to wear for the party, lies crumpled like a piece of rubbish in the middle of the floor.

He sits on the side of the bath and picks up the dress. He holds it to his face and breathes in the smell of it. It smells of damp and cheap washing powder. It smells like an old rag. He had spent ages trying to find the right dress for her. He knew she loved blue and he had gone up to the King's Road to have a look in some of the quirky little boutiques she said she liked. He had felt like a prat as he flicked through rail upon rail of dresses but he had wanted to surprise her. He had done something bad the week before and it had left him feeling empty; he wanted to make amends. When he saw the dress, it looked just right. He had imagined her walking into Ronnie's with him, looking like a movie star in that dress. But when he gave it to her she hadn't seemed that impressed. Sure, she had made all the right noises and said she loved it but he could tell she didn't, he could just tell.

She's with someone else, he just knows it. She's gone out with another man, that's what this has all been about. All this sulking and pushing him away and now he is left here like some cuckolded fool.

The anger coils up inside him and he starts to pull at the dress, ripping it apart from the seams and shredding it into thin strips of limp fabric. Then he throws them, like a pile of rags, into the empty bath.

'Fuck it,' he shouts, as he makes his way out.

He needs to calm his nerves and there is only one place left to go.

The evening is growing cooler and the sky is reaching the point Seb has often tried to capture in paint, when pink bleeds into blue and waning sunlight bathes the buildings in dark sepia tones. In this light, he can see all the Sohos of the past – from open fields to bedsit land – in the blink of an eye. The fresh air is making him feel light-headed and as he walks across Soho Square towards Greek Street, he feels the blood rush from his head to his groin. Hearing her voice in his head has left him feeling charged. He can feel her body pressed against his, feel her legs curled around him, while he kisses her velvet mouth and disappears into the darkness of her hair . . .

He thinks back to that bleak November afternoon when he took his sketchbook to the pebble beach at Rotherhithe thinking he would spend a few hours drawing. Looking up from his book, he saw a dark-haired young woman walking towards him carrying a pile of driftwood. She was the most glorious thing he had ever seen, so calm and assured, like a medieval sculpture emerging from the fog and the half-light on that dreary grey day. She stopped as she reached the spot where he was sitting, and then she spoke. 'Can I look at what you've done?'

The voice was raw and rougher than her appearance suggested. She placed the driftwood down by her feet and held out her hand towards him. He hadn't got into his stride that day, the images on the page were rough and scribbled, but he passed her the sketchbook all the same.

She took it and stared intently at the drawings, looked up at the skyline then at the page again before handing it back. 'I like your line. It reminds me of Stanley Spencer.' Seb smiled as he took the book from her outstretched hand.

'That is a big compliment,' he said, frowning at the erratic lines on the page. 'Although I can't see it myself, and certainly not on the basis of what I've done this after-noon. Anyway, I was just about to finish up; I can't seem to get my head in gear today.'

She nodded her head at him, picked up her pile of drift-wood and started to walk away. Then she turned and looked at him, narrowing her eyes as she spoke.

'If you're not going to be doing any more drawing, do you fancy helping me collect some more of this? There's a load of it further up the beach.'

'I'd love to,' replied Seb as he hurriedly packed his pad and pencils into his satchel. For two years he put his painting aside and fell hopelessly in love.

But she's not here, he tells himself as he looks at the empty square. She is not anywhere. She is gone and is never coming back.

Fuck it: he'll go to Henry's party. He'll dance and flirt with any woman he can find, he'll drink some more and forget about them all – his mother, his sister, that weird girl at work, 'her' . . .

His sorrowful erection leads him on as grey clouds blot out the light and an insipid gloom falls on Soho Square.

Chapter 11

Stella looks at the empty champagne bottle on the table in front of her. How long has she been sitting here? Hours? Years?

She realizes now, as she contemplates going back to the flat, to Ade and his chain-smoking, to the cockroaches in the kitchenette, why the news of Paula's reappearance made her lose all sense of perspective. Getting ready to meet her was a diversion. It meant that for just a few hours she could forget herself. She could forget her overdraft, forget her burgeoning student loan repayments, forget the pains in her chest that have been getting more and more worrying. She could drown out all the well-meaning voices. Everyone – from Ade to her parents, to the woman in the corner shop – seems to have something to say about her life and how she is living it:

'Isn't it about time you sorted out a career?'

'You look too thin, my dear.'

'Why don't you apply to the BBC?'

'I don't like that colour on you, Stella, it makes you look too pale.'

'You've got an English Literature degree, Stella, what are you doing with it?'

'Diet coke will rot your teeth.'

'Why don't you go travelling?'

'Why don't you do this? Why don't you do that?'

She is sinking under the weight of a thousand expectations and Paula was going to be the one to arrive at the eleventh hour and scoop her up, silence the dissenting voices and help her start again.

But now the hour has passed.

How could Paula have said those things to her? How could she have been so cruel? Of course, Ade had said far worse things over the years, but they never seemed to bother her, she could deflect his anger by simply turning away, blocking him out like an umbrella warding off the rain. But with Paula, it was different. Words were the very things that had bound them together. It was Paula's beautiful voice that had fired her into believing that anything was attainable, when she had sat there listening to it as a shy sixteen-year-old in an oversized hat. And it had been words that had cemented those feelings: pages and pages of carefully crafted letters, bouncing back and forth between Durham and London, thousands of words, hundreds of sentences, weaving in and out, carefully constructed to sidestep the glaring truth, that these were the words of two women in love. But now Paula has used them to rip apart whatever it was they had. She might as well have grabbed a knife and thrust it into Stella's chest, pulled out her heart, pulled out her entrails, pulled and pulled until nothing was left but an empty shell. That is what she must look like, to the people standing about her now: an empty shell, a thin whisper of a girl, hiding in the shadows, too afraid to step out into the world and take her place among the living.

It really is time she left the pub, but she can't bring herself to stand up. It feels like doing so will confirm what just happened and she will be forced to take the first step towards a new life, a life without the reassuring thought that one day Paula will come back. If she could block off her memories, all her memories, with some kind of cerebral brick wall, if she could put them in a sealed area of her brain that could never be accessed, then all would be fine. There would be no danger of a stray moment leaking out, a painful memory coming back unannounced and paralysing her with grief and despair. There would be no looking back, no asking, 'What if?' There would just be this moment, the moment she finds herself living through now, sitting at a sticky wooden table with a woozy head full of champagne; but instead of an aching heart there would be just a blissful feeling of indifference. Is it possible to erase the past and every painful memory picked up along the way? Is it possible to live the rest of your life as an empty shell?

The bar is beginning to empty now, it's getting near to closing time and the painted-faced crowds are heading out into the night to continue their celebrations in the night-clubs of Leicester Square. The straight-backed woman is still there. She has been joined by a puffy-faced man with a black 1950s quiff. He looks like an overfed dandy in his purple velvet frock coat and tartan trousers. They are huddled together, laughing at the expense of some unfortunate person called Angus.

'. . . and then he says to me . . .' drawls the man in a gruff, cockney accent which turns to a high-pitched squeak as he parodies Angus, '. . . he says, "Michael, stop, stop! That's the wrong font, the wrong font!" And I turns to 'im and I says, 'You want fonts, Angus? I'll give you friggin' fonts.'

The woman shrieks with laughter, throwing her head back so that her long red hair tumbles down her back like velvet snakes. She catches Stella's eye and smiles.

Stella smiles back then looks away.

Soho is a strange place. It can be the loneliest place, the coldest place, but then something small and insignificant will happen, like that woman smiling at her just now, and for a moment life will seem okay. Stella has always felt at ease here. No matter what raging emotions she may be harbouring, no matter how many conflicting thoughts may be rolling around inside her head, there is still Soho outside her window. There is still the beeping of horns, the hiss of espresso machines, the clinking of glasses, the hum of extractor fans and the wailing of sirens. There is colour and activity and all kinds of people from every corner of the globe. There is life in all its complexity going on about her. Most people see the brash exterior, the garish colours, the raucous clientele, the sex for sale, but Stella, like so many others who live in this strange twilit world, knows that this is just a front, a mask cleverly concealing the hidden streets, the haunting skyline and the infinite promise of morning.

She cherishes those Soho mornings. Stepping out onto a deserted Frith Street, two hours early for work but desperate to escape the claustrophobia of the flat and Ade's nicotine-induced snores, she will watch as a bleary-eyed Soho takes its first tentative steps into the day. She finds walking through the city far more invigorating than tramping across the countryside.

The open fields of her childhood always had a kind of melancholy about them; their remoteness, the great expanse of nothing but grass as far as the eye could see, seemed to tap into Stella's innermost fears. She used to have a recurring nightmare as a child about being trapped in a post-apocalyptic world where nothing was left but dead grass. She would have to walk through field after field of it and the grass would get higher and higher the further she walked, until eventually the giant blades would wrap themselves around her, squeezing the breath out of her. And that is how she always feels when she steps out of the city, like she can't breathe, like someone has switched off her oxygen supply. On her rare trips back home, she can feel her chest tighten as the train pulls out of Stevenage and heads for mile upon mile of silent, empty countryside.

She knows how to handle city living and has something of an inbuilt compass when it comes to navigating the streets of Soho. There is something so reassuring about

the layout of the streets, the knowledge that this one con-
nects to that one, that this little back street can get you
to where you want to be five minutes sooner than if you
take the crowded route through Shaftesbury Avenue or
Charing Cross Road. There is a continuity and order to the
layout of the city and you don't need a car to get from one
side of it to the other.

That is another reason Stella hates the countryside –
carsickness. When she was a child she would only have to
be in a car for ten minutes before the nausea kicked in.
Trips into the Dales with Caitlin and her parents would
take hours due to the frequent stops that would have to
be made en route so that Stella could throw up on a grass
verge. Caitlin used to call them 'sick stops'. Funny how the
thought of being sick made Stella panic back then, yet
now it's like second nature.

She winces as images of blood-splattered toilet bowls
and the splashing sound of bath water come back to her,
uninvited. See, even thinking about the countryside makes
her feel uptight. She rubs her chest as the sharp pain starts
to build up again. Even thinking about things that make
her happy – like walking through Soho – dredges up horrible things; not for one second can she just let herself
enjoy the moment, she has to spoil everything. Like earlier

with Paula, she could have just let things lie and had a pleasant evening; why did she have to be so defensive? So Paula looked different, so what? We all change, we all grow up. And now, as she replays the conversation in her head, she realizes that Paula was reaching out to her. She had sung her that song, the one Stella had played over and over in her little room in Durham; she had said she was her guilty secret; she had hinted that there might still be a future for them. But all Stella had allowed herself to hear was that word, that infernal word: *husband*. She had taken it between her teeth and refused to let go. And now there is no chance of any kind of reunion with Paula. She has ruined it. Ruined it all.

'Excuse me.'

She looks up to see Val the barmaid holding the crumpled up twenty-pound note.

'Is this yours, love?'

'Er, yes,' says Stella. 'I must have dropped it.' She smiles politely as she takes the money from Val's outstretched hand. 'Thank you.'

Val lingers. 'You want to be careful, there's plenty in here would have swiped that.'

'I know,' says Stella, stuffing the folded note into her pocket.

'I'll clear this away for you,' says Val as she leans over the table and picks up the champagne bottle and the two empty glasses. 'Can I get you anything else?'

'No thanks, I'm fine,' replies Stella.

'I'll just get a cloth and wipe up that spill,' says Val. 'You'll get your hands sticky and you don't want to spoil your lovely jacket. Half a sec and I'll sort it.'

Val goes off in search of a cloth, leaving Stella sitting at the empty table wondering what to do. She can't go back to the flat, not yet.

'Here we go, lovely.' Val returns with a large damp cloth and sets about cleaning the sticky champagne residue from the table. 'There, all done.' She stands back and admires the clean table. 'Now, are you sure I can't get you anything?'

'No thanks, I'm going now.' Stella has no idea where to go but she can't sit here all night and Val is starting to get on her nerves with her fussing. She stands up, picks up her bag and walks out of the bar.

Ade feels light-headed as he walks down Frith Street, past the Chiang Mai Thai restaurant with its chintzy Edwardian lampshades, past Ronnie Scott's, where a group of jazz virgins are trying their luck with Caleb who is territorially blocking the entrance with his clipboard.

He hears Caleb shout his name but he walks on. If he stops now he will lose his momentum. He'll go and see Alana and that will make him feel better, he will be able to think straight. Then tomorrow, he will decide what to do. He deserves a bit of a treat tonight and Lord knows there will be no close encounters with Stella later. It has been months since they last had sex, months of him cuddling up to her like some dog in heat. It makes him feel ugly and unlovable. He could handle all of it, all the banter from Ben and the guys in the band, if only she would hold him and make it better. She could shield him from all the comments, all the accusations that he is a sell-out. His jazz friends had sneered when he hooked up with Warren, and they were right. He tries not to think of the faded pop star standing alone among the ruins of his party, utter bewilderment etched across his face.

It is getting dark, just past nine according to the Bar Italia clock, the time when Soho starts to come into its own. When the neon lights merge into one giant kaleidoscopic blur and carry you with it, coasting along with the young, the old, the destitute, the landed, the whole scrap bag of travellers begging the driver not to stop, not to make them get off this ride.

He feels the power returning to his veins, life coming

back to his hands, his arms, his legs. This is his patch, his city, his world, and he needs someone to conquer, someone to take away the image in his head that won't go away – the look Rob Anderson gave him. A look that played right into Ade's darkest fears. A look of indifference mixed with disgust; it is the look Ade has been running from since he was a boy, the one that tells him that no matter how much he achieves, he'll always be a nonentity, a big fat zero fooling himself into believing he can ever be something.

But that look means nothing in this place, here in Soho, the land of jazz and hookers. Here he is a king, a man with power and reach. He can stand with the sax poised at his lips as the lights go down over the audience in Ronnie's and with the lightest of touches, the gentlest of breaths, mould the keys like a sculptor into shapes and forms that float out into the audience like so many ghosts, playing into people's memories, their hurt, their heartbreak. As the music flows through him and out into them, he knows that only he has the power to control this moment, only he can play with their minds. One by one, every jazz classic is greedily pounced upon by the frustrated housewives, the lonely singletons, the girls with frozen hearts waiting to be thawed. He can spot them from the stage, the ones vulnerable enough to fall for 'My One and Only Love',

'These Foolish Things' and the ultimate knicker-dropper, the Miles Davis classic, 'Tenderly'.

Under the forgiving low lighting, through the foggy eyes of wine-soaked women who have left their husbands tucked up at home watching TV in the suburbs, he is a hero, a star. On stage, he is John Coltrane, one of the greatest jazz saxophonists who ever lived. He is sharing the stage with Thelonius Monk on piano, Wilbur Ware on bass and Shadow Wilson on drums. And even if Ronnie's isn't the Five Spot Café in 1950s New York and the band is just Ade, his mate Ben and a couple of session players, who knows otherwise? Not these desperate housewives, that's for sure.

But they don't know his secrets. They don't know that he goes home every night to a ghost, that sometimes he lies there in the dark and cries about what he is doing to himself. Sex is everywhere in Soho, it's as accessible and normal as buying a pint of milk, that's what he tells himself. He can control it and he is always careful, he would never take chances, never put Stella at risk. The first time he had sex with Alana he had felt cheap and dirty. The room had smelt like bubblegum and bleach and the smell had lingered with him for days afterwards: he could smell it on his clothes, on his skin, and no matter how many times he washed and showered the smell remained.

He knows he should just turn around and go home but the loneliness of sitting in that flat while she is out with some man is too much to bear. If Seb had stayed in the pub tonight, he would have been fine. He would have got drunk and gone home and slept it off.

It's her fault, he tells himself. She is everything he could ever want but she is pushing him towards this. And sod it, she will never know. She's out having fun and he's meant to sit at home and wait for her like a fool. Sod it.

He turns onto Wardour Street and a route so familiar he could walk it with his eyes closed. Sometimes at three in the morning, that's exactly what he does. Eyes barely open, body shattered from playing jazz for six hours straight, mind pickled from copious pints of beer with whisky chasers, lungs filled with the acrid tar of cigarettes dragged on between songs, but a libido fit and ready and leading the way through Soho's labyrinthine streets.

Tonight, though, is an eyes-open night. Ade is high on a mixture of anger, lust and the bitter aftertaste of Warren's Baby Bellini. He wants to take in everything, even the fat lesbian staggering out of Candy Bar and puking on the pavement. It just reinforces what he loves about this place. It's raw, it's ugly, it doesn't try to cover up its blemishes with white drapes and scented candles; it keeps its freaks, its whores, its losers out in the open for all to see. This is life, in all its gruesome, lovely, neon-lit glory.

And that's one of the things he loves about jazz, how it runs parallel to every other music form. Number ones will come and go, boy wonders and sell-out stadium tours, Warren Craig and all that shebang, but jazz will remain. A saxophone solo screaming out into a smoke-filled world, standing alone, a 'fuck you' attitude that punk never came close to. You shut your eyes, it could be 1920, it could be 2020, but the jazz will remain, always out there, somewhere on the margins.

It is a pure, unadulterated piece of jazz perfection that plays now in his head, that carries him past Madame JoJo's and across Walkers Court where the crusty, dead-eyed zombies stand in the shadows waiting to drag some naive and horny tourist into their lair. Ade is never desperate enough for that and besides, living in Soho all these years, he knows the scams. The hostesses forced by their pimps to drag men in, give them a bit of banter then present them with an extortionate bill for a couple of lemonades and not a hint of sex. The men stupid enough to challenge them end up either having their wallets emptied or being frogmarched to a nearby cash machine by the bouncers who usually end up giving them a bit of a kicking. These unfortunate punters, who are typically in town on some dull business trip, are then left out on the street, with no money and a face full of bruises to explain to the wife. Those men are muppets as far as Ade is concerned, idiots who deserve everything they get. Paying for sex is like buying a pint at the bar, it's a service like anything else. And it's not a regular thing, far from it; he knows what he's doing. It's just a release, nothing more than that. It has been so long since Stella held him, really held him and gave him some affection. He knows he's not like those other men, those sleazebags who treat women like bits of meat. He loves Stella but this isn't about love, it's about sex, it's about feeling, for just a couple of hours, like he is not some loser.

On he walks, past Randall & Aubin, the champagne and oyster bar, where chinless city boys try to impress their bulimic girlfriends by ordering the most expensive thing on the menu then watch impotently as Annabel stumbles off to the loo to regurgitate a hundred quid's worth of Whitstable's finest; past the hardware shop where tourists flock to catch a glimpse of the former child actor who now spends his days cutting keys and flogging MDF.

A hundred metres along and there it is. A black shop-front with a barely noticeable set of steps leading down, a gentleman's club of the discreet, mannered, old school variety. And above the door, a tiny brass plaque telling patrons, in miniscule letters, it was established in 1960.

Ade stands on the top step and breathes in the smells of Soho: the restaurant waste that clings onto the air and the rotten fruit and veg left over from nearby Berwick Street Market. These smells never go away. Who knows when that cabbage started to rot. It is a perpetually rotting cabbage, perhaps even the ghost of a cabbage from a hundred years ago, when Berwick Street Market was alive and thriving, not just an inconvenient obstacle wedged in the heart of media land.

There is another smell lingering in the shadow of the decaying food and you need to have a discerning set of nostrils to distinguish this smell from the rest. To the tourist, the partygoer, the office worker, to the uninitiated, the smell can be compared to an overripe melon or a peach just this side of bruised. But to the connoisseur, it is the smell that hangs in the space between the first breath and the last, not shower-fresh and youthful but not yet rigor mortis. It is light and shade, it is life and death, it is food and hunger. It is the smell of sex and Ade takes a deep breath of it as he walks down the steps and into the darkness.

Chapter 12

Zoe has run all the way down Tottenham Court Road, wincing in pain as her shoes dig into her swollen feet. She slows down as she approaches a set of traffic lights. She has no idea where she is going so she just lets her aching feet lead her on. She presses the button at the traffic lights and waits for the green man.

There are tears running down her face and she wipes her eyes with the back of her hand. Even without a mirror, she knows what ten minutes of crying and running will have done to her face. A couple of Japanese girls in Hello Kitty T-shirts stand beside her as she waits for the lights to change. They look at her and start to giggle. Zoe tries to ignore them by staring straight ahead. She sees the theatre on the corner and that pub, The Spice of Life. She went there for a drink once with some girls from work. It sticks in her mind because it was the night before she lost her job. She remembers Dina had hugged her, told her everything would be fine.

The lights change and she lets the flow of the crowd carry her across the road. She doesn't know why she is walking this way. She knows she can't go back to the flat. Dina will be there by now. And what about her stuff, her clothes, her photographs, her mobile? Dina will probably burn it, or sell it. They are just things, she tells herself as she walks past The Spice of Life and onto Old Compton Street, just bits of junk really. And at least she has the money, thank God she has the money.

Old Compton Street is heaving, as usual. As she makes her way through the crowd, she can feel people staring at her. What a state she must look, and here of all places. She has always felt uneasy in Soho, and tonight even more so; everyone looks so edgy and streetwise. And what is she? Some idiot who fell for the oldest trick in the book. As she walks, she scans the names of the bars and restaurants looking for somewhere to go to fix her face. Once her face is done, she can think straight.

Café Boheme? Too scary-looking. Everyone looks so polished and preened and there are two security guards standing at the door. She will never get past them looking like this.

Although she has lived in London for six months, she has never been into this part of Soho at night. She prefers the clubs around Leicester Square because they are more like the ones back home. Soho has always seemed a bit too 'out there' for her, like you have to have a certificate in cool just to walk down the street. Her brother Mark came here once, on a stag weekend, and said it was full of shirt-lifters. 'Had to watch my back all night,' he recalled when he was safely back home.

Home. Zoe wonders what the girls are doing tonight; probably staying in, saving up for a big blowout on Friday night. She misses Middlesbrough. She knew what she was doing back then. She had a life and friends and money and as a trainee estate agent she had the use of a bright pink Mini Cooper. Who cared if it had 'Richardson Palmer Estate Agency' emblazoned across the side. Zoe had loved it. She still can't get used to travelling on the tube with all those sweaty bodies and elbows wedged in her side. Back in Middlesbrough, she had earned good money and there was plenty left over each month to spend in boutiques with names like Phizz and Joi, where she and her friends would spend their Saturdays trying on skintight Lycra dresses in lime green, fuchsia pink and, for those special occasions like New Year's Eve, silver sequins. Every Thursday, Friday and Saturday night they would squeeze into their dresses and head into town, to clubs like the Empire where they would stand nursing their Smirnoff Ices and checking out the stream of short-haired, short-sleeved young men as they filed past.

But it wasn't enough for Zoe. It had never been enough. She had always wanted to be looked at, to be admired and envied. At school, she had been the girl all the boys fancied, the one with the perfect hair and the best trainers. Her mother had entered her into bonny baby competitions when she was little and it was her mother's devotion that gave her the confidence to believe she could make it as a model. She had been signed to a little agency in Middlesbrough when she was seventeen and earned a bit of money modelling wedding dresses for local bridal fairs, but that was not enough either. She left school with a few C grades at GCSE and toyed with the idea of becoming an air hostess. Her mother told her that in her day all the pretty girls got jobs as air hostesses, it was a natural progression. The only problem was, Zoe was scared of flying. The estate agency was not her ideal job, but it did come with a pink car, which softened the blow somewhat. And for a couple of years, the dance floor at the Empire became her catwalk, the place where she could show off her body in a variety of skimpy, sparkly outfits.

She had met Declan in the Empire. She was in the middle of the dance floor, dressed in shiny black leather trousers and a silver crop top, when she saw him. He was standing at the side of the dance floor nodding his head to the music. He looked moody and serious and, unlike the other ninety-nine per cent of the males in the club that night, he wasn't wearing a checked, short-sleeved Ben Sherman shirt. Instead, he was dressed completely in black, which set off his big blue eyes and curly black hair. Zoe thought he looked like a gangster. He caught her eye and she moved towards him as the DJ slowed things down a bit with 'Wonderwall'. By the end of the evening, she had inter-rogated him enough to find out that he had just split up with his girlfriend of three years, that he had dropped out of university after the break-up, was working for his father's construction firm and that, like Zoe, he was nineteen.

After a few months of bumping into each other, Zoe managed to get him to commit and made it her mission to obliterate the ghost of girlfriend past from his mind. She helped choose his clothes and set about turning them into the Posh and Becks of Middlesbrough clubland. She even got her hair cropped like Victoria Beckham and started to cut out carbs. For a year she was happy in her world. Happy just being with Declan and knowing she was the most popular girl in town, but then she saw him holding hands with a girl in the park; they were laughing and cuddling up close. Zoe had hidden, like a fool, behind the public toilet block and watched them walk away. As they reached the corner, the girl turned to face him and he stroked her long dark hair then moved his hands around her waist. The girl's hand followed his and they stood there smiling at each other, lost in their own world, holding their secret in their hands. Zoe had stayed behind the toilets, watching them as they got smaller and smaller until they were just specks of blackness somewhere on the edge of her world.

Zoe's brother liked to read lads' mags. There was a huge pile of them in his bedroom. One afternoon, when he was out, Zoe found herself reading through his collection. There was an interview in one of them with Becky Woods, the chief model scout from Honey Vision. Becky said that all a girl needed to make it was a great personality and fantastic boobs. And Zoe had both. Three years after Declan's betrayal, she was still working at the estate agency, still trooping out to the Empire week in week out, trying to find someone to replace him. Reading the interview with Becky made her sit up and look at what she was doing. She was too good for Middlesbrough, she was too good for Declan and she was too special to be trudging all over town showing people round grim terrace houses. So, with encouragement from her mother who told her to follow her heart, she handed in her notice at work, withdrew a thousand pounds from her savings account and jumped on the coach to Victoria Station. Once in London she was determined to get onto Honey Vision's books and make herself so famous that every time Declan turned on the television or opened a magazine, she would be there looking out at him.

But it hasn't worked out that way.

Back on Old Compton Street, she is becoming increasingly paranoid about her face. Why are there no public toilets round here? Then she spots the familiar blue and black Caffè Nero sign. As she walks towards it she sees that, like everywhere else, it is packed with people, mainly men. Once inside, she squeezes herself through and looks around to see where the toilet is. A barista with a shaved head is wiping down one of the tables and he looks up at her as she stands there looking lost. 'Can I help you?'

Zoe goes to answer but the words won't come out. Her mouth feels heavy and a lump fills her throat. 'I . . .'

The barista comes towards her. 'Are you okay? Has something happened to you?' It is only then that she realizes how she must look. Her feet are bleeding, her face feels puffy . . . Then it hits her, the enormity of what she has just escaped. If she hadn't run away, what would they have done to her? Would she have been forced to smoke that stuff, be forced to do those things? She can feel everybody look at her as she stands there exposed in the middle of the floor. She suddenly starts to wheeze; she needs air. She pushes her way back through the hot sweaty bodies and out onto the street.

This street is quieter than the others. She starts to walk, breathing slowly, trying to calm herself. As she moves along the pavement, she hears the soft sound of a saxophone coming from somewhere up ahead. It sounds like jazz. A young girl with a 1960s beehive and a large baggy cardigan steps out of a car and walks up to the door of a black-fronted building. As Zoe draws near she hears the music again. The girl with the beehive is sharing a joke with the young black doorman and as Zoe walks past she looks up at the red neon letters above the door: Ronnie Scott's. So that's Ronnie Scott's, the one her granddad always used to go on about. It's a lot less fancy than she had imagined it, when her granddad used to play her his jazz records and tell her that they had been recorded in the 'famous' Ronnie Scott's jazz club. All Zoe can remember of those vinyl records were the scratchy sounds of whiny-voiced women, and crusty old men playing the clarinet. But for her granddad's sake, she had 'oohed' and 'aahed' and said how great they were. She has never really understood the appeal of jazz. It's a bit like Soho: everyone thinks it's so cool and cutting edge but really it's just a bunch of crumbling old buildings and weird people who dress like her gran.

As she draws level with Pret A Manger on the corner of Frith and Bateman Streets she catches sight of herself in the mirrored window, lit up by the blue neon of the restaurant opposite. Her hair has drooped into a pageboy style and her eyes are just two black circles. The red lipstick she so carefully applied is smeared across her chin like an open wound.

Two drunken men stop to gawp at her.

'Jesus Christ,' says one. 'It's the Joker. Where's Batman, love?'

If this were Middlesbrough, she would have taken them on, told them where to go, but now she just wants to run and hide. She looks around frantically. There is a pub called The Dog and Duck in front of her, a Nando's on the opposite corner, an Italian restaurant to the right and next to that a weird goth place called Garlic & something she can't quite read. The pub looks the least intimidating option. There are quite a lot of people standing outside but they look friendly enough and are too busy talking amongst themselves to notice her and her messy make-up. Putting her head down, she shuffles towards the side door and darts inside.

She finds herself in a little hallway with a gold-framed mirror and a set of red-carpeted stairs. There is a glass door in front of her that, by the sound of the loud voices and laughter behind it, leads to the bar. On the wall next to the stairs is a little gold rectangular sign saying 'TOILET' in black letters and an arrow pointing upwards.

Zoe looks up at the steep stairs and sighs.

'Here we go again.'

Seb stands outside the Union Club with its shabby-chic red facade and tries to remember why he ever thought this could be a good idea. But for as long as he can remember, all roads have led back to Henry.

Three years after they left school, Henry had blustered back into his life, full of ambitious schemes and big ideas. Seb was about to graduate from the Royal College with a

First Class Honours degree in Fine Art, and he invited Henry to come to see his graduation show. Seb had giggled as his old friend wandered around the exhibition hall looking utterly bemused. Henry was a practical person. He had been brought up in a military family where he was told to get on with things, not to wallow in sentimentality. At school he had excelled at Science and Mathematics. He felt at home in the world of logic and reason, solving puzzles and finding answers. To Henry, life was good when viewed from the clear perspective of black and white. He had little understanding of the creative world, the world of art, of intuition and dreams. He viewed it with suspicion, thinking it chaotic and disorderly. The same applied to religion, horoscopes and therapy – it was pie in the sky and there was no need for it in Henry's world.

Seb had felt good that day. For once, he was the strong one, confident and assured and on the brink of a dazzling career, while Henry was flailing, out of his comfort zone, out of his depth.

When Henry set up Honey Vision, Seb had laughed. What did Henry know about glamour modelling? Apart from an appreciation of the female form, the answer was, not much. Still, Henry was tenacious and saw potential where others saw empty space. When he heard that his old friend Becky Woods was planning to set up a model agency to supply girls for lads' mags, TV shows and sports events, Henry jumped right in. First, he and Becky went into partnership and then he managed to secure financial backing and a wealth of advice from Patty O'Connor, the legendary queen of Soho clubland. Another contact of Henry's leased them the premises on Shaftesbury Avenue and in the spring of 2003, after a year's hard slog, Honey Vision got its first big success story, a ballsy Liverpudlian tearaway who called herself Anna B. Her success in a high-profile lingerie campaign allowed the company to make a profit in its first year and, with Becky's eye for scouting new talent, by the following year there were over forty models on their books.

All this was not enough for Henry though. He was going to diversify. Honey Vision was just one strand of a huge, global media company that was already fully developed in his head. He planned to move into film production, music management, sport – you name it, he would incorporate it.

And now, as Seb's drawing career lies in tatters, Henry is the big man once more.

Seb goes to walk up the steps then stands aside as two women come out of the club. One of them, a pinched-faced brunette in a blazer and jeans, recognizes him.

'Oh, Sebastian, you made it,' she drawls, scraping back her hair with an oversized pair of Chanel sunglasses. 'Henry said you might be joining us. Although, I wish he wouldn't insist on having his parties in Soho,' she grimaces. 'I mean what's wrong with good old SW3?'

She starts to laugh and it's the strangest laugh Seb has ever heard – like a sneeze that she's been trying to keep in. The party will be full of people like her, the old school crowd that Henry just can't seem to break away from. It's a shame because Seb likes the Union Club, it's about as far removed from SW3 as this woman is. He smiles politely at her nonetheless. She looks familiar but he can't quite place her. The friend, a blonde mouse of a girl, has obviously had too much to drink. Her face is puffy, her eyes bloodshot and she is holding her head as though she is about to pass out. The brunette puts a hand around her waist and guides her to the edge of the pavement.

'Poor Gabby's going home,' she says in a school-matronly fashion. 'She just can't face everyone tonight.'

'Why, what's up?' asks Seb, wishing the two of them would get lost so he can go and have a drink.

Gabby goes to speak then dissolves into agonized sobs. The brunette lets go of her and turns to Seb with a frown.

'It's her little pug, Oscar,' she stage-whispers. 'He's

getting spayed tomorrow and poor old Gab's feeling guilty being out partying while he's at home all alone.'

Seb smirks. 'Guilty? Is that a new cocktail or something 'cause by the look of her she's had a few. Come on, a dog having the chop is hardly life-threatening, is it?'

He can't quite believe he is having this conversation.

'Oh, Seb, how insensitive,' snaps the brunette with a look that could curdle milk. 'Have you never had a cherished pet? Dogs are like family to some people you know.' She shakes her head, then returns to the snivelling girl who has managed to flag down a cab and is now stumbling into the back seat.

'Bye, darling!' brays the brunette. 'I'll pray to the Buddha for your dog.'

She blows kisses to the departing cab until it disappears into the pearly lights of Shaftesbury Avenue. Then she turns to Seb.

'Are you coming in then?'

He looks at her and it comes back to him. He *has* met her before. It was at Henry's house, a dinner party . . . His girlfriend had come with him. She had tied her black hair into a sleek plait and, with her long scarlet dress and pale skin, she had reminded Seb of a mythical Celtic princess, pure and strong, so out of place among the other party guests. And as they sat round the table, making small talk and passing around the Konditor & Cook olive bread, this woman, this harpy standing in front of him now with her ratty face and bulbous eyes, had tried her damnedest to put her down. He remembers it now. It had started with questions about school and descended into comments about Mulberry handbags, skiing holidays and a five-hundred-pound cut and blow-dry courtesy of some waste of space named Caspian. Then she had produced a bottle of champagne to toast the gathering and his girlfriend had commented that sixty pounds a bottle was expensive. The woman had leaned over the table with a look of vicious triumph and sneered: 'Sixty pounds. Expensive? Not in my world, dear.' She just couldn't get her head round this beautiful girl who bought her clothes in charity shops and cut her own hair. Within twenty minutes she and her cronies had made up their minds that she was not worth bothering with and regressed into the old public-school girls they were by huddling together and tittering at some vague, shared joke.

He was so drunk that night it hadn't really registered what they were doing, though she had tried to tell him afterwards. He thought she was being paranoid, he told her that they couldn't just hide away from the world, that it was healthy to get out and about, to socialize, that she owed him this. After all, she had her life, her separate life that she returned to each night. Coming out with him to these events showed they were a couple, a real couple. He had been angry, angry that she couldn't fully commit herself to him, that she refused to give up her other life and be with him, just him. Now, looking at this pathetic woman, the darkness returns: the guilt of that night and of all the empty ones since is creeping up his chest like poison ivy.

'Sebastian?' The woman moves towards him and places her hand on his arm. 'Sebastian, whatever's the matter? You look like you've seen a ghost.'

'I wish I had,' he hisses, yanking his arm away from her touch. 'I wish I fucking had.' He yells into her face and shocks himself at his ferocity.

'I . . . I'm going to get Henry.' She edges back nervously towards the club door. 'He said you weren't coping very well.'

'Yeah, you go and get Henry, you desperate old tart,' spits Seb. 'I'm out of here anyway. Do you know what you can tell Henry? You can tell him that I can't do this anymore.'

He is sick of Henry, sick to death of living his life as

some big payback to him. When it all happened, it was Henry who found him with the gas mask on, Henry who lifted him to his feet and spoon-fed him soup, like he was some colicky baby. Henry who found him the flat, paid for a new suit. Jesus, he even created his job for him.

'Come and work for me,' he said. 'I need a Creative Director; all the biggest agencies have Creative Directors. I've got the business head but I need someone to work on the look, the logo, the photo shoots, the arty-farty stuff. You'll be perfect.' And Seb had followed him like an obedient Labrador.

Now as he walks away to God knows where, everything around him seems to stop as if someone has hit the pause button. It feels like he is the only man left, the loneliest man in the world. He wants to go back to his old flat, see her standing on the doorstep with that naughty look in her eyes, the one that says she's got a reprieve, a couple of days to be with him, just the two of them. He wants to take off this bloody suit, scoop her up in his arms, carry her off to their messy bedroom and fuck her and make babies and laugh and cry and live. Jesus, he just wants her back.

He looks up and laughs an empty laugh. He is back on Shaftesbury Avenue, back where he started. But the noise and the traffic and the people are a welcome respite from the voices screaming in his head. He needs to get pissed, so pissed that he won't be able to think about anything.

He looks across the road and sees a group of attractive young men and women piling into an Australian theme bar. They look tanned and happy, like they haven't a care in the world. As they open the door a blast of tinny, early-Nineties rock music fills the air and carries Seb with it as he follows them in like a sleepwalker.

Inside, the place is just as grim as he hoped it would be, and he smiles to himself as he pads across the sticky floor towards the bar, past garish Perspex-clad posters advertising two-for-one shots of vodka and giant buckets of cocktails. It reeks of sweaty feet and cheap perfume and abandoned hope.

Perfect.

Anyway, what does it matter? After a few drinks it will all fade into a blur like some surreal postmodern collage, one with giant foam hands and cardboard boomerangs.

Behind the bar, the two skinny young barmen look flustered to death but Seb doesn't care. He can wait. There's no chance of Ade or Henry or anyone else finding him in here. He can stand back and enjoy the scenery, secure in his invisibility.

There is a lull in the music then the jangly guitar riff of Crowded House's 'Weather with You' starts up. Seb taps his foot and smiles at the girl standing next to him, an athletic blonde in denim shorts. He can't stop himself from looking at her legs. He doesn't usually look at women's bodies, and being surrounded by pneumatic, pumped-up breasts and bottoms at work all day has made them even less of a novelty. It is women's faces that fascinate him, they always have, even when he was a small boy: the myriad expressions, the contours of the cheekbone, the kaleido-scopic shades of eye colour and the softness of the skin. He could lose himself for hours just staring at a beautiful female face. It is like a perfect piece of foreplay, the appe-tizer paving the way for the main course. His girlfriend's face had been unconventionally stunning, like an ancient stone sculpture, strong, defiant almost, a face that would take a lifetime to fully reveal itself. Stella's face is pure Edward Burne-Jones, with her sad eyes and full, sombre mouth.

The girl standing next to him has a plain, almost mas-culine face, but her body, well, her body is like a foreign land. Little suggestions of it peek out from beneath bits of loose fabric. Here a glimpse of smooth, caramel midriff and an expanse of lean, toned thigh, there a slender wrist, white against its owner's tan and bound in red string bracelets. This is not the body of a glamour girl, this is unselfconscious sensuality, the kind that is honed in the great outdoors among the sea and the surf. It screams heartiness and Vitamin D.

'You like this song?' Her soft voice interrupts his fantasy of horseback riding along a rocky ridge.

'Sorry,' he stutters, then gathers himself. 'Oh yeah, they're great. Best Aussie band since INXS.'

The girl giggles. 'They're not Australian, they're Kiwis like me. Everyone knows that don't they?'

'Everyone except me obviously. I guess Antipodean music's not really my strong point.'

'I can see that,' says the girl. 'I'm Natalie by the way.' She extends her arm and the red bracelets fall forward. Seb shakes her hand and manages to get his thumb caught in the thin loop of material.

'I'm sorry,' he murmurs as he pulls his thumb free.

'No worries,' laughs Natalie. She leans across Seb to put her empty beer bottle down on the table behind him. As she does so, her shirt hitches up to reveal a daisy tattoo on the base of her back. Seb holds back from reaching out and touching it. It looks so smooth and enticing. He would like to get his paintbrush and add his own touches to the daisies: a creeping vine, some thorns jutting out here and there, pluck the petals out one by one: *she loves me, she loves me not . . .*

'Sorry, I didn't catch your name,' she says as she returns to his side.

'I'm Seb,' he says, swallowing his words. He doesn't want to get into all this 'names' business. He doesn't want to talk, he would rather just look at her body, let his imagination flow. Next, she'll be asking him questions and he'll have to lie or embellish and he just hasn't got the energy.

He needs a drink.

'So what do you do, Seb? Do you work round here?'

There it is.

'Oh, this and that,' he replies, noticing a gap at the bar. 'Come on, I think we can get served now. Let me buy you a drink, Natalie.'

'Oh that's really sweet of you; I'll have a Budweiser please.'

'Right,' says Seb sharply. He is on a mission now. Drink. Fuck. Blackout.

He squeezes himself into the gap and shouts his order to the barman as the music pauses. He hears his voice ricocheting around the room. It sounds ridiculous, like hearing himself on an answerphone. He sounds like someone else, someone plummy and nasal and obnoxious.

Christ, he sounds like his father.

Natalie giggles behind him. 'I think that got his attention.'

Seb passes her the bottle of beer then lines up six shots of vodka on the bar in front of him. Without asking her to join him, he downs them one by one.

'Jeez,' exclaims Natalie. 'Six! You must have a strong constitution.'

'Oh, Natalie, my dear,' he smirks, feeling the alcohol burning his gullet. 'That's just for starters.' He picks up a bottle of red wine from the bar and tells the distracted barman to keep the change.

They move away from the bar and stand near the front door. The air is still warm outside and there is a bare light above them that gives the scene a grisly seediness.

'Cheers,' he slurs, raising the wine bottle in the air.

Natalie frowns at him. 'Aren't you going to put that in a glass?'

Seb can't help himself now. He doesn't care whether she notices him staring or not.

'Can I just say, Natalie, your legs look like they could crush a man to death, like a python.'

She laughs nervously. 'Is that supposed to be some kind of joke?'

Seb takes a swig from his bottle then coughs as the wine goes down the wrong way. 'A joke,' he splutters. 'Oh, no, my darling, your legs are not a joke. *I'm* the joke.'

He can feel his lips moving, hear a muffled sound come out but he is no longer in control of what he is saying or doing. He sees Natalie come into focus then move back out again, like a spotlight in the theatre being turned on and off.

'Look, I'm going to go and join my friends,' she says. 'I think you're drunk and I'm not very good at making conversation with drunk people.'

'Oh that's such bullshit,' he spits. 'I don't need you to make bloody conversation. I couldn't give a shit what you have to say, I've had all the conversations I will ever need. I'm not interested in talking. I don't care about New Zealand and Australia and rich and poor, that's just bollocks isn't it. At the end of it all, we're either alive or dead. Now, I've got a hard on, you've been throwing yourself at me all night, so let's just go and fuck, eh?'

Suddenly the lights appear to go out. He feels sticky liquid seeping into his eyes, he smells the stale aroma of beer and a man's voice spitting venom into his ear.

'Come on, you tosser, you deserved that. Out you go.'

He hears laughter as he is thrown down the steps and when he looks up, he is crouched on the pavement as a dozen pairs of animated eyes bear down on him.

'Look, he's completely out of it.'

'He's still got his wine.'

'Nice one, mate!'

'Hardcore.'

He picks himself up, wincing at the thudding inside and outside his head, and starts to walk, hoping that each step might just bring him closer to something resembling peace.

Chapter 13

Zoe pushes the metal door of the ladies and edges her way through the tiny space between the sinks and the entrance. The room is empty apart from a skinny, dark-haired woman who is leaning over the sink, looking at herself in the grubby mirror.

'I'd better breathe in,' says Zoe. 'It's a bit of a squeeze in here, isn't it?'

The woman looks at her through the mirror and smiles. 'Yeah, it's what's known as small and bijou.'

Zoe laughs, though she has no idea what she means by 'bijou'. She shuffles in beside her and looks in the mirror. 'Oh sweet Jesus, look at the state of me!'

Tipping the contents of her tiny handbag onto the counter she rummages through her only remaining possessions.

Then she turns on the tap and frantically splashes her face with water.

'Are there any paper towels in here?' She lifts her head and looks at the woman pleadingly, her face dripping with water.

'Er, I don't think so,' the woman replies, looking around. 'Just a hand dryer.'

Zoe looks desperate. 'I can't stick my face under a hand dryer,' she cries. She stumbles into the nearest cubicle and, grabbing a handful of toilet roll, starts to dab-dry her face. Returning to the mirror she lets out a resigned sigh. 'Oh no, that's just made it worse.'

The woman looks at her sympathetically then reaches into her handbag and pulls out a packet of wet wipes. 'Here, these should do it,' she says, handing the pack to Zoe.

Zoe takes the pack gratefully. 'Oh you're a life saver. Thank you, thank you, thank you. I've already scared half of Soho walking down the street like this.'

'Oh, I think they've seen worse round here.'

'These are great,' Zoe mumbles as she furiously cleans the black from her cheeks. 'Water's no good for getting this mascara off 'cause it's waterproof you see.'

She waves the tube of mascara at the woman who is

now standing by the hand dryer with her arms folded across her chest. She looks at Zoe quizzically.

'Are you from Teesside?'

Zoe stops scrubbing and turns around with her mouth wide open, still contorted from her frantic make-up removal.

'Yeah, I am,' she says. 'How did you know? Most people down here think I'm a Geordie. I mean, as if.'

She turns back to the mirror and continues to wipe the mottled black gloop from her face.

'I grew up near there,' says the woman, 'in the country-side just outside Northallerton; out in the sticks really.'

'Northallerton,' says Zoe. 'We used to go to Northallerton when I was a kid. My granddad used to get his shirts from Barkers, on the high street. Wow, you're the first north easterner I've met since I've been down here. I can't detect an accent though.'

'I've never had one,' replies the woman. 'I was always determined that no matter what I would never have a Teesside accent.' She smiles awkwardly at Zoe. 'No offence.'

'None taken, love. You're entitled to your opinion. I just happen to think the Teesside accent is lovely – it's warm and friendly.'

There is a frosty silence as Zoe unzips her bag and starts pulling various tubes and pencils out. She can sense this woman is trying to think of something to say, that she is lingering for some reason. Finally after what seems like an age, the woman speaks.

'You're right though, people down here do get confused by Teesside and Tyneside.'

'Yeah they do,' says Zoe, squeezing dark beige foundation out of a pink tube. 'And there's bloody miles between Newcastle and Middlesbrough. It's like, I don't confuse London with Surrey; they're two completely different places. Sometimes I think people down here are just thick.' She continues to pack her face with thick pasty goo.

'That's a huge generalization,' says the woman. Zoe can see her in the mirror standing behind her. She is very pretty but far too thin; it makes her look cold, like one of those Dickensian waif figurines Zoe's mother collects to display on her mantelpiece. But despite her chilliness, there's a vulnerability about her. She can't quite figure her out, it's like she's drawing Zoe in with one breath and pushing her away with the next. But it's quite obvious she wants someone to talk to, even if they have conflicting opinions, and Lord knows Zoe has nowhere else to be right now. So she tries to open up the conversation.

'So, do you get back up north much? I'm from Middlesbrough; gets a lot of bad press but it's home to me. Fantastic nightlife as well, that's what I miss the most. I mean, yeah this is London and it's supposed to be a great city and all that but I just don't get it.' Zoe pulls a comb out of her bag and starts pulling at her hair, trying to drag it back into its style. She looks at the girl and shrugs her shoulders. 'I know you probably think that's a sad thing to say but that's just me. You probably think I'm just some oik.'

The woman smiles. It's a warm smile. 'No, I don't think you're an oik. I think it's nice what you just said, it must be wonderful to feel so connected to your home. I wish I did.'

There is a long silence before Zoe tries again. 'You must know the Empire?' The girl looks at her blankly. 'The Empire. It's a club in Middlesbrough.' The girl shakes her head but Zoe is on a roll now. 'The Arena? Looking at your style, I'd say you were definitely more of an Arena girl.'

The woman's face lightens. 'Oh God, I remember that place,' she says. 'I sneaked in with my sister when I was thirteen to see Oasis just before they became famous.' Her eyes brighten momentarily but then fade as quickly. 'But really,' she says, her voice lowering, 'I don't know Middlesbrough that well at all.' She looks down at the floor and her face crumples, like she is going to cry.

'Oh,' says Zoe. She had been about to mention people from Middlesbrough that the girl might know: Kelly Barker who worked in the coatroom at the Arena, Jim Brady, a friend of her cousin who used to book the bands, but there seems no point now, so she asks her name.

'It's Stella,' she replies.

'That's a nice name. Better than mine, I hate my name. It's Zoe by the way.'

She holds out her hand; Stella shakes it then reaches over and picks up the wipes. 'Are you finished with these?'

'Yeah, I am,' replies Zoe. 'Thanks again, Stella.'

'No worries, you're as good as new now,' says Stella, looking at the freshly made-up Zoe in the mirror.

'Aw, well I don't know about that,' says Zoe, blending the lip pencil around her lips with the tip of her finger. 'So what are you up to now? Are you off out?'

Stella stuffs the wipes into her bag and pulls it onto her shoulder. Sighing heavily, she places her hands on the counter and addresses herself in the mirror.

'No I'm not. I don't know where I'm going to be honest,' she murmurs.

'Well you can't stay here, Stella, they'll be closing up soon. I'm all for pub lock-ins but I don't fancy a night in the loo.' Zoe laughs a little manically then stops, noticing

Stella's serious expression. She has turned from the mirror and is standing with her arms folded, looking at Zoe with her head cocked to one side.

'Do you miss Middlesbrough, Zoe?'

Zoe really doesn't want to think about this now. Stella's vulnerability has allowed her to be the strong person for a while. Now it's all coming back to her: Dina, Marty, those two girls, that wretched, horrible feeling as she ran down Tottenham Court Road clutching stolen money.

'Yes,' she whispers, looking at the floor. 'Of course I miss it, it's my home and it always will be. In fact, it's where I should be now instead of standing in a stinking toilet. And anyway, what about you? You don't look very happy, to be honest you look like you need a good meal, you need your mam to cook you a few bacon sandwiches.'

Stella frowns then starts to laugh. It is a strange, uncertain sound, somewhere between a laugh and an aching cry.

'A bacon sandwich! Ha. Yeah that will solve all my problems,' she says, addressing her image in the mirror again. 'What you don't understand is that Northallerton's not my home, it never was. And my mother has never made a bacon sandwich in her life. And even though it doesn't make sense, Soho is my home now. Whatever shit I may be doing to myself, no matter how much goes wrong, this is the only place I have ever wanted to be.' She seems to be having a conversation with some imaginary person, somewhere beyond the mirror.

Zoe doesn't know what to say so she gathers her make-up into the bag. It seems like a good time to get going. 'Listen, Stella, I better be off. I was just joking about the bacon sandwich; you have a good night, yeah, and thanks again for the wipes.'

She walks out, leaving Stella as she found her, staring into the mirror, lost in her own world.

'This is my home,' repeats Zoe, as she walks down the stairs. 'She's right: it doesn't make sense, not to me anyway.' How can this strange, dirty, unfriendly city be anybody's idea of home? Home is soft water in the taps, it's eating a bag of chips in the freezing cold at 3 a.m. on Linthorpe Road, it is the transporter bridge, the beach at Redcar and the Cleveland Hills. Home is everything she thought she needed to run from, everything she thought was wrong. 'But it was him,' she cries as she slumps on the bottom step and stares at her reflection in the smudged mirrored door. 'It was Declan that was wrong.'

She reaches into her jacket pocket and pulls out the money. Laying it out on her knee, she slowly counts it. Two hundred pounds, more than enough to get to King's Cross and buy a ticket home.

'What do you mean she's not in?'

Ade glares at the plain-faced girl who is standing behind the bar looking bored.

'I mean, she's not in,' she drawls, sarcastically.

'I don't believe this,' mutters Ade. He is starting to sweat and the wet patches underneath his arms are chafing, making him even more irritable.

'Look,' he says, leaning over the bar, 'I know this place. Alana is always here. Always.'

'Well sorry, mate,' says the girl, folding her arms across her chest. 'Tonight's her night off. What can I say? U-n-lucky.' She turns her back to him and starts switching channels on the giant flat-screen television that hangs on the wall.

Ade is starting to feel on edge again. He leans over and taps the girl sharply on the shoulder.

'Oy,' he hisses. 'I've just spent fifteen quid coming in here. You know me. You know I only come to see Alana.'

'I've never seen you before in my life, mate,' says the girl, tying her dark hair into a messy ponytail. 'Look, why don't you chill out and have a drink, go and see the floor show downstairs. Get your money's worth.'

246

'Oh I want my money's worth,' he snarls. He draws a roll of twenties from his back pocket and waves it in the girl's face. 'I have all this money to spend on an hour with Alana. I'm not interested in bloody lap dancers, do you understand?'

He glares at the girl; his face is red and his eyes are bulging but the girl isn't intimidated. She's seen worse.

Ade realizes he is getting nowhere. He walks away from the bar and tries to think of something. Then he remembers: Patty O'Connor, the woman who runs this place, owns Honey Vision as well. Seb's always going on about her. He was telling him only last week how she's commissioned him to paint her portrait. Brilliant. He feels confident as he walks back to the bar.

'I want to talk to Patty,' he says, making sure his voice is calm but firm.

'Oh, will you get out of my face, mate?' The girl slams her hands down on the bar. 'God, I thought tonight was going to be a quiet one.'

'I'm asking you to please call Patty.' His voice sounds so menacing that he surprises himself. 'I have been sent here by a very good friend of hers and I'm sure she'll want to know I'm not happy about this service.'

The girl shrugs her shoulders and sighs. 'Alright, alright,

I'll give her a call.' She tuts loudly. 'Won't make no difference though, Alana still ain't here.'

She walks over to the red cordless telephone at the other
end of the bar. Picking up the receiver, she gestures to Ade
with her hand. 'Look, mate, why don't you sit down, yeah?
You're making me nervous standing there staring.'

She points to a violet-coloured chaise longue that
is wedged against the wall about a metre from the bar.
Above it, hanging on the wall, is a gigantic red velveteen
heart.

Ade walks to the sofa and sits with his hands on his
knees like a naughty schoolboy waiting outside the head-
mistress's office. He doesn't normally linger in this part
of the club. More often than not, he is so drunk he can
just about stumble through in a blur before he reaches
Alana. Looking at it through sober eyes, it's a strange old
place. The bar is tiny and looks like the counter in a 1950s
ice cream parlour, one with strange clashing styles. There
is a large sign spelling out the word 'bar' in pink neon but
this is almost hidden by a large red chintzy lampshade
hanging from the ceiling. It's probably meant to lend an
air of sensuality but it just looks weird, like the backdrop
to a seance. Ade shudders. The whole room feels tight and
oppressive, like it's closing in on him.

This is madness, he tells himself, utter madness. He doesn't want to sit here waiting, people will see him. All he wants is to just slip quietly into Alana's room, do the business then get the Hell out of here.

The fact that he only ever uses Alana makes all this seem less sleazy to Ade. She's a nice girl, soft and decent, not like some of the horrors you see out on the street. When he's in the room with her, he switches off, it's like getting a massage or going to see a therapist. He never looks at her face, he just uses Stella's trick and keeps his eyes closed. He tries not to think of Stella when he's in there but it's difficult not to. More than anything in the world, he would like to have a proper physical relationship with Stella. He gets turned on just by looking at her but she won't let him near. In a strange way, having sex with Alana is like having sex with Stella by osmosis. He just closes his eyes and thinks of her beautiful face, her small, pert breasts and her voice, that husky, sexy voice that made him fall in love with her when they first met.

But sod it. Where is she? He doesn't want to imagine what she might be doing right now.

He looks up at the television. A music channel is playing the new Shakira video and he sits transfixed, following the contours of the Colombian songstress's body as she thrusts her hips back and forth against a background of stampeding wild horses.

The blue double doors open and a middle-aged man walks in. His clothes scream out 'lonely man on business trip' and he straightens his cheap suit jacket as he scans the room nervously and stands there frozen between the door and the bar, not wanting to commit to either coming in or going out again. The man looks surprised to see Ade. He keeps his eyes down and mutters something as he walks towards the bar, pulls out a tall gold coloured stool and sits down.

Ade looks at him. Is that how he must look? Like a sad old man sitting here under a giant velvet heart? He needs a cigarette, maybe he should just go.

'Oy, matey.' The girl has reappeared and is shouting something over the man's head. The man at the bar goes to say something but the girl leans over him and shouts to Ade again. 'Excuse me. You with the creased shirt! What did you say your name was? I've got Patty holding on the phone.'

Too late. He has to go through with this now. This is just an obstacle, a delay, and in an hour or two he will walk home feeling calm and sated. It's all fine.

'Er, tell her I'm a friend of Seb Bailey,' he replies, trying to sound nonchalant.

'Seb Bailey?' repeats the girl. 'Hang on a tick, mate,' she says to the man at the bar. 'I'm just gonna sort this out and I'll be right with you.' She returns to the phone.

Ade looks at the other man awkwardly. The wait seems to last an eternity as they both sit there pretending to be engrossed in the MTV news bulletin. In his head, Ade rehearses what he is going to say to Patty. He will have to sound commanding, in control. He doesn't want her to think that he's just another punter.

'She's on her way down.' The girl's bored voice interrupts his thoughts and he looks up to see her leaning over the bar. He thanks her. She looks at him blankly then turns her attention to the man in denim. 'Now, mate, what can I get you?'

Ade sits there cracking his knuckles and staring at the floor. He tries to think about Stella and her smooth, slim body, but every time he tries he gets the image of her lying in that bath. He puts his head in his hands, tries to shake the image away. What has she done to me? I'm a nervous wreck.

He looks up at the screen. There is a music video showing a striptease. Ade stares at the TV, watching the pert breasts unhooked from their bra, the naked arse grinding towards the camera and as he watches his eyes start to glaze. This is all that exists, this moment, the naked girl on the screen and his erection which is growing harder. There is no Stella, no Warren Craig, no worries and no emptiness. All that matters is here, right now. And all that stands between him and his pleasure is a woman with a reputation as a ball-breaker.

When the video finishes, he sinks back into the sofa and laughs to himself. The queen of bloody Soho, that's what they call her. Patty O'Connor. He's heard the name countless times but he has never met her; this titan, so powerful that he's heard stories of grown men pissing themselves after she's finished with them. He's heard she doesn't need henchmen, she sorts out her enemies with her bare hands. And her presence can be felt in almost every establishment from one side of Soho to the other – brothels, drinking dens, gaming rooms, massage parlours, she's got the lot, as well as a substantial stake in Honey Vision.

Seb seems to think she's alright, but then Ade has never managed to work Seb out. He never seems to have a girl-friend, though Ade has noticed the way his eyes light up when Stella walks in. One night at a gig, Seb had been flirting outrageously with her but Ade had put it down to drunken banter. He was a mate wasn't he? A good bloke. But he could switch it on and off. One minute, he was everyone's friend, getting the round in with that big smile of his, the next he would kind of shrink into himself, and he had a temper on him, Ade had seen it a few times these last couple of months. One night in the pub, he completely lost it when Ade had jokingly said that Patty might want to turn Honey Vision into a brothel. He got all uppity and defensive so Ade had dropped the subject.

The doors open and he looks up to see a tall dark-haired woman dressed in black skinny jeans and a tight fitting Rolling Stones T-shirt walking towards him. From a distance she could be in her thirties but as she comes closer, he sees the deep lines around her mouth and eyes and, that scourge of middle-aged women, the saggy turkey neck. Ade stands up and wipes his clammy hands on his trousers.

The girl looks up from pouring out a measure of whiskey.

'Oh, Patty, that was quick,' she says, wiping her hands on her jeans.

'I was on my way down when you called,' Patty drawls. Her voice is surprisingly genteel. 'And anyway,' she says, looking around, 'I wanted to see Sebastian's friend. Where is he?'

'He's just there by the wall,' she says, pointing at Ade.

Patty turns round.

Ade tries to speak but no words will come out. She is not what he was expecting at all. What was he expecting? He's not sure, someone more rough and ready than this. Someone with bad teeth and a foul mouth, like Hogarth's procuress in *A Harlot's Progress*. He certainly wasn't expecting this cool, refined creature. She looks like she would be more at home in The Groucho.

'Patty O'Connor,' she says, extending a bony hand towards him. 'I take it you've come about the portrait? Are you Seb's agent? How's it coming on?'

Ade suddenly finds his voice. 'I think we must have our wires crossed, Miss O'Connor,' he says. 'My name's Adrian Ward, I'm here to see Alana.' He holds out his hand towards Patty. 'The girl behind the bar said she's not in but I know she works on Wednesdays. If you could discreetly sort this out for me that would be great, you see I'm in a bit of a rush.'

Patty is looking at him with a puzzled expression, as though she can't quite believe one of the punters would even attempt to address her. After a few moments, her curiosity turns to irritation and she calls over to the girl, who is now engrossed in an episode of *The Osbournes*.

'Julie, for God's sake.' She points her finger at Ade, like he's a bit of shit on the bottom of her shoe. 'I thought you said it was a friend of Sebastian's. Sort it out will you.' She goes to walk away but Ade catches her arm.

'Listen, Patty,' he says, the desperation rising in his voice. 'I've come to see Alana, is she here? Look, I know she's here. You gotta let me see her.'

Patty removes her arm from his grasp and proceeds towards a set of stairs with a velvet rope tied across the top. The stairs lead to the lap dancing section of the club, a fact that is proclaimed by the word 'Heaven' written in blue neon on the wall above.

'Julie! I said, can you deal with this please.' She turns to Ade, who is standing in front of her with his arms folded across his chest. 'Julie will help you with this,' she says. She is smiling, but her eyes are cold. 'If one of our girls is not working tonight, there are plenty of others to choose from, or you can go and enjoy the show. Now if you will excuse me.'

His heart is racing. There is something about this woman's face that he can't work out. It is like she's egging him on, deliberately trying to play games with him. Why won't she just go and get Alana for him? He has to see her.

'Look, please just tell me where I can find her,' he says, grabbing her arms. 'You see you don't understand what kind of night I've had. And I've got money, look.'

He pulls out the money and pushes it into Patty's hands.

'I've got this money for Alana. I've got to see her, do you understand? I have to see Alana,' he yells.

Patty presses the money back into his hand, holding her arm out against his chest, keeping him at bay, like a frantic dog on a lead. Then she takes her hand away and speaks in a low whisper.

'Now, it is quite clear you are in the wrong place, my love, so unless you want to be escorted out of here like a prize prick, I suggest you turn around and leave my club.'

Ade staggers backward. Now Soho is turning its back. Who is he? Where is he? He feels like punching someone, like kicking the door in. He leans in towards Patty who has turned to unhook the velvet rope.

'Who do you think you are? You're a fucking ponce, that's what you are,' he snarls. 'Standing there with your Joanna Lumley voice when you're making money out of young girls. You're nothing but a pimp.'

She unhooks the rope but doesn't walk down the stairs. Instead, she stands with her arms folded, looking at Ade, daring him to carry on.

'Anyway, love,' he continues. 'I know people, important people. I'm talking big time. Vice Squad. You wanna be afraid, very afraid.'

He nods his head and sneers.

There is a pause then a loud snort, followed by machine gun bursts of high-pitched laughter.

'Ha!' she shrieks. 'That's the best laugh I've had all year. You "know people". Oh dear, oh dear, I'm so scared.'

She continues to laugh hysterically and Ade can feel himself start to erupt. He won't be laughed at. He can put up with anything but that.

It gets louder and louder until it feels like all the laughter – Patty's, Rob Anderson's, Caleb the doorman's – is bearing down on him in some macabre mega-mix with the Jackson Five medley that's now playing on *MTV*.

'Ha ha ha . . .'

'. . . *won't you please let me back in your heart . . .*'

'Ha ha ha . . .'

'. . . *oh, darling, I was blind to let you go . . .*'

'I said, shut up!' roars Ade and he grabs Patty's bony shoulders, shaking her violently. In a matter of seconds, he is surrounded. Burly black-clad security guards grab him from behind, their walkie-talkies crackling and spitting. But he is up for a fight; the pent-up sexual frustration has turned to aggression as he wrestles with the two men at the top of the stairs. He hears Patty's voice telling Julie to call the police, he hears the music from the floor show downstairs, a slow, warped noise that sounds like a forty-five vinyl record being played on thirty-three. He kicks out with his arms and legs, trying to extricate himself from the headlock the guard has now got him in. Then one of his kicks reaches its target; with one clean shot he manages to smash the guard right in the bollocks, but his triumph is momentary as the second guard jumps on top of him. He can't see anything. His face is pressed into the carpet, and its smell of vomit mixed with booze and God knows what is making him gag. He doesn't see the police arrive, he just feels the tight grip of the handcuffs as they click them onto his wrists. He doesn't see Alana standing by the bar, watching this unexpected floor show, and as he is read his rights, he doesn't see her float past him and disappear down the spotlit stairs, back down to 'Heaven'.

Chapter 14

Seb has found his quiet place, a nice lone bench in Soho Square Gardens, right by the statue of Charles II. He raises his wine bottle towards the merry monarch, a distant ancestor on his mother's side.

'Just you and me, eh, Charlie.'

He takes a swig of wine and looks around. The square is deserted except for a couple of winos huddled up asleep under the bushes by St Patrick's Church. They usually lock the gates at nine but when Seb had arrived he saw they were still open and slipped inside. He doesn't care if he gets locked in, he tells himself, he's got nowhere else to go.The elegant Georgian houses that surround the square look confused and out of place, like they have lost their way en route to Fitzrovia and somehow ended up here amongst the FA headquarters and the drunken over-spillage of the Astoria nightclub.

Seb leans back and stares at the red-black sky. Peace, solitude, clarity. And right in the middle of one of the busiest cities on earth. You can't put a price on this kind of peace. Still, it is only a matter of time before someone does. In London, they're bound to corner the market one of these days. He can see it happening: little pockets of peace sold off to the highest bidder, negotiated by lanky twenty-somethings in oversized pinstripe suits, driving around town in brightly coloured Mini Coopers with their company name splashed across the sides, 'Foxtons Peace Agency'. It has a certain ring to it and, after all, London estate agents will have to diversify someday once the market for one-room cupboards dries up.

He takes another swig of wine from the bottle and closes his eyes. Why can't London ever grow dark? The glowing yellow street lights and neon shadows are making him squint. He wishes for real darkness, pure black nothingness that he can wrap himself up in and disappear, like he does in his dreams. Sometimes when he sleeps, it feels like he has been swallowed up, like he's fallen through the earth's core and is lying on the edge of a great void. These dreams don't scare him, in fact he finds them rather comforting.

It's as though they are taking him to the very place he wishes he could get to in his waking hours, the place he tries to find when he drinks. These are not vivid dreams, the kind you have when you fall into a deep sleep and every voice, every face, every gesture can be recalled the next day as clearly as one would see a photograph. No, these dreams are the product of night upon night of restless sleep, the kind that brush against your consciousness like a feather and leave behind only a shadow. Like a wave coming towards you then freezing, suspended in mid-air over your head, you are aware of its presence, of what it could do if it started to melt, and though you can't see it, the ghost of the dream stays with you long after you wake, clinging to you like a second skin.

He knows he shouldn't be here. He knows his mother and Claire will have finished dinner hours ago and be sitting gloomily over the Philippe Starck dining table. But he has no choice. His mother is the very person he has to avoid if he is to get over this grief. He can't face her tidal waves of emotion, her analysing of every little thing, her insistence that she knows how to help him because she is his mother and he is, and always will be, her baby boy. As much as he loves his mother, he knows that some hurts can never be healed, that there is a huge chasm of pain that cannot be filled no matter how much love and hugs and bottles of champagne she throws into it. He knows what he needs and he knows he will never find it, not in his mother's dining room, not on a psychiatrist's couch, not even in that hole deep in the Kent countryside. What he needs has ceased to exist, it has gone, leaving only dreams in its wake.

He remembers reading Vera Brittain's *Testament of Youth* – the story of young public schoolboys like him sent to their deaths in a futile war – when he was at school. There was a line in the preface written by Brittain's daughter that had particularly affected him. She said her mother didn't have much of a sense of humour because, after losing her brother, her fiancé and her best friend in the war, she could never escape the rows of wooden crosses that were embedded in her mind. He didn't know at the time why this image made such an impression. He had never suffered loss within his family; death had not yet touched him. His mother would have put it down to his artistic temperament, but he felt, even then, the whispers of something cold blowing down his neck, warning of some unformed event somewhere in his future.

Now death is all he knows, all he can think about: the darkness of the deep earth, the suffocating stench of soil and corpse, the worms eating away at love and beauty. But there are no rows of crosses for him, there isn't even one cross, there is just a big empty space spreading back as far as the eye can see, as wide and as deep as time.

He feels cold despite the warm evening and it has been hours since he has eaten. Has he eaten today? Who knows? Who keeps an eye on those things now? Looking down at his feet he sees fag ends, empty cans of Special Brew, a half-eaten Pret A Manger sandwich – the detritus of the wretched creatures that lie in the bushes over there, under the watchful eye of the Catholic church, sleeping away whatever demons have brought them here. As he kicks the rubbish around with his foot, he feels light-headed as though his body is somewhere else, floating above this scene, watching the futility of it all.

What sets him apart from those drunks in the bushes? he wonders. Public school? An illustrious heritage, thanks to old beardy over there? A gift for drawing pictures? What use is any of it if he can't get off this bench, make the short walk to the tube station and get on a train? Isn't it just a matter of time before the Rioja becomes Special Brew?

Every morning as he stares at his bloodshot eyes in the mirror, he tells himself it won't happen again, but come evening the drink has an answer to every doubt. The drink tells him he is in control, it tells him not to worry, that this is Soho and everyone here is hiding something. Come on, it urges, just one more glass and you won't even remember her name. He can slip amongst the crowds, pretend that he is partying too, that the glass wobbling in his hand is his first not his seventh. And why should he stop? So he can go home to a tiny flat that belongs to someone else, full of someone else's furniture, someone else's stories.

He remembers an old Swahili proverb he saw on the wall of a museum in Tanzania when he was fifteen. *Usisafirie nyota ya mwenzio*. It roughly translates as: 'Don't set sail following someone else's star.' He wrote it down in his teenage notebook of drawings and doodles and decided that those words would be his motto, his philosophy to guide him through life. What a joke. All he's done since the age of fifteen is follow other people's stars – his parents', his art tutor's, Henry's.

When Seb met Henry as a thirteen-year-old boarder at their illustrious school in Wiltshire, it did not seem likely that theirs would be a lasting friendship. Seb was the artistic one, happy to be holed up somewhere with a sketch-book and pencil. He would stand for hours in the little art gallery in town, looking at the paintings so closely his nose almost touched the canvas. It wasn't enough for him just to look at the drawings and paintings, he had to smell them, breathe in the oil paint and charcoal and let his thoughts wander freely. He always felt at ease in the gallery, walking from room to room as life opened its eyes in a blur of brushstrokes and smudges of light. The feeling stayed with him as he grew up and discovered the great galleries of the world: the National Gallery, the Museum of Modern Art, the Musee d'Orsay, the Uffizi. Nothing else offered him the sense of anticipation and unconditional promise as the cool open space of a gallery.

Henry, on the other hand, was the loud, brash would-be entrepreneur, head of house and captain of the hockey team. The other boys may have found him overbearing, but Seb needed him, he needed his strength. As a shy new boy, Seb had fallen victim to the sadistic initiation ceremonies implemented by a weasel-faced bully called Summersby and his grinning band of sycophantic thugs. It had started with pretty tame stuff, a bucket of water balanced on the top of the door, hiding his sports kit on match days, sticking rude words on his back and so on, but then things took a more sinister turn and Seb had woken one night to find his face pushed into the pillow and a sharp elbow digging into his back. Someone was holding him down. He was small back then, skinny and asthmatic, and he could feel his chest tighten as his attacker started to pull at his pyjama bottoms. If it hadn't been for Henry getting up in the night for a glass of water, who knows what would have happened. Seb remembers Henry's voice, clear and authoritative, as he pulled the boy's hair and grabbed him off the bed. It was an adult voice that came roaring out of Henry, like a warrior hurtling across some ancient battlefield. Seb lay there like a corpse, trying not to move, not to breathe, trying to disappear into the rough grey sheets, silent, as this voice of safety stormed the walls and freed him from his darkest nightmare. From that point on they were brothers, but Henry would always be the warrior king, the strong man, and Seb, though Henry would never say it, would always be the victim.

'Ssh.' He hears her voice again. It's telling him to slow down. It's singing him a lullaby, an Irish lullaby. 'Ay de doo, ay de doo de doo . . .' The wind sings with her through the plane trees and behind the church, a great silver moon peaks behind the rooftops, like a shy girl hiding her beauty behind the thick velvet curtain of night. He can feel her, he can feel her everywhere; she's beside him now. His hands shake as he reaches out and touches her. As tears dampen his face he clasps her hand.

266

'Sophie.' The name flies out of him, out into the night and off into the sky, rising above the rooftops like a bird carrying a message to a far off place.

He looks down at his clenched fist, at the empty space on the bench next to him and he smiles. His love, the love he will keep with him always, had come to say goodbye.

'Are you finished with that?'

A young man is standing in front of him. He is pointing at the half-eaten sandwich that Seb has spent the last twenty minutes kicking into a mulch under his feet. Seb looks at the pile of squashed bread, coated with fag ends and soil, then he looks at the young man. His black hair is greasy and matted with filth and as he stands staring vacantly at the food, he scratches both his arms so vigorously Seb almost reaches out to stop him from hurting himself.

'You can't eat that, mate,' says Seb, shaking his head. 'It's been thrown away, it's rubbish.'

The young man continues to stare and the scratching intensifies.

'Look,' says Seb, feeling around in his pockets. 'Here's a fiver, go and get yourself a burger, yeah.'

The man frowns at the note as though he's not sure what it is.

Seb holds it out towards him again. 'Here, take it and don't fuck yourself over buying crack with it; go and get some food, okay?'

With a swipe, the man grabs the note and tucks it into the pocket of his stained T-shirt, then he looks at Seb and smiles a wide, almost mocking smile.

'He humbled you.'

The man's voice is sharp and piercing as it cries into the night.

'He made you feel hunger, he fed you with manna which neither you nor your fathers had known.'

Seb tries to stand up. This guy is obviously a psycho with a knife and . . .

The man pats Seb's shoulder and nods.

'Thanks, my friend, let the Lord God fill your heart with love, let Him remove you from this wilderness of sin . . .'

He stops. Seb doesn't move, he is trying to gauge the man's next move, but then a group of men file past the railings on their way to Oxford Street. They are singing and chanting and the noise seems to unsettle the young man. He stumbles away, muttering to himself, something about 'Moses' and 'manna' and 'bread'.

As the men troop past, high on booze and happiness and ignorance, Seb laughs, and once he starts he can't stop. He laughs and laughs as he clutches the wine bottle to his chest. He laughs at the young man, he laughs at the stupid revellers, and the ridiculous figure he must cut sitting here singing lullabies to himself on a piss-streaked bench.

Sod it, why shouldn't he stay in Soho and drink? Real life is out of reach, he's sailed too far away from the bloody stars now and if he is honest, he prefers it that way. No, he will stay where he is, create his own island right here on this bench in Soho Square, like Robinson Crusoe. He will live for cocktail hour, wear a velvet jacket and dance with the ghost of Francis Bacon over on that little patch of grass. He tips his head back as he drains the bottle. He will stay here and recreate the Soho of the past. Back when men and women would argue and dance and fuck, and together they would change the world. The French House, the Colony Club, the Coach & Horses, the carousel going round and round like the alcohol in Seb's veins, pulsing, warming, spinning, clouding his mind with purple stains and drawing a veil over his tired eyes. Yes, this is where he will live and die, right here on this bench where love once sat.

Zoe steps out of The Dog and Duck and looks at her watch. Eleven o'clock. There is still time to get the tube to King's

Cross, but she can't face it. After the horrors of the party, the last thing she needs is to be trapped in the darkness of the underground. No, she will stay out here in the open where it's bright and noisy and alive. She will find a nice, busy McDonalds to sit in for a few hours; then when morning comes she can begin the long journey home.

Soho is still open for business. She can hear raucous laughter coming from the jazz club end of the street, so she decides to take a chance and walk the other way.

As she walks, the street opens up into a large Georgian square and the noise of Soho dies down into a distant hum. There are a couple of people chatting on the pavement and beyond the square she can see the yellow headlights of the night buses running along Oxford Street. She decides to walk in that direction, thinking it will be safer with more people milling around. Oxford Street's a twenty-four-hour place, she reasons, and there's bound to be a McDonalds there.

She knows it is silly and that it would be better to stay on the pavement with its street lights and people but she can't resist taking a peek at the little garden square. The gates are padlocked, but she stands with her hands on the railings and looks inside. There are benches dotted around and in the centre is a pretty little black and white hut with a pointed roof. It looks like the gingerbread house in *Hansel and Gretel*. As she stands there, she is consumed with a sense of longing. She wants to taste the air inside that garden, to walk through the grass. As she looks through the railings, she senses someone moving on the bench to the right of the little hut. Looking closer she sees a crumpled figure lying flat out. She starts to walk on, thinking it must be a tramp, then something makes her look again. It is him, it is definitely him. She recognizes the navy blue suit, the blond hair and the brown Paul Smith satchel. What is he doing, lying sprawled on a bench like this? It's none of my business, she thinks as she goes to walk away, but it is not in her nature to do that. He might be ill or worse. He's hardly the type to sleep on benches. Something about the chat with Stella has emboldened her. Something of her old self has returned, the one that knew no fear; the one who climbed onto the school roof on the last day of term, gripping onto the drainpipe while the teachers pleaded with her to come down.

The locked gate is not too high, but its railings are sharp and she doesn't rate her chances. Looking around she sees a bike chained to the bars. If she could use that as a pulley, she could haul herself over. She looks around to see if anyone is passing. The street is quiet, so she takes off her shoes and puts them under her arm then grabs hold of the bike's handlebars and hauls herself onto the seat. The bike wobbles and she grabs hold of the railings to steady herself. Regaining her balance she pulls herself into a standing position and jumps into the garden with a thud.

'Zoe, you are crazy,' she tells herself as she looks around the square. She walks towards the centre and it feels like she is stepping inside a fairy tale. She walks slowly, each step taking her deeper into the story, and it's a good story full of good people with good intentions. With each step, she leaves behind the prostitutes and the fat madam, the cheating boyfriend and the rancid smell of Marty's breath. The square is like a little piece of Heaven with the gingerbread house its palace of peace, and as she walks towards it she feels her breathing slow down, her hands stop shaking. Keeping to the path that cuts through the patches of grass, she reaches the bench.

She edges closer to check if he is breathing and he lets out a loud snore. He stinks of booze and an empty wine bottle is tucked underneath his arm. She leans over and gently taps his face.

'Come on, Seb, wake up,' she says gently. 'You'll get yourself mugged lying out here.'

He makes a contented groan and holds her hand against his cheek.

'Seb, wake up,' she repeats, in a louder voice. 'You've got to get yourself home, you've had too much to drink, love.'

She yanks her hand away from his grip. He mutters something and curls up with one arm over his face.

'What did you say?' Her voice echoes in the empty night air.

'I love you,' he whispers. 'Come back to bed and screw me you gorgeous wench.'

Zoe laughs. The daft bugger. His girlfriend's probably at home spitting feathers 'cause he's stayed out drinking. She takes hold of his shoulders, pulls his upper body into an upright position, then taps his face again. 'Seb!' she shouts. 'C'mon, mate, wake up.'

His eyes open but they are glazed and he looks around blankly. 'What's going on?'

He rubs his neck then sees Zoe standing above him. She looks larger, standing in the half-light like that, and all he can see are a pair of glossy lips bearing down on him.

'Oh no, not you again,' he snaps. 'I've told you she's not in.'

He picks up the wine bottle, sees that it's empty then throws it onto the ground.

'Charming,' she cries. 'I've just found you here asleep like a bloody tramp and that's the thanks I get. I should've left you to get mugged.'

'Oh please, can you turn your volume down? My head's throbbing,' he mutters, rubbing his temples with both hands. Then he looks up at her and sees the concern in her face. 'Look, thanks for waking me up. I'm fine honestly, just had a long day that's all.'

'Yeah it looks like it,' she says, nodding at the wine bottle nestled amongst the empty cans of Special Brew.

He follows her look and quickly springs to his own defence. 'Those aren't mine. What do you think I am? I've just had a bad . . . Oh fuck it, I don't need to explain myself to anyone, least of all . . .'

He puts his head in his hands.

Zoe sits on the bench and takes her voice down a couple of notches.

'What is it, Seb? Have you had a fight with your girlfriend or your . . . boyfriend?'

Seb gives a hollow laugh. 'Zoe, you think that because I wasn't interested in your glamour photographs then I'm gay, is that right?'

'Not necessarily,' she replies. 'You just seem, well, you seem like you're in touch with your feminine side, that's all.'

274

'Oh Jesus Christ,' he exclaims. 'Where have you just beamed in from? 1950? Listen, no I'm not gay and if I was I'd be open about it, but in answer to your question, no I haven't had an argument with my girlfriend. I wish I had. I wish I could scream and shout and yell at my girlfriend and I wish that she could yell back at me and shake me and wake me up but she can't, Zoe, because she's dead.'

He puts his head in his hands again and starts to sob. The noise he makes is not of this world. It seems to come from another place, somewhere outside this little garden square; the pain of it rips through the pages of Zoe's fairy tale. It makes her think of her mother. That time she found her sitting at the kitchen table with a carrier bag full of letters. Zoe had stood in the doorway and watched as her mother revisited her teenage years through a pile of yellowing papers filled with the proclamations of a love that never had the chance to grow old, a time and place that Zoe had never been part of and would never know. It was the same sound as she is hearing now, a hopeless, childlike ache.

The sight of Seb and the thought of her mother makes her even more determined to go home tomorrow. Why did she ever think it was a good idea to travel all this way in pursuit of such an impossible dream? Declan doesn't care what she does, she could streak naked across the Riverside Stadium on match day and he wouldn't bat an eyelid, he's moved on. She can see the past six months for what they have been now – a complete waste of time, a waste of her life, her precious life – and it is magnified by the sight of this broken man sitting on a bench. She puts her arm around him and tries to stop the shaking.

After a minute or so, he sits up straight and gently shrugs Zoe's arm from his shoulder. He looks like a little boy with his tear-stained face and runny nose. Zoe has never seen a man cry like that before and it has shocked her.

'It's just too much, all this,' he says quietly.

He takes out a handkerchief from his suit pocket, blows his nose then looks at Zoe despairingly.

'I'm trying to get on with things, Zoe, but I can't.'

He sits back in the bench, looks into the starless sky and whispers:

'I just can't.'

Chapter 15

Ade slumps in the back of the police car and whispers her name over and over.

'StellaStellaStella . . .'

She will leave him once she finds out where he has been, once she finds out his guilty secret.

Five years. Five years he has been with her and still it feels like he is living with a ghost. Everyone said she was out of his league, that she was too beautiful for him, but it wasn't about looks, it wasn't even about sex; they had connected in a way he had never connected with anyone in his life. At the beginning, when it was just the two of them, they would sit for hours, him playing the sax, her singing. He had loved that. And they made plans, big plans for the future, for when they made their millions. That should have been enough but there was a gap, a huge empty space, that had grown bigger and bigger.

Sex with Stella always left him feeling empty. Sometimes, she just lay there like a piece of wood, and she always closed her eyes. He used to wonder where she went to in those moments, who she was thinking of. Going with prostitutes is just about release, it makes him feel in control for a few hours. Same with the one-night stands, it's just sex, easy, uncomplicated sex.

When he found her in the bath that night he was scared, not of what she could have done, but because in some way he was expecting it. She was fragile, more fragile than he had realized before, maybe too fragile for him to cope with.

He could have been stronger, he could have made things better but she had let him down, hadn't she? Left him standing at that party, made him look stupid. All these years he has given her. He gave her a place to stay, he worked on her songs, he gave and gave. Why couldn't she just be there for him, just once? If they had been together tonight there would have been no question of going to the brothel. If she had been a normal girlfriend they would have gone to the party together, they would have come home together, they would have gone to bed and had sex, like normal couples do.

Why did he go there? He should have just stayed in the pub, then all he would be facing in the morning would be a sore head. And the way he had laid into Patty O'Connor. That wasn't him; he doesn't know where that came from. He has never hit a woman in his life. He knows it was wrong but she was taunting him, she was giving him that look.

He has tried to place it, this look that has haunted him all evening. Where has he seen it before? Now, as he is ferried through the urban sprawl like a corpse laid out in the back of a blacked-out hearse, he locates it. He sees it as they speed along Shaftesbury Avenue, past the theatre hoardings. It is there bearing down on him from the poster of *All My Sons*, right there in the middle, his brother's face, full of anger and disgust and that look, the look Ade grew up fearing. One glance and he is back fifteen years, staring into those eyes, their unbridled hatred simmering beneath a veneer of amiability. He was ten years older than Ade and he bullied him from the moment Ade could talk. He remembers it now, the Chinese burns on his arms, locking him out in the backyard for a laugh, a relentless stream of abuse. Now he sees his brother's bloated face in every passing car, every neon light, every drunken fool stumbling about in the semi-darkness. They are just like him, all these people;

like mangey birds they fly in from crappy satellite towns with pointless names – Bromley, Slough, Epping – until they reach their Mecca, this promised land of eternal night. Hadn't he done the same? Ran away from Southend, with its closed-down shops and chain pubs in search of a lifestyle he imagined into existence by playing too much jazz.

He hears the policeman mutter something and it's his brother's voice cutting through the clammy air:

'Useless little prick! It's what I always said, innit? You waste of space, ha ha, look where you've ended up.'

Ade wants to scream, he wants to rip the cold metal that links his wrist to the stranger beside him, and run for it. Run back to Soho and the safety of his flat. He wants to run for his life, run to Lenny.

Lenny Morris, his mentor: legendary jazz musician and the greatest man he has ever known. He was the one who took Ade in when he didn't have anywhere to go. He had believed in little Adrian, hadn't he? Given him a safe place to run to, given him a reason for living. Lenny had sat him down in the window of that little flat on Frith Street and showed him how to take on the world using the only method he knew. Lenny's language was jazz and he taught Ade how to live and breathe it while, outside, Soho nodded in time to every syncopated note.

Ade had made a promise to him, as the old man lay in the hospital saying his goodbyes to the great and the good of Soho's jazz fraternity. He made a promise that he would make something of himself, that he would make him proud. And he had almost done it, he had almost made a name for himself as a jazz musician. When Lenny died, Ade had stood in the Coach & Horses and raised a glass to his memory then he had walked back to the flat, picked up his sax and played the most difficult tune he knew. He played until morning and the tune was nailed. Lenny had given him this life. That had been his legacy. He had introduced Ade to that little square mile of streets that others knew as Soho but he would always know as home. He had taught him to believe in the tainted beauty of a jazz chord and the perfect redemptive moment that only comes when you take up your sax and let your fingers transform every pain, every sorrow, every punch into a beautiful collection of sounds.

The first night he played Ronnie Scott's he thought he was going to throw up. As the lights went down and the collective silent expectation of the audience crept up his spine, he had almost fled the stage. But as he played the first note, as he led the band to a series of encores, he drowned out his brother's voice. Every last note was a steel-toed boot in the bastard's face. The world was his for the taking; his life was going to be worthwhile. He was going to be a somebody. Jazz, music production, management . . . nothing was beyond him. He was riding the crest of his ambition the day a little skinny girl called Stella knocked on his door.

'Stella.'

The police car has stopped outside Charing Cross Police Station and Ade waits for the policeman to open the car door.

'Watch your head,' he says as he bundles Ade out of the car. The yellowing brick walls of the police station rise up around him. He looks up and sees hundreds of tiny windows illuminated in artificial light. The other policeman gets out of the driver's seat and together they lead Ade across the forecourt towards the side entrance. There is a thick set of metal grilles, like a caged tunnel, that connect the door to the outside world. The policeman leads Ade through it, like a jockey leading a reticent horse towards the starting block. Ade takes one last look at the clear London night sky. Somewhere out there life is going on, somewhere out there his band mates are playing jazz to a packed audience. Somewhere out there, Soho is carrying on without him. He takes one last gasp of the cool night air as they guide him through a thick metal door into the station.

Stella comes out of the pub and as she steps onto Frith Street she hears sirens in the distance. Nothing remarkable about that; sirens in Soho are as ubiquitous as birdsong in the suburbs, but even so, something about that noise cutting through the city like a knife through metal makes her speed up towards the flat. The lights are on up there, and some drunken woman is screeching out a bastardized version of 'Bittersweet Symphony' in the karaoke bar underneath. She hopes Ade is still out; she can't face him, not yet. As she walks up the steps to the flat, she hears someone call her name.

She turns and sees Paula, illuminated by the lights of The Dog and Duck, and as she walks towards her, she sees she is smiling, a real smile reflected in her pixie eyes. Stella stands in the middle of the street and watches her approach, so lovely and pure, so out of place in this filthy evening. Her dress is billowing slightly in the evening breeze and her hair falls about her shoulders like a veil. She can forgive her. She can forget everything that has happened if Paula will just hold her like she did that first night, if she will let her drink in all her goodness. She can make her better.

Paula reaches her and they stand looking at each other. 'I'm sorry,' she whispers into Stella's ear, 'I'm sorry . . .'

Then they kiss; they kiss as if they are the only two people left in this world. They kiss until they can't breathe and Stella closes her eyes and thinks of Dean Street and the love that has been put on hold for so many years, the hunger that has never been sated.

'Come upstairs with me,' she says, lightly removing herself from Paula's embrace.

'What about him?'

'Don't worry about him, I can get rid of him if he's there, he's not going to suspect anything of two women, but I don't think he will be.' For some reason, she seems to know that Ade will not be home tonight, that some great benefi-cent being has given her this night, that after so many years, so many heartbreaks and disappointments, this is her happy ending, her gift from Heaven.

Ade stands by the door and holds out his arms as the policeman removes the hard metal cuffs from his wrists. They release with a spring and Ade squeezes his hands open and shut, feeling the blood return, the numbness subside. Out of habit, he stuffs his hands in his pockets.

'Hands out of pockets, please,' demands the first policeman, looking at Ade sternly.

Ade does as he is told and, not quite sure what to do with his hands, folds them across his chest.

'We're going to book you in with the custody sergeant now, okay?'

Ade nods at the policeman. He is young, late twenties, early thirties, and his face is alert, like a springer spaniel. He asks his question like he is delivering a speech; it is obviously a line he has recited many times.

They walk across the dim, beige waiting area towards a small hatch. It reminds Ade of the serving hatches they used to have at school, as he stands flanked by the two officers like a ten-year-old waiting in line for his fish fingers and chips.

A policewoman with a hawkish face and cropped grey hair stands behind the hatch. She looks at him not with any sense of contempt, just complete indifference. To her, he is just another figure, another statistic to add to her list.

'Arrested in Club Zero on Brewer Street, one charge of affray . . .'

Ade hears the arresting officer give the monotonous details of his crime, but he cannot focus. He looks around at the ugly square room with its wooden benches and stained, linoleum floor. The clock above the door strikes the hour.

Midnight. Six hours ago he was on his way to the party, buoyed up with excitement...He starts to panic. He shouldn't be here. He should be out celebrating with Stella. This was going to be their big night. Why did he do it? Why did he go to that bloody club? If he had just waited for her back at the flat, they could have sorted it all out. He rubs his eyes. They are dry and stinging and the yellow strip lighting is making his head throb. The blandness of the room is so oppressive, it's starting to make him feel faint.

'Could you empty your pockets, please?'

The custody sergeant is holding out a blue plastic tray. They are going to take his things. His chest tightens. This is real; he is going to be trapped inside this Hell hole.

She repeats the question and shoves the tray closer to him. He rummages in his pockets, like a naughty child giving over contraband, and pulls out his wallet, his phone, his keys, a packet of cigarette papers, two lighters and a handful of loose change. One by one, he drops each of them into the tray.

The woman takes it and walks with it to the other side of the hatch. He hears his phone start to ring inside the tray, and he goes cold. Stella. He turns to the policeman who is still by his side. The other one, the driver, has disappeared.

'My girlfriend,' he says. 'That call, it'll be my girlfriend trying to get in touch with me. She'll be worried. I should take the call; I should let her know I'm okay.'

The policeman nods his head.

'We can inform your girlfriend of your arrest,' he says, almost gleefully. 'If you give us a telephone number we can let her know where you are.'

Ade rubs his temples. Stella would have a heart attack if she got a call from the police. Then they would tell her where he had been arrested. No, it's best if she is kept out of all this. She would never forgive him if she found out about Alana, never.

He turns to the policeman. 'Nah, don't do that. There's no need to let her know.'

The policeman goes to reply but he is drowned out by a screeching female voice coming from the entrance.

'Fucking get your hands off me, I said!'

Ade turns to see a young woman coming through the door. She is flanked by two heavy-set policemen. They are gripping onto her tightly and they shake their heads at Ade's policeman as they approach.

'We've got a mouthy one here,' says one of them. His radio crackles inside his jacket and Ade hears a muffled robotic voice and a stream of disjointed words: 'Male, mid-twenties . . . Meard Street . . . suspected . . . dealing . . .'

'She fucking slapped me first,' the woman slurs. 'That's why I glassed her: she's a fucking whore!'

She is young, no more than twenty, and very short. The two policemen tower over her. Her flimsy lilac dress is covered in wet patches and has ridden up around the tops of her legs. She is obviously extremely drunk. As the policemen guide her to the hatch, she loses her balance and falls onto her knees.

'Get off me,' she yells, as they try to get her onto her feet. 'I said, get off me, you pervert.' She catches Ade's eye and leers at him. 'Did you see that, mister? Did you see that filthy copper try to feel my tits?'

She is in a bad state. Her hair is stuck to the side of her face and she has a patch of dried blood on her arm. As the two policemen bring her to the desk, Ade can smell the alcohol on her breath and her clothes. It is a stale, rancid smell: cheap booze mixed with cigarette smoke and sweat. He edges away from her and as he does she lets out a deep moan. Ade leaps aside as a splat of vomit lands on the floor, centimetres from his feet.

'Jesus Christ,' shouts the policeman who has been holding her up. 'You could have warned me, Shelley. You could have warned me that was coming. Thanks for that, I just love getting covered in vomit.'

288

The custody sergeant is back behind the desk and is standing looking at the scene blankly.

'Is she capable of answering questions?'

It seems quite obvious to Ade that the girl is not, but still the sergeant has her lines to recite and she will do so despite the chaos.

The second policeman extricates himself from the girl's arm, gingerly steps over the mound of vomit and shakes his head at the custody sergeant.

'I can give you the arrest details, but I don't think we'll get any sense out of her until she's slept the booze off.'

The custody sergeant tuts.

'Take her to Cell 22, and have someone stay with her. We don't want her to choke on her vomit.'

As they escort the girl away, a thin duty officer appears with a bucket of water and a sponge. As he sets to cleaning up the girl's vomit from the floor, the custody sergeant turns her attention to Ade.

'Now, your name?'

Chapter 16

Seb composes himself by focusing on the faded features of Charles II's stony face. On the bench beside him sits Zoe. He is glad she is there. Despite everything he may have thought, it seems that tonight he needed human company after all.

'What happened to her?'

Zoe's question breaks the silence.

Seb takes a deep breath and looks down at his feet.

'You don't have to tell me if it's too hard,' she says, gently.

'No, no, honestly, I want to tell you,' he says, but he directs the story to his royal ancestor all the same.

'She was driving back to Kent to see her husband.'

He looks at Zoe. She doesn't seem shocked. She just nods her head like a priest in the confessional.

'She was driving home to her husband,' he repeats, 'and I went to Henry's birthday party. Henry's my best friend. He runs Honey Vision; you might have seen him dashing about the place, he's got mad curly hair.'

Zoe smiles, though she has never seen this curly haired Henry.

'Anyway, we'd had this stupid argument, me and Sophie.'

'Sophie, that's a nice name.'

He is taken aback by the sound of her name on someone else's lips. 'Er, yes it is, was a lovely name. Where was I? Oh yes, it was Henry's birthday and as usual he'd persuaded me to go to his party at The Wolseley. I asked her to come with me but she refused. She'd always been intimidated by that lot. You see, Henry and I went to public school and . . .'

'You don't say?' Zoe interrupts him with a laugh.

Seb rolls his eyes and smiles. 'So,' he continues, 'instead of saying, "Sorry, H, I don't want to come to your party and spend an evening making small talk with a room full of vacuous social climbers, I'd rather stay in bed with my beautiful girlfriend, thanks all the same." Instead of saying what I truly felt, I just folded and let Henry talk me into it, as he always does.'

He sighs heavily then goes on.

'You see we had so little time together, every moment we could find was precious. She worked in a small gallery near Battersea Bridge and I was living in Stockwell, so we would meet in the park . . . Her husband worked away. I don't know what he did. You know, as time goes on I'm finding that I knew very little about her. I just knew that I couldn't live without her.'

'I can understand that,' says Zoe quietly.

Seb doesn't seem to hear. He is sitting forward, his hands clasped together, and he stares intently at his thumbs.

'She was an artist, you know, but not like me,' he says quietly. 'She was more of a sculptor. She would sit for hours working on these amazing pieces . . .'

He stops and closes his eyes. After a moment he continues.

'So, anyway, that afternoon when she rang me from the gallery and said she wasn't coming to the party I just lost it. I told her that she couldn't have the best of both worlds, that she would have to decide once and for all between me and her husband. She had cried and told me that it wasn't as easy as that, she couldn't just leave him, there were complex things involved, things that I wouldn't understand. And I had screamed and raged at her, told her she was taking me for a fool. I said that if she wouldn't leave

292

him then we were over, finished. She got hysterical, begged me not to say those things, but I wouldn't relent and I ended up putting the phone down on her as she was screaming. All I know after this is the little bits of information I've been given from her friend Nina who worked at the gallery with her. According to her, Sophie left the gallery at about four o'clock, cleaned the snow and ice from her windscreen, got in her car and drove away. By five o'clock, while I was nicely sozzled in The Wolseley with a bottle of champagne in my hand, she was lying in pieces on the side of the M20.'

Zoe puts her hand to her mouth. 'Oh, Seb, you poor thing.'

'No, not poor thing,' he replies brusquely. 'She's the one who deserves sympathy, not me. Why the fuck did I say those things to her? It was just a party; it wasn't the end of the world if she didn't come.' He leans forward and presses his hands together. 'John Riley, that was his name,' he says, bitterly. 'Such a dull name. Never would I have believed that someone called John would ruin my life. He ran a marketing agency in Deptford. I found this out later from the newspaper reports. Apparently, he was on his way home from a work lunch . . . three times over the limit.'

Zoe shakes her head and tuts.

'But the thing is, Zoe,' he says, looking up. 'I'm no better. I killed her just as surely as John Riley did. I sent her off into his path. If only I hadn't insisted she come to that bloody party, things could have been so different. She would still be here now. And why did I think I could convince her to choose me over her husband by demanding she come and listen to a roomful of pretentious hoorays? Wouldn't it have been better just to blow Henry out, to bloody stick up for myself for once? Wouldn't it have been better to go and meet her at the gallery, take her out for dinner, go home and make love to her, show her that I was someone worth sacrificing a marriage for? Instead, I pushed her into that bloody car. I chose Henry over her that night. I chose that group of so-called friends over her and that's something I will have to live with for the rest of my life.'

His voice cracks and Zoe goes to comfort him but he politely brushes her hand away.

'You know, I couldn't understand why she felt so uncomfortable around those people but I should have seen it. I should have noticed them asking her which school she went to every time they met her, just so they could smirk when she told them it was a comprehensive in Margate. Then they would ask her where she worked and she'd try, she'd really try to explain to them but they would never understand, not in a million years. Galleries meant nothing to them unless it was one they had read about in *Vogue*. A little non-profit-making collective in south London was so off their radar it might as well have been on the moon. Oh, she was extraordinary, Zoe, she really was. She just did her own thing: sculpting, dancing, she wrote poetry, beautiful poetry. Christ, she was only twenty-nine. Why shouldn't you do all that when you're twenty-nine, why shouldn't you just follow your heart, be a free spirit?' His voice breaks and he sits up straight, trying to compose himself again. 'You know, I thought they were all tossers too, but I put up with them for Henry's sake. He's always been there for me and I felt I owed him.'

'It really wasn't your fault, Seb,' says Zoe. 'So you went to a party, you can't beat yourself up over that for the rest of your life. And, yes, there is nothing wrong with being a free spirit but not if by being like that you end up hurting people. I'm not being funny, but it sounds to me like she did want the best of both worlds.'

Seb should be annoyed with this, some stranger casting judgement on his dead lover, but weirdly it doesn't upset him. 'You're a good person, Zoe,' he says, pulling out a packet of Marlboro Lights. He takes out a cigarette and offers her one. She shakes her head. 'No, I don't blame you,' he says, as he strikes a match. 'Bloody cancer sticks, they kill you in the end but then again, doesn't everything?'

'I guess it's just the way you look at things,' replies Zoe, folding her arms around her chest. 'I mean, yeah life can be crap and things happen that just don't make sense, but what choice do we have? You can either take life by the balls or give up.'

Stella lies on the bed. The room is in darkness, there is no sign of Ade and the latch is safely up on the door. She looks at Paula lying beside her, and can't quite believe it. They got here in the end.

'Hey, you,' whispers Paula as she gently nuzzles her neck. 'Come here.' She pulls Stella towards her and kisses her, gently at first, then stronger, more urgent as she slowly makes love to her.

There is a purity about the night, even the noise seems to be dulled, like it is somewhere apart from this room, this bed. She buries her face into Paula's neck; her hair smells of orange blossom and fresh air. As Paula's body curves around her own, she realizes that she has lived this moment before. Little snippets of memory flicker before her eyes: sitting in the garden looking up into the sun at

Paula's shadow, crouching in the darkness under that table at the party and feeling Paula's fingers go deeper and deeper inside her. As they are now.

Stella feels emboldened. She is not frail, weak Stella anymore. She is not the victim, she is the victor. She feels in control as she climbs on top of Paula.

As they become one, Stella cries out. This is what she has waited for, her whole life. All those painful one-night stands, all the waiting, all the loneliness – they have all been worth it because they have led to this moment. She wants to lie here forever, she wants to submerge herself in this woman, to dive down deep into the very fibre of her. She takes Paula's hand and gently kisses her fingers as she comes. Then they lie there silently, wrapped around each other, safe in their own world.

'I wish I could be like you,' says Seb, taking a deep drag of cigarette. 'You see the best in everyone, you don't care what people think. If something goes wrong, you pick yourself up and get on with it. Christ, look at me, I've spent the last six months ringing my dead girlfriend's phone.'

'Oh, Seb,' whispers Zoe.

'I know, I know. I may as well book myself into the funny farm right now,' he says, stubbing out his cigarette. He waves the pack at Zoe as he puts it back into his bag. 'See. I only need a couple of puffs. I'm *so* not an addict.'

'You're not crazy,' she says, looking up at him. 'God, when I split up with Declan – he's my ex and a lying, cheating scumbag by the way – I used to sit in the car outside the office where he worked just so I could catch a glimpse of him. Sometimes I would sit there for hours; it's a wonder I wasn't arrested.

Seb laughs. 'I think you probably just trumped me there on the crazy, bunny-boiler scale,' he says, pretending to back away from her. 'You make me look quite sane by comparison.'

'You cheeky sod,' she cries, slapping his arm. 'Still, if I felt like that after breaking up with Declan, I dread to think how I would have coped if he'd died. You remind me of my mam actually. She's really strong. You see my dad died when I was a baby and she had to look after me and my brother Mark on her own. Well, she had my granddad but he wasn't really that helpful, God bless him.'

'Oh, Zoe, I *am* sorry,' says Seb. 'It must have been awful losing your father.'

'I was too young to remember him,' she says. 'I was only two when he died. All the memories I have of him come from stories and photos. He was a bit of a legend in Middlesbrough, so people tell me. Apparently he was the champion arm wrestler in The Two Brewers – that was his local pub. I'll be walking through town on a Saturday and someone will stop me and say, "You're Charlie Davis's daughter, aren't you." Still now after all these years, people remember him. That's why he'll never really die. And that's why Sophie will never die because she'll always be in here.' She taps her hand against her forehead. 'You're stronger than you give yourself credit for, Seb. After all that's happened you're still here, still trying to make things work. She would have wanted that, I'm sure of it. And look at it this way, you had two years of real love. Some people don't get that in a lifetime.'

She stares at him and he feels uncomfortable. He really shouldn't be doing this. 'You're right, Zoe,' he says, 'but you don't want to be hearing all my woes and I shouldn't have unloaded them onto you like that, it wasn't fair of me. Why don't you get off home, eh? I'm fine now, really.'

'I don't actually have a home to go to,' she says. 'Not here, anyway.'

'What? Surely you must . . . I mean, where have you been living all this time?'

'You don't want to know,' she says. 'Anyway, I'm packing

it in. All this London stuff is just not for me. I realize that now. I'm going to get the train home tomorrow.'

'So you're giving up on the Honey Vision dream?' He laughs.

'Come on, Seb, be real,' she replies. 'Becky's never going to take me on, is she?'

'I don't know, Zoe,' he sighs. 'But then, why would you want her to? You're worth more than all that, you really are.'

'You don't think I'm an idiot then?'

'You're not an idiot, Zoe,' he says. 'Far from it.'

Zoe looks down at the ground and smiles while Seb shuffles uncomfortably on the bench.

'So anyway, what time's your train?'

'Dunno,' she replies. 'I'm just going to get the first tube to King's Cross in the morning and then see what time the next train to Darlington is. I'll change at Darlington and get another train to Middlesbrough, then I'll be home. Oh, I can't wait. I don't know what I've been doing down here.'

'You've just been working out who you are, Zoe, there's nothing wrong with that,' he says, fiddling with the straps on his bag. 'That's what people do: try on different identities, different careers, until one fits. I don't understand this obsession with having to have your whole life sorted by a certain age, it's crazy. Look at it this way, if you hadn't come to London, you'd probably always wonder what might have been.'

'I've never thought of it like that before,' she says with a shrug. 'I can't wait to see my mam and granddad though. I'll give them the biggest hug.'

'Sounds like you're a close family,' says Seb.

'Yeah, we are,' she replies. 'Well, we were before I moved down here.' She folds her arms across her chest and sighs. 'Soon as I get back, I'm going to get my mam to cook roast beef with Yorkshire puddings and vinegar salad,' she drools.

Seb screws his nose up. 'Vinegar salad? Sounds interesting.'

'It's delicious.' She laughs and nudges him in his side. 'I tell you, there's so much I miss about home. Roast dinners, proper fish and chips with curry sauce, lemon tops.'

'What are lemon tops?' asks Seb, with mock incredulity.

'They're an ice cream, a whippy ice cream with bright yellow sorbet on the top. They sell them at Redcar beach. My granddad used to take me there when I was little and we'd sit on the seafront with fish and chips and a bottle of Dandelion and Burdock . . . we'd always finish with a lemon top.' She stares into space, off in a little reverie somewhere on the north-east coast.

'Sounds like you've made the right choice, going home,' says Seb. 'Your family sounds lovely. It must be nice to be so close.'

'Are you not close to yours then?'

'Not really,' replies Seb. 'I mean I was at boarding school from the age of seven until I was eighteen so I guess I never really had much quality time with the family. Though, saying that, I've always been pretty close to my mother.'

'What was boarding school like?'

'Oh God, where do I start,' he replies. 'Well, the first place they sent me to was on the south coast and so draconian it would make a Victorian prison look soft. I couldn't believe it when they dropped me off.'

'How old were you?'

'I was seven, still a baby really. My father just patted my head, told me to keep out of mischief, then got back in his car and drove off. I was terrified. Anyway, that was my home for almost five years until they packed me off to prep school. I always remember my first night there: they served up purple undercooked meat and it looked like it still had a valve attached,' he says, frowning. 'I spent the rest of the

302

evening throwing up in the toilet. Probably explains why I'm vegetarian now.'

'Sounds awful,' says Zoe, screwing her nose up. 'I loved the dinners at St David's, they were lush.'

Seb smiles. In completely missing the point, she somehow gets right to the truth of a situation. He yawns as he stretches his legs out. 'I'm supposed to be having dinner at my mother's now as it happens,' he says.

'Ooh, I think you might be a teensy bit late,' says Zoe, raising her eyebrows.

'It's okay, I'll phone her tomorrow, take her some flowers to make amends,' he says. 'Sometimes, I think she only invites me to dinner out of pity. We used to get on well before the accident; now she can't be herself around me. She's treading on eggshells all the time, trying not to say something that will upset me, when all I want is for her to make her silly jokes and be the madcap mother I know and love.'

'She'll get there,' says Zoe. 'So will you. It just takes time.'

He gets up from the bench and smiles. 'So then, how are we going to get out of here without breaking our necks?'

Zoe laughs as she stands up and takes off her shoes. 'Better prepare myself, eh?'

They walk across to the gate. The bike is still chained on the other side of it.

'That's how I got in here,' says Zoe, pointing at the bike.

'Why *did* you climb in here, if you don't mind me asking?' says Seb.

'I saw you on the bench. I was worried . . .'

They stand looking at each other awkwardly, then Seb puts his bag down on the floor and cups his hands together. 'Come on then, I'll give you a lift.'

'Don't be daft,' she giggles. 'I'm too heavy, I'll hurt you.'

'Of course you won't,' he says, 'you're tiny. Now come on, let's get out of here.'

Zoe gently places a foot onto Seb's cupped hand. She wobbles as she reaches out for the railing.

'Get your other foot onto my hand,' says Seb. 'I'll count you in. One, two, three . . . up you go.'

With a heave he lifts her over the railings.

'Now, my turn,' he says, handing her his bag across the top. 'This may take some time,' he laughs.

'Oh, be careful, Seb,' says Zoe, as he wedges one foot onto the base of the railing. 'Do you want me to grab your arms?'

But Seb is busy counting. 'One, two, three . . .' He hauls himself to the top; one foot is wedged precariously between two closely positioned spikes. 'I'm out!' he shouts as he lands on the pavement on his haunches.

'We made it,' giggles Zoe, passing him his bag.

He takes it and slings it across his chest. 'Yes, we made it, and not a missing limb in sight,' he says. 'Listen, are you going to be alright? You shouldn't really be walking around by yourself at this time of night.'

'Oh, I'll be fine,' says Zoe. 'I'll just go and sit in Maccy D's, read the paper or something.'

They stand facing each other awkwardly.

'Well then,' he says, putting out his hand. 'It's been an experience, eh?'

Zoe smiles. He looks different. His eyes are brighter.

'I'll never forget it,' she says, shaking his hand. 'Craziest night of my life.' She crouches down to put her shoes back on. 'I'm just pleased you're okay.' She stands up and looks at him and her stomach flips. He is a beautiful man.

He smiles, then pulls her towards him with a hug. 'You take care of yourself, Zoe,' he whispers into her ear. 'Don't settle for second best, eh? You promise me?'

She squeezes him tightly and mumbles into his chest. 'I promise.' She feels tears coming as she releases herself from his arms. 'Go on, you silly bugger,' she says, wiping her eyes.

He leans forward and kisses her cheek. 'Bye,' he says gently. 'Good luck with everything.' He goes to walk away, then turns and smiles.

'Oh, and one day I might get up to Middlesbrough and try one of those famous lemon tips,' he says.

Zoe laughs as he walks away. 'It's a lemon top, you daft bugger,' she whispers, but there is no one left to hear her.

Chapter 17

As Seb walks down Frith Street, he feels energized. Talking to Zoe has sobered him up. He has a plan. There is some unfinished business he has to attend to in the office and it cannot wait. He strides on past the pub, past Stella and Ade's flat where he sees the lights are off. He doesn't linger on thoughts of Stella though. There is only space in his head for one person tonight, the person whose face is already threatening to disappear from his memory forever.

He crosses Shaftesbury Avenue and as he gets to his office building he fumbles around in his pocket for the key fob that will let him in. Finding it, he holds it up against the large electronic pad, the light flashes green and he goes in. As he crosses the dark empty reception area towards the lift, he thinks of Zoe. What a great girl she turned out to be in the end. He makes a mental note to be less hostile with people. There is a life waiting out there for him and thirty is no age to give up on it. Once he has done what he has to do, he can begin again, he can find out what he is meant to become.

The lift doors open at the third floor and he walks along the empty corridor towards his office, stopping at the little kitchen on the way to grab some things. He turns the light on and picks up a couple of mugs, a pint glass, some kitchen roll and a bottle of washing up liquid, then goes to the office.

There is a beautiful stillness about the evening. He has no idea what time it is; it must be getting close to three o'clock. The night is creeping towards that opaque moment when the world pauses in a sort of no-man's-land between one state and another. He turns on the light in his office and sees what he has come here for. There, in front of him, standing four feet tall, is Sophie's faceless form. The painting he created the day of her funeral. The funeral that had taken place in a country church in Kent with hymns and flowers and psalms – all the things she hated. She had told him, one night when they had just finished making love, that when she died she wanted a happy funeral. She wanted to have The Monkees'

'Daydream Believer' playing as her coffin was taken away, she wanted everyone to sing along, and then when it was all over, she wanted her ashes to be scattered on the pebble beach at Rotherhithe on the very spot where they met. He had told her not to be so morbid, she had years left and they were going to grow very old and very grey and very fat together. How wrong he was. The worst thing was, he never got the chance to say goodbye, how could he when – to her husband, her parents, her brothers and grandparents and friends – he didn't even exist? So, on New Year's Eve 2004, instead of watching the woman he loved being lowered into her grave, he had stayed up all night and immortalized her in paint, captured the moment he had first met her, walking along the beach carrying a pile of driftwood. He had allowed himself a bit of artistic licence, swapping the black jeans and cardigan she had been wearing that day for her favourite red dress and leaving her dark hair long and loose. But when it came to drawing her face, he found he couldn't do it. He tried over and over again to get it right but whatever he drew ended up looking odd, it was as though in the two weeks since her death, he had forgotten what she looked like. In the end he had drawn himself into the painting, lying there on his side with an old gas mask over his face, while Sophie remained unfinished.

Until now.

He takes his suit jacket off and rolls up his sleeves. There is a lot to do and he wants to get it finished before the cleaners arrive. This will be her eulogy and he wants to do it properly. He goes across to his shelves and flicks through his CDs, taking out a well-worn copy of Mozart's *Requiem*. This is the piece of music he has always painted to, ever since he was at college, and now it will be even more fitting. He puts it into the CD player and presses play, then sets about getting his things together.

He reaches behind his desk and tears out a sheet from a large A3 pad of cartridge paper. He hasn't drawn properly for so long, he wants to loosen up his hands before attempting to paint on the canvas. Sitting at his desk, he takes the first pencil that comes to hand and starts to draw. He sketches the outline of a face then rubs it out. He starts again but soon becomes frustrated; his hand movements feel restricted by the size of the paper, but still he has managed to create something. He takes the drawing of the emerging face and sticks it onto the canvas, close to eye level. Then he takes a few steps back. Stops. Turns his head from side to side, walks up to it, stands back from it. Then he walks back to his desk, opens his drawer and pulls out a piece of charcoal from the old cigarette tin his grandfather left him when he died. He returns to the canvas and begins to add looser marks to the paper, this time with more confidence and speed. He can feel himself coming back to life, feel his hands start to work as they should.

He goes to his jacket that is draped across the back of the chair and pulls out a packet of cigarettes. Leaning across to the CD player, he turns the music up as loud as he can bear and suddenly the room is full of life and sound and movement. He stands beside the CD player and lights his cigarette, looking at the painting. He breathes in deeply, pulling the smoke down into his lungs. He is ready.

He goes over to the small cupboard at the back of the office and takes out a wooden box of paints, a square palette, a bunch of paintbrushes tied together with string and a bottle of white spirit. As he walks from place to place, his feet moving in time to the gloriously sombre music, he can feel something leaving him; he is ready to let her go. He takes the two mugs that he brought from the kitchen and pours a double whiskey-sized drop of white spirit into each. Then he opens up his box of paints and selects the colours he will need to recreate her face: Burnt Siena, Raw Umber, Yellow Ochre, Cadmium Red, Alizarin Crimson, Ultramarine. He tries twisting off the lids but they are stuck with congealed paint, so he takes them to his mouth and pulls the lids off with his teeth. Then, after squeezing a mound of each colour onto the palette along with a dollop of white, he sets about sorting out his brushes. He takes the elastic band from round them and sticks them into the pint glass. First the square-ended brush, then a slightly more rounded one, then several finer round-tipped brushes. They all look pretty weathered, their bristles stiff from lack of use. He dips them into the white spirit to soften the bristles then wipes them on a piece of kitchen roll. He is almost ready to begin, almost ready to see her again.

Zoe looks around her. The square seems very big and empty now that Seb has gone. The temperature has dropped and she shivers as she zips up her thin jacket and walks towards Oxford Street. This is what it must feel like to be homeless, she thinks, as she steps out of the square and crosses the road.

As she walks, she thinks about Seb. She thinks about the things they talked about. She thinks about broken hearts and shattered dreams, the hopelessness but also the resilience of the human heart and what it is capable of. The love that Seb felt for Sophie, well she is capable of that, she knows she is, and that is all that matters now:

love. She wants to find someone who will love her, someone who will talk about her the way Seb had talked about Sophie, someone who will never see her as second best. She wants to feel the stillness in the pit of the stomach that comes from being truly loved. For a few minutes, as she sat holding Seb's arm and listening to him talk, she felt something close to that. Seb was born to be with the Sophies of this world, of course he was. Yet, for those few minutes, he had made Zoe feel special too, like she mattered. All the bullshit, all the betrayals from Declan to Dina had been cancelled out just by sitting next to him on that bench, by being strong for him. She will never feel lonely again, she tells herself. For the rest of her days, she will surround herself with the people she loves. These last few months have taken her to places she never thought she would go, but they have given her something else, an inner strength she didn't have before. In a matter of hours, she will be on the train. Until then, she will just have to keep being strong.

Thank God, she says to herself, as Oxford Street comes into view, pouring its colour and light onto the dark little street she is exiting, thank God she took that money. She looks at her watch as she steps onto the wide street. Three-thirty. The tubes start running at five. Not long now. What's a couple of hours out of a lifetime's worth of days and weeks and years? Oxford Street is still very much alive: there are groups of people waiting at the bus stop, sharing boxes of chips and drinking from bottles of beer; the traffic is still thick with the throb of black cabs and double-decker buses ferrying people home. As a convoy of night buses trundle past, bound for Willesden and Hammersmith, Archway and Notting Hill Gate, she wishes she lived in one of those places, wishes she could climb on board and be taken away from here, for despite the lights and the activity, she feels desperately alone.

As she walks, she sees the familiar red and blue underground sign up ahead. It must be Oxford Circus. When she first arrived in London the tube had daunted her, it seemed like some giant unfathomable algebra equation. But over time she has got used to it. A few Sundays ago, at a loose end, she had boarded the Circle line train at Victoria armed with a bag of sweets and a copy of the *News of the World*. Though she had never been to Blackfriars or Temple or Aldgate, their names became familiar as they flashed past her once, twice, three times. When she got off, it had been quite dark and her eyes had taken a while to adjust to the daylight after three hours sitting in the yellow gloop of the tube train. But this is her little secret. She will never tell a soul that she did it, they would think she was mad. She can hear her brother laughing: 'You're a right Billy no mates, our kid,' he would say. 'You'll be talking to yourself next.' No, when she gets home she will tell her friends about the parties, the clubs, the heaving social life. She will tell them she has been so busy partying she has had to come back to Middlesbrough to have a rest.

As she walks on towards the underground sign, she sees another more comforting one: a giant red 'M' looming above the street on the opposite side. Her salvation has arrived; she can sit and get warm for at few hours, at least until it gets light. She crosses the street quickly, imagining a piping hot cup of tea warming her hands, and she half runs, half walks towards McDonald's. When she gets there, she pushes the door but it is stuck fast. Through the glass she can see a man mopping the floor. She knocks on the window to attract his attention but he either doesn't hear or pretends not to. She presses her face against the glass and sees that, apart from the man, the restaurant is empty. The counter is in semi-darkness and black cloths have been placed over the tills. 'No,' she cries, slamming her fists onto the reinforced glass. She looks around her. There is nothing as far as the eye can see but steel grey shutters.

Seb mixes the yellow ochre with the raw umber until he gets a muted sepia colour and starts to fill in her hairline, her brow line, the almond shape of her eyes, the line of her nose, the subtle curve of her lips. Then he adds the tiniest amount of crimson and white to the brown mixture to achieve a more fleshy tone and starts filling in the side of her cheeks. He adds some blue to the jaw line to give a hint of shadow. Once the face is loosely covered in fleshy tones, he returns to the eyes, moving from one to the other to keep the balance.

As the choral voices rise behind him, so his brushstrokes speed up, become more fluid. He stands back and watches as the face starts to take shape. He adds a drop of linseed oil to loosen the paint and, as the consistency thickens to his liking, he feels his teeth start to tingle. The magic is starting to happen. He can feel it in the smell of the paint and the loose oil, in the texture of the brush flowing with the paint as it gently strokes the canvas.

As he starts to fill in the colour of her eyes, those pale hazel eyes that would change from yellow to brown to green depending on the light, he can feel, once more, that something is departing. He wonders where she is going. He knew that she had been brought up a Catholic – her parents had insisted on a full requiem Mass at her funeral – and he hopes that, despite what the Catholic Church says about adulterers, there might still be a place for her in Heaven. He hates the thought of her being trapped in some eternal purgatory, having to be stripped of all her wrongdoing. That surely isn't fair. She was a good person – her only sin had been loving him. When he finds himself gripped by these dark thoughts, he likes to imagine other outcomes for her. The Ancient Greek idea of purgatory is an appealing one and he finds it comforting to think that she could be lying in an asphodel meadow somewhere, her beautiful black hair spread out behind her on a bed of wild flowers. That is the image he sees in his head when he thinks of her: lying back in a state of bliss, as though she has just woken up or just finished making love. He refuses to let the other images in: the corpse, the broken body. He can't bear to think of what happened to her beautiful face; he won't let himself think.

Instead, he takes the crimson, the blue and the white and mixes them to form a pinky-purple hue, like her favourite lipstick: Aveda's Dusky Rose. He remembers it smelt faintly of Parma Violet sweets; he could always taste them when he kissed her. He takes his brush and starts to fill her mouth with Dusky Rose, gently filling in each curve of the lip. This is how he will remember her, a beautiful girl with her whole life ahead of her, walking in her favourite place in her beautiful dress. This has been their last night together and as he steps back and sees her in all her glory, he feels vindicated. Life can go on from here, from this moment. He goes over to the soft chair by the door and sits looking at her. He will look at her for as long as he can keep his eyes open.

'Think,' Zoe tells herself, trying to stem the panic that is rising from the pit of her stomach. Her mother had told her so many times not to put herself in dangerous situations and here she is walking the streets in the early hours of the morning in one of the most dangerous cities on earth. What would she do if she was in Middlesbrough? Well that would be easy, she would hail the first taxi that came by and she would go home. She feels like a lost child in a supermarket, looking imploringly for someone to rescue her, silently screaming into the night air: 'Help me.' She tries to pull herself together, knowing that she is even more of a target if she starts crying, she may as well stick a sign round her neck saying 'victim'. She tries to think. There must be some clubs round here. Clubs stay open all night in London, don't they? But she doesn't move. Somehow, staying here next to the light of McDonald's makes her feel safe; she can't bear the thought of walking away into darkness. Instead, she stands and does the one thing that always made her feel better when she was a child. 'Hail Mary, full of grace,' she begins, and with each word, makes a silent wish to the dirty grey pavement that everything will be alright. When she looks up she sees a middle-aged couple walking towards her.

'Excuse me,' she asks, as they draw level. The woman looks at her suspiciously. The man beams at her jovially. He has a grey beard and is wearing a smart overcoat, the kind her granddad used to get from Barker's. His face is kind and open.

'Yes,' he says, as his wife tightens her grip on his arm.

Zoe tries to sound respectable. She is aware of the wife's eyes boring into her, taking in her short skimpy dress, her messed-up hair.

'I just wondered if there was anywhere still open up there,' she says, pointing to the eastern end of Oxford Street. 'Any clubs or anything.'

The man laughs. 'Well we're not really the best people to ask, a pair of old codgers like us.' His wife frowns. 'We've just been to see a friend of our daughter. She was singing at the 100 Club. I think it might still be open, if that's any help.'

'What kind of club is it?' Zoe can't believe she is having this conversation with a pair of fifty-somethings.

'It's a jazz club,' says the woman, curtly. 'Probably not your kind of thing.'

Probably not. Still, she is in no position to be picky. 'Where is this club?'

'Back in that direction,' says the man, pointing behind him. 'It's a bit of a walk but if you stay on this side of the street, you won't miss it. It has a big red sign outside with its name on. There's a couple of side streets to cross before you get to it; I'm afraid I don't know their names. We're just up for the evening from Kent, on our way back to the hotel now, aren't we, Kate?' He smiles broadly at his wife and hugs her towards him. Zoe thinks he may have had a bit too much to drink; she can't imagine that he would be this chatty if she had approached him in the day.

'That's great, thank you,' she says. 'I'm sure I'll find it.'

The man pats her shoulder, like a father waving off his daughter. 'Have a good night,' he says as they walk away.

Zoe shivers as she makes her way up the street; it really is freezing now and the cold air is making her need to pee. She looks at the names of the shops as she passes – Sports World, Super Babe Fashion – this seems to be the shabby end of Oxford Street. Any minute now she is expecting to see a pound shop. Really, you'd find classier shops in the Dundas Arcade back home. She gets to a side street and stands on the kerb waiting to cross. Maybe she should hail a cab, she thinks. After all, it does seem a bit pointless trekking out all this way to go and sit in a jazz club. She stands watching as one cab after another passes by with lights out, carrying tired, contented passengers back to their homes; to their beds. In the distance she sees something, like a hologram glowing in the inky black night. It's a yellow light, as faint as a whisper and it's coming towards her. She stares at the light as it grows stronger, as it separates itself from the red and green of the night buses and the traffic lights. It is, she tells herself. It's an empty black cab. She can go home. She takes her hand out of her pocket and lifts her arm to flag the cab down but, before she has the chance, someone grabs her by the shoulder and pulls her up the narrow street.

He has his hood up, but she recognizes the ratty face. His eyes are cold; he looks different, more menacing.

Marty.

'I can explain,' she begins. But before she can finish, he pushes her against the wall.

'Where is the money?' he hisses, squeezing her face between his fingers. He looks wrecked. His eyes are bloodshot and there is a grey pallor about his face that she had not noticed in the flat. She tries to scream but no sound comes out. He takes her arm and marches her up the side street, holding her in what passers-by would think an embrace, his arms locked around her shoulders.

'Bad move, little girl,' he whispers into her ear. 'That was my money you stole. You drank my booze, enjoyed my hospitality and that's how you repay me, huh?'

'You can have the money back,' she cries. 'It's all here, I haven't spent any of it.'

He pushes her hard in the small of the back as the narrow street curves round into a small courtyard. 'Oh, I'm gonna get my money back, sweetheart,' he spits. 'But first, I'm gonna get what I paid for.'

Chapter 18

Ade sits on a hard wooden bench in Cell 27. It is bare but for this sorry excuse for a bed and a filthy, shit-streaked metal toilet in the corner. Behind his back, he has wedged the blue plastic lilo that is supposed to somehow constitute a mattress. The temperature has dropped and as he shivers, half from the cold, half from pure terror at being caged in this appalling place, he listens to the shouts and screams of his new neighbours.

'Give me my pipe back, you hear me,' screams a male voice in the next cell. 'Do you hear me, Mr Hitler. Give me my fucking pipe back or I will kick this door down.' It sounds like he is going to carry out his threat as a series of thuds and crashes follow. Ade hears the sliding hatch open and a monotone voice addresses the angry man.

'What's the problem?'

'What's my problem? My problem is you, you wanker, that's my problem. I been in here eight hours, you took my pipe, I ain't had no food since this morning. You starving me to death, ain't you. Gonna find my corpse in the morning, innit?'

Ade tries to block out the noise, but it is impossible. Somewhere along the corridor, another door slams shut and the familiar thud of footsteps echoes through his head, like a mallet cracking open his skull.

They had brought him up here to this row of cells on the second floor after he had been booked in. 'Adrian Patrick Ward,' he had replied to the custody officer. 'Date of birth, the fourteenth of the eighth, nineteen-seventy-three . . .' He had been fingerprinted, a long arduous process that involved various prodding and pressing until they got what they wanted. Next, he had endured a foul plastic stick being scraped against the inside of his mouth in order to extract his DNA. That had almost made him gag. He had felt like a guinea pig, trapped by mad scientists hell-bent on stripping him of his sanity.

So here he is, caged in this tiny cell that stinks of piss, aching with exhaustion and freezing to death in a thin cotton shirt. They said they would come back with a solicitor but that was hours ago. He has no idea what time it is but it must be somewhere in the early hours. The sky outside has changed from thick black to a lighter grey; morning must be on the horizon. He wonders where Stella is now. Sleeping? If that was her on the phone then she must be worried. He wants to reach out and touch her, tell her he's okay, that everything is going to be okay. He had been so angry earlier when he had found her dress all crumpled on the floor that he didn't know what to think. What if she hadn't been with another man. Jesus, what if something had happened to her. Did he even think of that? Being in this place with all these nutters shouting and screaming is making him jump to all sorts of conclusions. Fuck, he thinks, what if someone had broken into the flat. It was in such a state and her dress . . . it was lying on the floor. What if some weirdo had broken in and . . .

He jumps up from the bench and smashes his fists against the door. He has to get out. He has to go and find her.

But he knows it is a pointless waste of energy to continue, and any feeble noise he makes will be masked by the banging and crashing from the rest of the cells. He walks back to the bench and sits down, whispering reassuring words to calm himself.

Stella will be at home. She will be curled up in her usual

position, with one arm over her face. She might not even realize anything is wrong. He thinks of Ben and the band. They would have played Kettner's tonight. He was pencilled in for that gig, but he had blown them out for Warren's party. Will they have missed him? Who knows. Sitting in this bare room, stripped of his possessions, he feels invisible, empty and alone.

The noises along the corridor are becoming weirdly normal to him now, as familiar as his heartbeat, and as he sits, he starts to drum his fingers on the wooden bench. As long as he keeps drumming his fingers, he tells himself, he will stay safe. The fear that is coursing through his body right now will be kept at bay if he just keeps drumming. He starts to hum a melody: a syncopated melody with a jazz beat. If only he had a pen, he could write this down. He hums the melody over and over; it's a sticky 'ticka-tay, ticka-tay' rhythm. He feels his blood start to warm up, feels the familiar exhilaration of songwriting stir up inside him. Suddenly, he is not in this place, he is outside of it, out on the periphery observing it all. Out on the margins, where he has always felt safest. Those people shouting and screaming in the cells, they are not like him, they are his audience. They can't hurt him if he is not really here. He can hear Lenny telling him to 'sort himself out'. He would have been fine in here, old Lenny, he would have had the custody sergeant eating out of his hand. Something of Lenny's strength fills the cell, while outside the window, light returns. He can transcend this; he can strip away the smells and the noise and the terror and turn it into something else, something wonderful. Jazz. This is what he is made for. This is what he promised Lenny. What the fuck had he been doing with Warren Craig? It was all madness.

He is going to get back on that stage, he tells himself. When he gets out of here, he's going to go home and play the sax until his fingers bleed. This is his wake-up call. He's going to show everyone – the boys in the band, Stella, Rob Anderson, all those who ever doubted him – just what he can become. He will never be in this position again, he will never feel the fear that he has felt tonight, never have to endure those screams and the oppressive blankness of these four walls. He is going to honour his promise to Lenny and he's going to make Stella love him again.

Stella is crouched amongst sharp spikes of barley. She is hiding in the field at the back of the house. The sun is just beginning to fade and the air smells of fireworks and damp earth. Somewhere in the distance a dog barks, a car door slams shut and footsteps crunch down a gravel driveway.

She looks up from her well-worn copy of *The Magic Faraway Tree* and sees a golden streak of light coming from the kitchen. She can see her mother's silhouette darting across the room, lifting a heavy pan from the hob, draining the steaming hot vegetables into a colander. The windows will soon cloud over with condensation, the kind you can write your name in. Her sister will be hurrying about, setting the table, warming the plates in the hostess trolley while her mother lifts the enormous wedge of beef out of the oven before letting it rest in its blood-soaked juices.

She gets up from her hiding place and walks through the vegetable garden. It opens up before her like a maze. In the half-light, the wooden stakes look like watchtowers standing guard over the leek trenches, the rows of lettuces and the beds of sleeping onions. She draws closer to the house and sees her red bike lying on its side by the kitchen door. Her mother is standing in the kitchen; her face looks translucent, she is smiling, her eyes are shining and she's holding a string of pearls up to the light.

'Stella!'

It's Caitlin. She's running towards her, holding a white plastic carrier bag with 'Duty-Free' written across it in red and gold.

'He's back, Stella. Wait till you see what he's got us.'

She is almost at the kitchen door when she hears the voice. The voice that says everything is going to be just fine, the voice that lulled her to sleep as a baby with 'The Lake Isle of Innisfree', the voice of safety and warmth and unconditional love.

Stella runs towards her father's voice just as the scene shifts. Years become moments and she's sitting in the passenger seat of a battered old Vauxhall Nova, looking out onto the vast golden expanse of barley field.

It's a cool August evening. She is with Michael. They have driven home from some forgettable film at the cinema and are parked up at the side of her parents' house. The air is filled with the muddled aroma of peppery aftershave, vanilla musk perfume and the minty fresh zing of chewing gum. His hand is on the gearstick and the engine is still running. The tinny sound of his compilation tape cuts through the space between them as Richard Ashcroft sings into the empty night a song of 'memories' and 'sonnets'. She fiddles with the collar of her coat. It is pulled right up to her face, almost obscuring her mouth, another thing to hide behind. He says something and she looks up; her eyes are the only things he can see.

Michael.

SOHO, 4 A.M.

He will fill the house with flowers, he will make her feel safe for a short while, then leave her with a new life burning inside her. It is Michael's voice she can hear, calling her from the shadows of a dying century.

'Stella.'

She can hear it now, an insistent voice, searing through her consciousness.

'Stella.'

She is standing on Palace Green as a grey cloud drifts across the night sky. It has never been like this. The cold air feels colder, seeking a kind of vengeance on her already frail, worn body. She looks up at the black armoured bulk of Durham Cathedral bearing down on her like a giant chess piece, a giant that is waking from its nine-hundred-year sleep. The ground trembles as the mighty structure rises off its haunches like an arthritic old soldier, and slowly moves towards her. She starts to run towards the city as the huge shadow advances upon her through the narrow streets, clinking and screeching like Marley's ghost. She runs past empty lecture halls, empty pubs, empty sandwich bars, places where she had once lingered like an afterthought. She daren't look back, she has to keep running, but her way is blocked by a group of people wearing rugby shirts and loafers. They are huddled together con-

330

spiratorially, speaking a language she doesn't understand, clutching books she hasn't read and laughing at a shared joke, one she will never get, because she will never be part of their world.

She has to keep going, so she edges past them and runs across the road, past the Royal County Hotel and down Old Elvet. She feels like she is running against a wall of steel but she carries on through the darkness. A light in the distance illuminates a side street. The hulking monster is still on her heels as she takes the shortcut and finds herself on a small bridge. The moon comes out from behind the grey clouds and casts a sickly glow on the green-black water. There are hundreds of papers floating across the surface. She looks closer and sees her name written on them, sees the detritus of a life long gone. She has nothing left to give, no strength inside her to fight back. She's just a series of broken parts lost within a sea of bodies. She watches as the papers drift away downriver and feels her shoulders lighten. The need to create has been taken out of her hands and she feels at peace in this void. She doesn't want to bring anything to life, she wants to silence it, to stop its breath like her baby stopped. Without a struggle or a fight for its life, it simply drifted away silently, not disturbing anyone. It was a polite death, the only sign of animation a slight reflex of a tiny blue hand. They had taken it away, far away to the place where stillborn babies go. No grave, no headstone, no memorial, just a big empty space. Babies are supposed to be warm, she had whispered, but nobody heard. She feels a breath on her neck and a cold hand touch her shoulder. As she climbs over the metal frame, she takes a deep drag of the sharp northern air. She hears someone call her name but she is gone.

'What have you done?' Zoe's voice gets fainter as she lies crumpled on the floor like a wounded animal. She had angered him, put up too much of a fight. She had bitten him and he struck out.

A few metres away, Warren Craig sits in an all-night Chinese restaurant with his entourage. He laughs; it's a high-pitched laugh, frivolous and empty. His people have flocked to his side and helped him rise intact from the ashes of his party. As they sit drinking jasmine tea and sampling the delicacies of the £300 taster menu, they are unaware of what is taking place in the deserted courtyard next door.

Zoe doesn't see the blade as he plunges it into her, and at first she thinks she has been punched. The first blow has knocked her to the floor, the second will make her choke up blood, bubbles of deep red liquid that will stain the front of her pink dress Alizarin Crimson. The third will suck the breath out of her. The fourth will take her life. She screams a desperate scream, like the first cry of a newborn screeching out into the night, but who will hear her above the traffic and the sirens, the shouts and the laughter, the smashing of glasses and the ringing of mobile phones? In this city of twenty-four-hour noise, lives slip away silently.

As Zoe takes her last breath, London carries on as normal.

Stella is flying through space as a hundred and one images flash by in freeze frame: her red bike lying on its side; her father placing a green bound copy of *The Collected Works of W.B. Yeats* on her desk; a perfect baby girl; Ade's fingers as they caress the saxophone; Paula. Words and voices spin through the air with her. Loud, insistent voices telling her to wake up. She is back in the barley field; she can smell its sweet scent under her nose. She opens her eyes. Somewhere in the distance, a door slams. She looks around at the room. She looks at her clothes crumpled in the middle of the floor, at her phone sitting on the rickety old table by the window, and she remembers. She turns and sees the empty space in the bed next to her and a piece of paper with her name on it lying on the pillow. Sunlight bathes the room in barley-coloured light. The day has come at last.

Chapter 19

Ade wakes up to see an unfamiliar face standing over the bed. He is so stiff he can barely move. He has no idea what time it is. His mouth feels dry and clammy and his back has seized up. He pulls himself up into a sitting position. As he does this, the blue plastic lilo that he had folded up to use as a pillow flips back into shape and falls off the bench. The policeman asks if he wants a cup of tea. He shakes his head. He just wants to know what is happening and when he can get out of this wretched place. Along the corridor, a cell door is being opened. In a matter of seconds the occupant of the cell is effing and blinding, making an almighty din. The policeman says something but Ade can't quite hear him above the noise. He just catches the end of the sentence, hears him say something about a formal warning, that he just has to sign a form then he is free to go.

Free to go. Is he serious? The policeman nods and beckons Ade to accompany him out of the cell. But Ade's brain has turned to putty and he feels disorientated as he follows the policeman down the corridor.

When they get to the front desk, Ade looks at the clock. 8:35 a.m. He shivers and folds his arms across his chest. When he finally got to sleep, sometime near dawn, he had been plagued with nightmares. Stella was in danger and he couldn't save her. He could hear her screaming outside the cell window but he was trapped inside and he couldn't get to her. He looks at the desk sergeant. It is a man; the hawkish custody sergeant must have finished her shift.

'Have there been any reports,' he asks the sergeant, 'has anything come in, any news of a girl, er, of a girl being attacked . . . or robbed in Soho?'

The man puts his head to one side and speaks to him in a loud voice as though addressing a senile pensioner.

'I'm sorry. I just need you to sign this form for me then you're free to go.'

Ade looks around the room. It is empty. What is he looking for? A murderer, a rapist, some evil cartoon character? He has to get home; he has to get back to her, see if she's okay. 'Please, God,' he mutters, as the desk sergeant pulls out the tray and hands him back his belongings. 'Please, God, let her be okay.'

Seb is in the kitchen next door to his office, making coffee, when Henry arrives. It is nine-forty-five, late for Henry.

'Make mine a double, will you,' says Henry, taking a large mug from the draining board and passing it to Seb. 'I've just had a nightmare bus journey from Fulham. It was horrendous, packed to the rafters and stinking of BO. The tube's down – power failure apparently. The whole lot's gone down, it's absolute chaos out there.'

'What a nightmare,' says Seb, as he adds another spoonful of coffee into the machine. 'Still, I'm sure it will all be back to normal by home time.'

'I hope so,' says Henry, crunching a Rich Tea biscuit. 'They really need to do something about the underground. Here we are, one of the greatest cities in the world, and we can't even get our transport system to work properly. God help us in 2012.'

Seb pours two mugs of strong black coffee and hands one to Henry.

'Thanks, Seb,' he says, taking the mug. 'I must say, you're looking a lot brighter this morning. I was worried about you last night. Mags came running into the Union saying you were having a nervous breakdown on the street, but when I came out there was no sign of you.'

'I think she must have been having you on,' says Seb, taking a sip of coffee. 'I spent the night working. I've finished the Rotherhithe painting.'

'Oh.' Henry puts his mug down on the kitchen worktop then places his hand on Seb's arm. 'Are you okay?'

Seb nods his head and smiles. 'I am actually,' he says. 'In fact I'm more than okay. It's time to get on with life, H, and for the first time in ages, I feel excited. I think we should arrange a catch-up, talk over all the plans we had for this place – you know, moving into the art world and all that. I'd like to form a subsidiary company to focus purely on the arts.'

Henry stands back and looks at his friend. 'Seb, that is the best news I have heard all year. You know what, I'm excited too. Let's do this, let's really do this.'

'There's just one stipulation,' says Seb.

'What's that?' asks Henry.

'I want to call the company Asphodel.'

'Asphodel,' says Henry. 'I like it.' He smiles and holds

out his hand towards Seb. 'It's a deal,' he says as they shake on it. 'Welcome back, Seb.'

Stella sits up in bed and takes the letter in her hands. Her stomach lurches. Please, not again, she thinks, as she opens up the carefully folded note. She smiles as she sees the formal structure of the letter. She would expect nothing less of Paula. As she reads, she feels the colour coming back to her cheeks.

Soho, 4am
7th July 2005

Hello, sleepy girl,

Now don't start worrying. I haven't disappeared again, I just have a few things I need to sort out this morning. Also, I didn't want to be there when Mr Jazz Man arrived home, so I have called a cab. I am sitting on your window seat waiting for it as I write, and I am looking at your beautiful sleeping form.

There is so much to tell you and lots to plan. Why, there is a lifetime ahead of us now, my love. I have got a place for us to stay while we work out what we want to do. It's my granny's old flat in Ealing – not as bad as it sounds, I promise you. Anyway, the plan was to do it up and sell

338

it. Now we can do it up together, we'll have so much fun, then we can sell it and go on from there.

As I sit looking out onto the street I can see little bursts of activity despite the lateness of the hour. And the noise, I don't know how you have managed to sleep at all these past few years. The street cleaners have just arrived and they are making the most infernal racket. Yet still you sleep on. I can see why you have loved living here and I can see that it will be hard to give up, but I promise you that together we are going to do and see the most wonderful things. I don't know where we will end up, but we will have each other and that, for me, is enough.

I love you, I love you, I love you . . . have I told you that? I think I must have told you a thousand times in my head, but I'm going to tell you every single day for the rest of our lives. (If you don't mind.)

Now, darling girl, will you come and meet me at South Ealing tube at midday? I will show you the flat – it's just a few streets away from the station. Text me when you are on your way.

I love you more than life!

Yours, forever,

Paula x

Seb is sitting at his computer, searching through the list of names registered with Companies House. He needs to see if Asphodel has already been taken. He has got as far as 'Ae' when he hears Henry shouting to him from the next office.

'Jesus Christ! Seb, get in here and look at this.'

He runs into the office and sees Henry standing in front of the widescreen television, the words 'BREAKING NEWS' flashing across the screen.

'What's happened?'

'They've blown up the tube,' says Henry, his voice quivering.

Becky comes running into the office. 'Turn the TV up,' she shouts.

Henry turns and puts his arm around her. 'Becky, thank God you're okay.'

She shrugs his arm off gently and sits on the edge of the desk, frantically tapping out numbers on her phone. 'Who's arrived?' She looks round the office.

'Just us three, so far,' says Seb. He can't take his eyes off the screen. There is a graphic of a tube map with various stations highlighted. He turns up the television again and the voices of the newsreaders compete with those of Henry and Becky on their respective phones.

'Dad,' booms Henry. 'Dad, can you hear me? Hang on a sec, I'll just turn the volume up. There, is that better? Yes,

340

I'm fine. We don't know what's happened, looks like a bomb by all accounts. You're where? Scotland. What are you doing in Scotland?'

'Leila, it's Becky. Could you call me urgently when you get this message? There's been an explosion on the tube and I want to make sure you're okay. Call me on my mobile and if that's busy call the office and leave a message with Callie.'

'Callie,' she shrieks. 'Shit, has Callie called yet? She gets the Piccadilly line, doesn't she? Oh my God, this is horrendous.'

Stella is sitting on the window seat reading Paula's letter for the fifth time, running the words over and over in her head.

'. . . *going to tell you I love you every day . . .*'

'. . . *granny's old flat in Ealing . . .*'

Ealing. Stella repeats the word, she practises using it in a sentence: 'Hello, I'm Stella. I live in Ealing.' It doesn't feel quite right, but it doesn't have to. As long as she can start and end each day lying beside Paula, she doesn't care where they live.

She looks out of the window. The street is quiet. The sky has clouded over and it looks like it might rain. There is something different about the street, something she cannot quite place. It seems to have lost its lustre overnight. All of a sudden, it is no longer the place where the world begins and ends, it is just another London street.

Her love affair with Soho has always been bound up with her feelings for Paula. It was the place they had first got together, and as long as they remained apart, Soho had been the thread that held them close. Now that they have found each other again, Soho is no longer relevant, it has served its purpose.

She feels awkward. It feels like she has no right to be here, like she is an intruder, sitting here in Ade's flat, with all Ade's stuff around her. Looking around, she is suddenly aware of his absence. It is like she has been on some potent drug for the last few hours and is slowly coming down. Where is he?

She gets up from the seat and goes into the kitchen. She could really do with a strong coffee. Her head feels a little woozy from the champagne, and the new options that have sprung up overnight, though exciting, are quite a lot to take on. She opens the cupboard and sees a mouldy loaf of bread, a box of Cup a Soup and a sachet of mayonnaise, but no coffee. Ade must have drunk the last of it. She closes the cupboard and goes back into the room to get her purse. She will go and grab a coffee from Bar Italia, then come back and pack her things.

But as she walks towards the door, she hears a key in the lock.

He is back.

Chapter 20

In Henry's office, the crossed phone conversations continue as one by one, each of the Honey Vision team arrive.

'Callie, darling,' cries Becky as the young receptionist walks into the room. 'How did you get here?'

Callie goes to answer then Becky's phone rings again.

'Hannah,' she cries into the phone. 'Thank God. Have you heard from Lou and Carly? You have. Oh brilliant. You take care, yeah? Bye. Bye.'

Henry holds up his phone. 'That was Kelly. She's at home. She's safe.'

Becky nods and holds her hand to her chest, mentally crossing Kelly's name off her list.

Seb gets up from the chair.

'Does anyone want some water or a tea?'

The office is full now; everyone has been accounted for – almost everyone.

As Seb walks out of the office he sees someone walking up the corridor towards him. It is Adam Fraser, from the accounts department. His face is grey; his eyes look dazed as he walks into the room.

'Adam,' says Henry. 'Come and sit down, mate. Are you alright?'

'I'll get some water,' says Seb.

Adam sits down on the arm of Henry's soft chair and takes a deep breath. Becky comes over and puts her hand on his shoulder.

'I walked from Camden,' he says, falteringly. 'There were no trains or buses, everyone was panicking.'

Seb comes in and hands him a plastic cup of water. Adam's hands shake as he takes the cup and holds it in his lap.

'I got to Tavistock Square and . . .' His voice falters. His hands are now shaking uncontrollably. Seb grabs the cup of water before it spills. 'I got to Tavistock Square and there was this almighty bang; I was almost knocked off my feet. I looked up and there were bodies on the road . . . a bus. I just carried on walking till I got here. I didn't know what to do.'

'Here it is,' shouts Henry, pointing at the screen. 'My God, my good God.'

The picture has changed. The focus has shifted from the frantic rescue teams outside the underground stations to the golden sunlight of a pretty tree-lined square where a red London bus stands with its roof blown away.

Ade is sitting on the bed watching Stella as she stands folding clothes onto the table. His head is throbbing but it feels good to be back in the flat, to see Stella, to know she is safe.

'I'm sorry, Stel,' says Ade, 'I've been an idiot.'

She had wanted to avoid all this. She had hoped to make a clean break without any confrontation. She had even written him a note.

'Look, Ade,' she says, as she pulls a black suitcase from under the bed, 'it doesn't matter anymore.' She zips open the case and starts filling it with the folded clothes. Next she goes to the bookshelves by the window and removes the first two rows of paperbacks.

Ade looks at her, suddenly aware of what she is doing.

'What's the case for?' He stands up from the bed and walks towards her. 'Where are you going?'

346

'I'm moving out, Ade. I'm going to live with a friend of mine,' says Stella, not wanting to bring Paula's name into the conversation. 'She's got a place in Ealing.'

'Moving out,' he cries. 'Stella, what are you talking about? You can't move out, let alone to a shithole like Ealing, you belong here. You belong in Soho, with me.'

'I know what I'm doing, Ade,' she says softly. She carefully distributes the books across the top of the clothes, then wedges a hairdryer into the neat folds of woollen jumpers. She zips up the case and looks up at him.

All the pent-up anger she had towards him has gone. Looking at Ade now, she feels protective of him. She wants him to be happy, wants him to have a good life. Her grandmother used to say that when you looked back on life, you wouldn't see a smooth, unblemished road, you would see all the potholes and patches, all the corrections and repairs. But rather than spoiling the view, these patches just add to its charm. It was wrong to think of Ade as a patch, but he had been a kind of bridge, carrying her from one world to the next.

'Stella, please,' he says, holding her by the arms. 'I'm begging you. I know I've upset you by not coming home last night, but don't do this. We can sort it out. I can get help. I'll go and see someone, a counsellor or something.

You see, I've been doing some thinking, and you were right, you were right about Warren and I know that all our problems started when he came along. I'm going to focus on jazz again, get back with the lads. It can be like old times again, Stella, making music for the love of it. Do you remember our toast: "To London and music"? I promise, Stella, they'll be no more crappy parties, no more Warren. I love you, baby, I love you so much I'll do anything, just don't leave me, please don't leave me.'

Becky is pacing up and down the office, talking to various friends and relatives on the phone. Henry has taken Adam to a meeting room. He needs to rest but he won't be able to go home yet.

'Do you think he needs to go to hospital?' asks Seb as Henry comes back into the office.

'He's in shock,' says Henry. 'But the hospitals will have their hands full dealing with the seriously injured. The best we can do for now is keep him calm and let him rest. What an appalling thing to witness.'

'Horrendous,' says Becky as she puts her mobile down and comes to sit next to Seb and Henry in front of the television. 'All those people just trying to get to work; it could have been any one of us.'

'And yesterday was such a wonderful day,' says Henry. 'It's like we've descended into Hell.'

Seb hears his mobile ring. He looks around the room, trying to locate it, then sees his bag sitting on the sofa outside the office. He must have flung it there this morning in his haste to go and get started on the painting. He brings the bag into the office and pulls out his phone. It stops ringing.

He scrolls through the phone to see who was calling him. 'It's my mother,' he says. 'She'll be frantic.'

'You've dropped something,' says Becky, pointing at the floor.

He looks down and sees Zoe's photographs.

'King's Cross.'

'What's that?' Henry looks up from the television.

'They said King's Cross, didn't they?'

'Yes,' says Becky. 'A Piccadilly line train.'

'Oh God.' Seb feels the blood drain from his face.

'What?' asks Henry.

Seb puts the photographs on the desk. 'This is Zoe,' he says to Becky. 'She gave me these to give to you. She was waiting to see you yesterday. She had an appointment.

Becky takes the photographs and looks at them. 'Oh, shit. I forgot all about it. I got delayed at that shoot on Brick Lane. Callie should have called me. Oh, she's lovely.'

'Well she got tired of waiting,' says Seb. 'She was going home to Middlesbrough today. She told me she was going to get the first tube to King's Cross this morning.'

'Well if that's the case, she will have missed all this,' says Henry, pragmatic as ever. 'The trains start running at around five, don't they? She will be safely back at home by now. And we still don't know what direction the train was going in, whether it was going to or coming from King's Cross.'

'I just hope she's okay,' says Seb. 'She is a nice girl.' He remembers the phone in his hand. 'Listen, I better go and call Mum,' he says as he walks out of the room. 'She'll be worried.'

As he leaves, Becky is still looking at the photographs.

Chapter 21

The rubbish collection comes late to Hanway Street this morning. Gridlocked traffic on Tottenham Court Road has meant that Bob Gardener, the driver of the truck, has had to sit for forty minutes, watching the traffic lights go from red to amber to green over and over without being able to move his truck so much as a millimetre.

He doesn't know, as he reverses into the little alleyway off Hanway Street, that the exultation he felt when the lights turned green and he put his foot on the accelerator and glided up Oxford Street will be shot to pieces in a matter of moments, and that for him, fifty-eight years old and a council employee of twenty-five years, this will be his last collection.

'My turn,' he says to his young partner, Kelvin, who is

sitting in the passenger seat. He climbs out of the truck and prepares to collect the black bags that are piled up at the far end of the alley. He picks up the nearest one and throws it into the back of the truck. Then he turns around. He expects to see a pile of bulging black bags; he expects to pick up another one and put it into the back of the truck. He expects to repeat this over and over until the job is done. What he does not expect is this: a crumpled mass of blood, a pink dress, a pale, lifeless body and a pair of dead, staring eyes. He lurches back. He goes to shout, to alert Kelvin, but no sound comes out. He turns back to the pile and instinctively holds out his arm, tries to extend some comfort, some humanity to this poor, wasted girl.

Within seconds, Kelvin is by his side, the police are called, witness statements taken. He will be asked over and over to recount how he found her, what position she was in, what time it was. But Bob Gardener will never forget. So traumatized by the sight of that broken body, those haunted eyes, he will sign off on permanent sick leave and spend the rest of his days growing flowers in his window box, drinking cups of tea, tasting the endless round of cakes baked by his wife. He will book himself on a cruise ship and smile at comedians on TV but nothing will ever make him forget, nothing will ever take away the sight of her from his mind, that poor lost girl lying there among the rubbish.

'Do you remember when we first met?' Ade is still holding Stella's arms.

'Please let me go, Ade,' she says. 'I've got to go.' She looks around the room to see if she has forgotten anything. She spots her demo CDs stacked in a neat pile on the bookshelf. They can stay, she thinks. Ade is still pleading with her, but she can't look at him. This is too much; she did not want to do it like this.

'You asked me if you were what I was looking for. Do you remember that, Stella?'

'Yes, Ade. I remember.'

'You were everything I was looking for. You were beautiful and talented, you were my best friend,' he sobs. 'And I've tried to be the person you want but I'm not. I never will be.'

Stella's phone starts to ring.

'I have to get that, Ade,' she says, wriggling herself free from his arms.

She picks up her bag and takes the phone out but before she can answer Ade grabs it and flings it onto the bed.

'Ade, what are you doing?'

'You've got someone else, haven't you?' His eyes are red and wet from crying and he wipes them with the back of his hand.

'Ade, don't do this.'

'Just tell me the truth, Stella, and I'll stop making a fool of myself. What's his name?'

She shakes her head.

'What's his name?' he yells.

'Paula,' she shouts back. 'Her name is Paula. Are you happy now?'

Ade sits back down on the bed.

'Paula?' he says slowly. 'You're leaving me for a woman?'

She sits down next to him and puts her hand on his arm.

'Ade, I don't know what to say.'

He pushes her hand away.

'Can you please go now?' he says, quietly.

She picks up her bag and the case and stands in front of him.

'I'm sorry, Ade.'

He pulls himself up from the bed, takes her arm and marches her out of the room. She opens the door then turns to say something but he stops her.

'Just go, Stella. Please just go.'

Stella stumbles down the stairs, almost dropping the suitcase as she goes. Tears sting her eyes as she opens the front door. Putting the case down onto the step, she slumps onto it and tries to stop herself from shaking. It is over, she tells herself. But it wasn't supposed to have happened like that. She never wanted to hurt him, she wanted to just slip away, leave him quietly, let him get on with his life. Now, it feels like she has destroyed him. That silence, the way he had looked at her when he asked her to leave. She would give anything to take it back. She didn't have to mention Paula; why had she mentioned Paula?

She looks at the Ronnie Scott's sign and its neon lights now dulled by the morning light; she looks up the street at The Dog and Duck, at Garlic & Shots and Pret; all the familiar landmarks that have defined the last five years.

Tomorrow she will wake up in Ealing. She will look out onto rows of suburban gardens with neatly trimmed hedges and potted plants. She will go to sleep in a darkened room; her dreams will not be disturbed by crashing glass and the glare of pink neon.

But she will have peace and with peace comes clarity. All this noise and colour, it's not conducive to healing, and that is what Stella needs now. She needs to start the lengthy process of recovery. She will go to the doctor and get the chest pains sorted out. She will stop hurting herself. Some day she will look back on these five years and, with the benefit of hindsight, she will hopefully be able to make sense of it all.

She looks up at the flat. He will get on without her; Soho will carry on without her. There is nothing left for her now.

She looks up the street and sees that it is almost eleven o'clock. There is still time for a coffee.

She picks up her case and gets up from the step.

Inside the flat, Ade stands frozen in the middle of the room. Suddenly everything feels wrong in this place. This was where he had escaped to, this tiny flat with its thin walls and draughty windows; this was where he had found safety and a purpose. He had trusted it, like he had trusted Lenny and the guys in the band . . . and Stella.

He looks at the clothes rail, empty now but for a row of thin wire coat hangers. It is like she never existed, this woman who shared his life for five years; it is like she has evaporated and left behind no trace. Maybe she *was* a ghost all along; maybe he had imagined her into existence like he imagined Soho and Warren Craig and multimillion-pound record deals.

He sits on the bed and lights a cigarette, trying to gather his thoughts. It feels like he is losing his mind. He needs the day to start as it should; he needs to feel the ordinariness of a Thursday morning. Any other morning he would be sitting at the mixing desk, headphones on, adding the finishing touches to Warren's latest track. Now the mixing desk stands there in the corner like a redundant block of defunct machinery. He looks at his saxophone, gleaming in its stand like an ancient sword, and wonders if he will ever be able to play it again. No, music is the last thing he needs. Right now, he wants dull noise, empty vacant background soup to mask this unbearable silence.

He gets up from the bed and switches on the television. No doubt there will be some banal daytime chat show on. That will do; that will be enough to fill the void. But as the screen flickers to life, there is no comforting, aimless chat, no lurid pink sofas and frothy hosts. Instead, there is a solemn newsreader and a thick red line flashing on and off the words 'BREAKING NEWS'.

Ade turns the volume up and hears the newsreader talk of 'rush hour tube trains', and 'suspected terror attacks'. He sees ambulances parked end to end outside King's Cross station and yellow-jacketed paramedics rushing inside with stretchers; he sees people stumbling towards the cameras with bandages across their faces, terror and confusion in their eyes.

Ade sits back on the bed and stares at the screen, trying to make sense of the barrage of news, trying to work out what has happened on the tube, what has happened to his city.

Stella has never seen Bar Italia so packed. It is heaving. A crowd of people are gathered round the TV. Is there an Italian football match on or something? She pushes her way to the front, hauling her case with one hand. She is still reeling from the confrontation with Ade and desperately needs a coffee to calm her nerves before she gets on the tube.

But there is no football match, no excited Italian fans, there is just deathly silence. The TV screen is switched to BBC News 24 and Stella cranes her neck to see what is going on.

'Something terrible's happened,' says the man behind the counter.

Slowly, bit by bit, the news sinks in.

Aldgate.

'Who would do this?' whispers a woman in a purple beret.

358

A Circle Line train that had just left Edgware Road.

'They need to bring the SAS in,' says a grey-haired man, stirring his espresso.

Russell Square.

'They'll target the West End next,' says a young man in cycling shorts and sunglasses. 'My boss just called and said he's seen army tanks lining up in Leicester Square. Looks like we'll have to stay the night, Marco.'

The café is packed with people. Pale faces, redundant briefcases, mobile phones ringing. Shock and disorientation permeate the small space as more people arrive, some with news, others still unaware of what is happening. They stand, unable to move, transfixed by the horror unfolding before them.

Stella's phone beeps. She can barely take her eyes from the television but she opens it and reads Paula's frantic message:

Are you okay? Tell me you are safe!

Stella types out a quick text, telling her that she is fine, that she is standing in Bar Italia watching the news.

Ade leans across the bed and opens the window. The flat

feels stifling all of a sudden. He needs air. There are people clustered around on the street, huddled in groups. A man in a suit is gesticulating, pointing his finger in the direction of Soho Square and shaking his head. He looks terrified. What has he seen? wonders Ade.

A woman runs across from the other side of the street and joins the group. 'They're saying there's a bomb in Starbucks in Leicester Square. I've just heard it on the news,' she shouts.

Another voice joins in: 'Do you think we should get out of here? I mean, they've hit the tube; they're going to hit the heart, aren't they? They're going to get the centre. Soho's a bit of a sitting target right now . . .'

Ade steps away from the window. The panicky voices continue to speculate as he sits back down on the bed. He has always been able to read Soho's moods. Every hour of the day has its own character, so unique Ade could identify it blindfold: the early morning banging and crashing of the street cleaners, the nine o'clock clattering of hurried footsteps as they rush down the street from coffee stop to office. This hour, eleven through to noon, would, on any other day, be filled with the buzz of the restaurants getting ready for lunch; the smell of garlic would fill the air and hungry tourists would be dotted about, having followed the wafting smells of good food from Oxford Street or Leicester Square. Eleven-thirty in Soho is a happy place to be, a pocket of time in which anything seems possible, where the only appointment worth keeping is with a plate of antipasti and a glass of house red.

But now Soho wears the sorrow of the morning like a mantilla. It is as if the sun has been extinguished, leaving the city and its people suspended in darkness, scrambling around trying to make sense of it all, trying to find their way out.

Ade's eyes are heavy with tiredness. He lies down on the bed, his back aching from lying on the wooden bench, his exhausted brain unable to fully comprehend what is happening. He closes his eyes but the screams from the cells last night ring in his ears. He pulls the duvet on top of him, blocks his ears with his hands, tries to silence the screams, but they are everywhere: inside the room, outside on the street, he can even hear them crying out from the television screen.

He lies there, praying for sleep, for oblivion; praying for the screams to stop. Maybe it has all been some sick, twisted dream, he thinks, as sleep finally claims him. Maybe when he wakes up everything will be as it was.

As Ade sleeps, London scrambles through its darkest hour, and in a quiet side street the small body of a twenty–four-year-old woman is discreetly placed into a body bag and silently removed without ceremony. The lengthy process of identification will begin later. For now, she is simply a nameless girl, with no wallet and no mobile phone.

'A frenzied attack,' they will describe it as to her heart-broken mother. 'A punctured lung.' Her mother will try to block out the words and instead try to think only of that lovely smile. 'Severe heart trauma.' A month later she will stand in St David's Church and tell the congregation about her daughter's beautiful heart. The police will leave her then, leave her to her grief, leave her to piece together the last moments of her precious daughter's life. But before they go, they will give her something, a piece of paper that was found in her coat pocket. She will wait for them to leave then she will open it up and see a little girl's drawing and her heart will break into a million pieces.

Stella stands in Bar Italia as the clock silently records the passing hours. She stares up at the television screen, unable to move, unable to step away lest she miss some vital piece of news, some clue as to why this has happened, while outside sirens wail and the noise merges with the blue flashing lights on the screen. A great, unquiet darkness descends upon the city, engulfing it in sorrow and bewilderment and silencing the hearts of the living and the dead. Time stops, and all that is pure and innocent dissolves into a clear London morning, leaving in its wake the shattered pieces of a strange new world.

Acknowledgements

I would like to thank the following people for their amazing support and encouragement in writing this novel:

My agent Madeleine Milburn at Madeleine Milburn Literary, TV & Film Agency; my editor Jo Dickinson at Quercus; Kathryn Taussig, Lucy Ramsey and the Quercus team. Barrie Sherwood, Abi Curtis and Christopher Walker at York St John University; Ray Honeybourne; Andrea Semple and Matt Haig.

My incredible parents, Luke and Mavis Casey, for their love, support and unstinting faith in me and for teaching me the beauty and power of the written word.

My little boy, Luke, for giving me the strength to write this novel and for lighting up each day with his beautiful smile and magical stories.

My husband, Nick, for the rainy night in Soho that changed my life.

Soho, 4 am Songlist

1.	Summertime	Ella Fitzgerald/ Louis Armstrong
2.	J'ai perdu mon Eurydice	Maria Callas
3.	Yesterday	The Beatles
4.	New York New York	Liza Minnelli
5.	A Strange Boy	Joni Mitchell
6.	Bar Italia	Pulp
7.	Total Eclipse of the Heart	Bonnie Tyler
8.	Morning Morgantown	Joni Mitchell
9.	The First Cut is the Deepest	Rod Stewart
10.	Waterloo Sunset	The Kinks
11.	You Really Got Me	The Kinks
12.	Falling	Kate Rusby
13.	Something Changed	Pulp
14.	Song 2	Blur
15.	My One and Only Love	John Coltrane
16.	These Foolish Things	Billie Holiday
17.	Tenderley	Miles Davis
18.	Wonderwall	Oasis

19.	Weather with You	Crowded House
20.	Underneath your Clothes	Shakira
21.	Bittersweet Symphony	The Verve
22.	Daydream Believer	The Monkees
23.	Mozart Requiem	London Symphony Orchestra
24.	Sonnet	The Verve
25.	Soho Square	Kirsty McColl

My favourite places in London

London is at its most fragile and atmospheric in the hour between seven and eight o'clock in the morning. To see the city as it opens its eyes and takes its first tentative steps into the day before the great commute begins is such rare treat, rather like the collective hush of the audience before the curtain rises. This is the hour of watching, absorbing and easing yourself into the mood of the day. For me, one of the best places in London to experience this is Soho, where the contrast between day and night is stark. As the street cleaners clear away the aftermath of the night before it feels rather like turning on the lights at the end of a party and seeing, in harsh light, the bleary eyes, the cracked CDs, the wine stains on the carpet. I lived on Frith Street, right in the heart of Soho, when I was in my early twenties and the early morning walk to work was always the most invigorating and inspiring.

One of my favourite places to eat at this time of the morning is the Star Café on Great Chapel Street, still open for business despite the disruption from Cross Rail digging up the road outside. This Soho institution with its red gingham tablecloths and movie-star memorabilia has been going strong for eighty years and is still the best place in town for a good hearty breakfast, coffee top-ups and a leisurely read of the papers. There's also the legendary Mario, whose father opened the café in 1933, and who will happily put the world to rights as he dishes up your full English.

If a fierce shot of espresso is needed, then I head for Bar Italia on Frith Street. Established in 1949 and immortalised in song by Brit Pop heroes, Pulp, this is the place to take your front-row seat outside and do some serious people watching.

Breakfast over, it's time for a spot of shopping and I can never resist a trip to Cecil Court, the little thoroughfare off St Martin's Lane, for a rummage in the second-hand bookshops. Marchpane is a particular favourite of mine and is the place I found a copy of *Little Grey Rabbit's Party*, one of my favourite books from childhood that I had never been able to find elsewhere. Cecil Court really is a book lover's paradise and with its Victorian shop fronts and boxes full of books, maps and prints displayed out on the street it feels like stepping into another age and makes for a delicious diversion from the bustle of neighbouring Covent Garden and Leicester Square.

Across the river, deep in the oldest part of the City is a little haven of peace where I like to spend ten minutes or so in quiet contemplation. Years ago, after reading Samuel Pepys' diary and being captivated not by stout old Sam but his spirited wife Elizabeth, I decided to spend an afternoon in Tower Hill looking at their former home in Seething Lane and paying a visit to the church where they worshipped, St Olaves's, just across the road. Unfortunately, the house had been swallowed up by development and the area seemed to be a mass of glass and concrete, part of the megalith that is London's Square Mile. So I headed for the church and was greeted warmly by the vicar who was putting a poster up on the noticeboard. Inside it was like stepping into the seventeenth century, everything was still intact – the dark wooden pews, the low ceilings, and I could imagine Samuel and Elizabeth dressed in their Sunday best. A harpist was playing a lunchtime recital and the music added to the tranquility and sense of history. After a few moments, I walked into the little church garden which had been used as a mass burial ground during the plague. I had expected to feel a sense of doom there but instead, just yards from the hub of the City, I felt a real sense of peace. Back inside the church I found what I had come here to see – the statue of Elizabeth Pepys. It sits just above the altar and true to its Baroque style it is animated and alive. The sculptor has captured her as if she is just about to fling her head back and burst into fits of laughter. I had a few moments quiet thought and then I left, saying goodbye to the vicar on the way out and feeling truly soothed and uplifted. It is still one of my favourite places to visit to experience a deep sense of stepping outside of time.

One place I always return to for lunch is Mildred's, the grand dame of vegetarian restaurants, nestled in a quiet(ish) corner of Soho on Lexington Street. I first came here when I was eighteen and couldn't believe a vegetarian restaurant existed that offered more than the standard pasta, quiche, and baked potato fodder that us veggies often get lumbered with. It's great in the winter for a good old hearty spicy bean stew as well as in summer where you are spoilt for choice with a range of delicious salads and soups. Mildred's is one of those places that I can't imagine not being there and I hope to still be eating lunch there when I'm eighty.

Nicely fed and watered, if I was in possession of a magic carpet I would fly across the river and land on the soft grass of another of my favourite places. But failing that I'll just hop on the tube to Sloane Square then catch the 137 bus which will deposit me at the gates of Arcadia – or Battersea Park as it's otherwise known.

I love this place and when I lived in Battersea I would try to walk here at least every other day. To me it is the best park in London. It doesn't enclose you like Regents Park or make you feel like you are trespassing on the Queen's rhododendrons like St James's, it's not as wild as Hampstead Heath or as sparse as Hyde Park. It is whatever you want it be – there's enough green space to run with the kids or the dog, yet there are also secret hideaways like the magical English Country Garden, with its trickling fountains and wisteria-clad trellises. Winter is a particularly beautiful time in the park – the exotic plants get bound up in protective padding to save them from the frost and as you walk towards them they look like the frozen fawns and elves of Narnia. In summer, you can take a boat out onto the glassy lake and eat ice-creams in Le Gondola, the gloriously retro café, or stroll down to the giant Peace Pagoda whose great gold Buddha looks out across the river towards the genteel Georgian houses of Cheyne Walk with a look that says: 'I'm glad to be on this side.' Memories blindside me whenever I return to the park

– the Pump House Gallery where I almost got married, the benches in the English Country Garden where I sat and wrote a letter to my unborn child, the zoo where the same child aged five whooped with excitement as he fed the pigs and drove a fire engine, the spot by the river where we stood and watched impotently as a beautiful, doomed whale thrashed and blustered to its death in the alien waters of the Thames. It's a beautiful place and whenever I leave, I can almost hear the park telling me to hurry back. And I always do.

My favourite places to spend the evening in London vary according to my mood, which oscillates between laid-back and flashy. Here I will describe to you my favourite bits of each. Let's start with flashy (always a good place to start).

There is something about the sun setting on London that makes me want to hail the nearest black cab and, in a near-perfect recreation of a Graham Greene rendezvous, direct the driver to The Savoy. Okay, so I might not be in the throes of an illicit affair but it's nice to play the part. The American Bar at the Savoy has the distinction of having served the first Martini cocktail in Britain. Each and every drink is beautifully presented with the Vodka

Martini being, quite possibly, the finest you will ever taste. To complete the mood of Gatsby-esque decadence, a jazz pianist plays from 7pm each night.

But, if I am not in a flashy mood, if I want to ease myself out a hectic day with a glass of red in a relaxed, bohemian haven then I head for the quirky little wine bar, Le Beaujolais on Litchfield Street in Soho. This place reminds me of those bars you stumble across in France and Spain, the ones with *jamon* hanging from the rafters, a surly bartender who ends up becoming your best pal and a simple menu of *plat du jour* that tastes like something your mother would cook when you're ill. I was introduced to it by a friend years ago and when I lived in Soho it became a local of sorts – far enough away from the centre of Soho to be intimate and private, but still central enough to feel the pulse of the West End beating underneath your feet. I took my brother here once for a quick drink and we ended up making a night of it, drinking far too much house red and eating huge chunks of French bread with slabs of butter. My brother then foolishly debated the merits of the English football team over the French national side with the cross French landlord. They ended on good terms, though, with pats on the back and a rendition of 'La Marseillaise' as we stumbled off down the street. Not all my evenings here have been as raucous . . . this was also the place I had my first date with the man I would go on to marry.

It might be tempting to stay and eat here, put my feet up and settle in the night, but for a vegetarian, the menu of beef bourgignon and spicy saucisson is not really for me, so after a glass of red and a dish of olives it's off for dinner in . . . Earls Court?

Yes, Earls Court, home to the exhibition centre and lots of Australians, apparently, but also home to the Troubadour.

As you approach the elegantly shabby green building on Old Brompton Road, you could be mistaken for thinking you are in Paris or Greenwich Village circa 1950. Bicycles with baskets line up outside and the dim light of the windows illuminates a row of mismatched coloured bottles, like some Elizabethan apothecary shop. Inside it's like stepping into a warm and welcoming bohemian house party. There is something about the Troubadour that reminds me of the Chelsea Arts Club, where I used to work when I first came to London. You don't come to those places for the food – though it is great – or to be seen, you come here to step into another world, to feel how Alice felt when she hurtled down the rabbit hole and emerged into a new world, with labyrinthine corridors and warm fires burning and doors leading to mysterious dark-panelled rooms. The Troubadour is one of the last remaining fifties coffeehouses in London; long before the homogenous slew of Starbucks and Caffè Nero took over our streets, there were places like this serving frothy coffees to would-be poets and rock stars. Today it is not just a coffee house, it is a restaurant and café, a wine shop and wine bar, a music club that has played host to everyone from Bob Dylan and Jimi Hendrix to Ed Sheeran and Adele, and a B&B – with a cosy garret upstairs offering accommodation for those who can't face a long trip home. There is a sense that you are allowed to linger here, to take your time and soak up the atmosphere without being rushed along by some harried waiter. Its cranberry walls, stained glass windows and dark wood panelling add to the contemplative mood. I like to eat by candlelight – to me, bright lights in a restaurant are the spiritual equivalent of a cold shower or an insensitive remark, cruel and unnecessary – and the end of a long day in London requires just the sort of ambience that the Troubadour offers. Like the best host, it takes your coat, hands you a glass of wine, feeds you heartily and makes you want to return again and again. It's the perfect place to end the day.

Reading Group Discussion Topics
Soho, 4 a.m.

* How important is the clock in Soho, 4 a.m.? Discuss the use of time as a device for pushing the narrative forward.

* How far does Ade with his attitudes, his jazz-playing and background represent 'old' Soho? Could you divide the characters into 'old' and 'new' Soho. Think about the media companies that now dominate the Soho landscape versus the jazz clubs, the family businesses, the brothels and drinking dens. How does Seb represent both old and new?

* How important is memory and the past? How far can you trust each character's recollection of his or her past?

* Discuss the characters of Stella and Zoe. Both grew up a few miles from each other, both left the north east to follow their dreams in London. How similar are they? What sets them apart?

* Discuss the importance of music in the novel. Did you feel the novel was playing to a soundtrack? What does each character's taste in music say about them?

* Seb, Stella and Ade all employ coping mechanisms to deal with the pressures of London life – binge-drinking, bulimia, sex . . . yet Zoe doesn't appear to have an addiction. How relevant is this and do you think, perversely, the other characters' addictions made them less vulnerable to the dangers of the city?

* Zoe, Stella and Ade all fled their hometowns to realise their dreams in London, while Seb was sent away to boarding school. How important is the idea of home and the search for belonging in the novel?

* The city is one of twenty-four-hour noise – discuss the importance of sound in the novel. What does it mask? What does it illuminate?

* Did you find that the tight, twenty-four time frame of the novel added to the intensity of the action?

* Discuss the character of Warren Craig. Does he represent the ugly side of the music industry or was he genuinely interested in Ade and his work?

* Is Paula simply a construct of Stella's imagination? Do you think their relationship will survive?

* Soho, 4 a.m. is written in the present tense. How effective did you find this? Would the action have been as immediate if it had been written in the past tense?

* Were you surprised by Zoe's death? What did you feel it symbolised?

* What do you think Stella's dream symbolises? Did it help you gain a better understanding of her character?

* Compare the way Stella and Zoe navigate the city. Stella knows every nook and cranny of the West End and she shows her disdain for the tourists who ignore the 'unwritten laws' of the underground by standing on the left side of the escalator or walking too slowly. Zoe ignores all of these rules when she sits on a Circle Line train and goes round and round to kill some time on an idle Sunday. What does this say about their respective attitudes to the city and to life?

* How far does Zoe's behaviour reinforce the idea of her being an 'outsider'? For example, the incident on the

Circle Line Train, her bemusement with Soho, and her trust in Dina and Becky.

* Which of the characters do you think is the most attuned to Soho and its moods?

* Contrast Ade's behaviour at the party with the descriptions of him performing on stage.

* Did you trust Paula? Was Seb's description of her and Stella as a lioness with her cub an accurate one?

* Discuss the symbolism of the garden square. What do you think it represents in terms of Zoe and Seb's relationship and what happens later?

* Could Soho be described as the fifth character? How far does the location permeate the novel and do you feel you got a sense of the 'real' Soho by the end of the novel?

* How far do the inner thoughts of the characters merge with their external environment? Were there times where they clashed?

* Did you find the inner dialogue effective or distracting?

* Discuss the nature of the friendship between Seb and Henry. Do you think it is a healthy one?

* The characters in Soho, 4 a.m. are torn between their 'regular' jobs and their true passions. How far do you think this is reflective of young people in 21st-century Britain?

* Discuss the framing of the novel – between the announcement that London had won the bid to host the 2012 Olympic Games and the terrorist bombings of 7/7 – did you get a sense of the change in mood from one of jubilation to one of horror and devastation?

* How far does Stella's love of water reflect her inner world? Discuss the relevance of the bath as her 'think tank', her immersion in the Serpentine as a child and the river in her dream – is Stella the most fluid and unknowable of the four characters?

* How convincing was the relationship between Stella and Ade? Who do you think had the upper hand?

* How far did the book give a sense of the hidden Soho – the drinking dens masquerading as Chinese restaurants, the discreet brothels? Is everybody hiding something in the novel?

* The novel takes the reader on a journey via an invisible street map – how effective did you find the various characters' walks across Soho? Did you find it helped build up a picture of Soho in your mind?

* How convincing is the friendship between Ade and Seb? Is it mutually beneficial? Do you think Seb's drinking problem has contributed to the friendship, would he even speak to Ade when sober?

* Soho, 4 a.m. shows us London from four different perspectives – all very different. Discuss these differing views and attitudes: are there areas where they overlap? What values, if any, unite the four characters?

* How did you feel at the end of the book? What did it leave you with?

* What images did you find the most poignant or striking in the novel?

* *'A strange new world'* Discuss the various ways in which London has changed in the years since 7/7?

* Was the jubilation of 6th July reflected in the Olympic Games of 2012? Do you think the novel conveys the mood of those two extraordinary days in 2005 accurately?

THE LAST DAY OF SUMMER

BY NUALA CASEY

London, 2012

PhD student Stella is returning to London for the first time in seven years. As she revisits her old haunts, she is troubled by the voices of the past and wonders if she will ever be able to leave Soho and its ghosts behind.

Seb has moved on from his wild days at Honey Vision and is happily married with a young daughter and a thriving art gallery. As he helps his wife, a glamorous chef, prepare to launch her restaurant in Soho, he feels that his life is truly blossoming. But a chance encounter with a stranger brings back tragic memories and puts the lives of his wife and daughter in serious danger.

The characters come together to celebrate the launch of the new restaurant, but little do they know they're being watched.

The dog-days of summer are about to come to a shocking end.

COMING SOON

www.quercusbooks.co.uk

Quercus
Join us!

Visit us at our website, or join us on
Twitter and Facebook for:

- Exclusive interviews and films from
  your favourite Quercus authors

- Exclusive extra content

- Pre-publication sneak previews

- Free chapter samplers and
  reading group materials

- Giveaways and competitions

- Subscribe to our free newsletter

www.quercusbooks.co.uk
twitter.com/quercusbooks
facebook.com/quercusbooks